"You would have me ruin you, willingly?" Night Thunder demanded.

"No, but I . . . but you saved my life and I—"

"Is it this that causes you to come into my arms?"

"No," Rebecca said, "it is only because I cannot marry you, but I feel strongly about you and we have to share a sleeping robe and . . . " She glanced away from him.

"Know you this," he said, gently putting a finger beneath her chin and bringing her face around to his. "If we make love, you will be my wife in every way. My people already think it. All we have to do to make it so is consummate it."

She stared up at him. "Do you truly *want* to be marrying me?"

"Surely you do not question that I want you."

"But do you love me?"

For an answer, he pulled her into his arms where he proceeded to kiss her; her cheeks, her nose, her eyelids . . .

And she might have melted right then and there. But she didn't. Not when even having an affair with this man meant marriage . . .

KAREN KAY

NIGHT THUNDER'S BRIDE

Lodi
Memorial
Hospital
Complementary Book

AVON BOOKS ◆ NEW YORK

AVON BOOKS, INC.
1350 Avenue of the Americas
New York, New York 10019

Copyright © 1999 by Karen Kay Elstner-Bailey
Map by Trina C. Elstner
Inside cover author photo by Take Two Portraits
Published by arrangement with the author
Library of Congress Catalog Card Number: 98-94824
ISBN: 0-380-80339-9
www.avonbooks.com/romance

First Avon Books Printing: July 1999

AVON TRADEMARK REG. U.S. PAT. OFF. AND IN OTHER COUNTRIES, MARCA REGIS-
TRADA, HECHO EN U.S.A.

Printed in the U.S.A.

WCD   10   9   8   7   6   5   4   3   2   1

This book is dedicated to some of
the kindest people I have ever known.

For my friends,
Becky Johnson-Hillman,
a true inspiration, who first
introduced me to romance novels

Mary Bridges-Thompson,
whose loyalty and friendship
I will always treasure

Christine Pickens-Milliman,
how could I forget
our many adventures in high school?

Also to my daughter, Alyssa Elstner-Howson,
who celebrates her first year of marriage

HAPPY ANNIVERSARY

Acknowledgments

Because one never really writes a book "alone," I would like to acknowledge the following research sources: to Chief Buffalo Child Long Lance and his book *Autobiography of a Blackfoot Indian Chief*, from which I received the information on the seven tents of the medicine man and many other interesting facets of Blackfoot life.

To James Willard Schultz and his book *My Life as an Indian*; what an adventure in reading.

Also to L. Ron Hubbard for his books *Buckskin Brigades*, a truly unusual book of the Blackfoot Indians, and *Assists Processing Handbook*, specifically, data on the "Bring Back to Life" Assist and the "Unconscious Person" Assist.

This book is dedicated to some of
the kindest people I have ever known.

For my friends,
Becky Johnson-Hillman,
a true inspiration, who first
introduced me to romance novels

Mary Bridges-Thompson,
whose loyalty and friendship
I will always treasure

Christine Pickens-Milliman,
how could I forget
our many adventures in high school?

Also to my daughter, Alyssa Elstner-Howson,
who celebrates her first year of marriage

HAPPY ANNIVERSARY

Acknowledgments

Because one never really writes a book "alone," I would like to acknowledge the following research sources: to Chief Buffalo Child Long Lance and his book *Autobiography of a Blackfoot Indian Chief*, from which I received the information on the seven tents of the medicine man and many other interesting facets of Blackfoot life.

To James Willard Schultz and his book *My Life as an Indian*; what an adventure in reading.

Also to L. Ron Hubbard for his books *Buckskin Brigades*, a truly unusual book of the Blackfoot Indians, and *Assists Processing Handbook*, specifically, data on the "Bring Back to Life" Assist and the "Unconscious Person" Assist.

Note to the Reader

The year is 1833, a time when the Blackfoot Indians held control of their country and patrolled it with unmerciful vigor. The white man is the invader in this land, and from the Blackfoot viewpoint, the white man is the interloper. With his weapons and snares, the trapper purges the land, taking more than he could ever use. With his whisky and wine, the trader further weakens the more feeble spirits within the Indian tribes, and with his lack of conscience, the white man begins a practice of taking Indian women as wives, only to cast them soon aside.

Most of the Blackfoot chiefs urge their people to trade with their Canadian allies in the north, rather than risk the dangers of bartering with the newer, more savage "Americans"; men who will ply whisky in their trade in order to cheat the Indian out of his hard-earned goods. At Fort Union, such a man was Kenneth McKenzie, who encouraged whisky to flow freely under the cover of darkness.

It is this period in history which is most condemning to the newly founding country of the United States. The white men who first met the Indians were often no more than criminals escaping justice in the east. Here these men felt free to dramatize their antisocial acts upon a people who had no recourse with the new American government. Such people as these first white men often placed themselves above the law and held little respect for the life and well-being of others, often writing, when they could write at all, of the savage aspects of the Indian—perhaps to atone for their own wild conduct. But careful research of unprejudiced, firsthand accounts, reveals an entirely different scenario.

They (the Indians) were friendly in their dispositions, and honest to the most scrupulous degree in their intercourse with the white men. . . . Simply to call these people religious would convey but a faint idea of the deep hue of piety and devotion which pervades the whole of their conduct. Their honesty is immaculate; and their purity of purpose, and their observance of the rites of their religion, are most uniform and remarkable. They are, certainly, more like a nation of saints than a horde of savages.

—GEORGE CATLIN,
from the writings of Captain Bonneville

Never in the history of the United States have unspeakable injustices been carried on amongst an entire people who knew so little of such things. Rarely has such information as what truly transpired in the west been so suppressed and hidden.

We have no other mode of accounting for the infamous barbarities, of which, according to their own story, they were guilty—hunting the poor Indians like wild beasts, and killing them without mercy—chasing their unfortunate victims at full speed; noosing them around the neck with their lassos, and then dragging them to death.... A great number of Shoshokies or Root-Diggers were posted on the opposite bank, when they (the white men) *imagined* they (the Indians) were with hostile intent; they advanced upon them, leveled their rifles, and killed twenty-five of them on the spot. The rest fled to a short distance, then halted and turned about, howling and whining like wolves, and uttering most piteous wailings. The trappers chased them in every direction; the poor wretches made no defense, but fled with terror; neither does it appear from accounts of the boasted victors, that a weapon had been wielded, or a weapon launched by the Indians throughout the affair.

From these, and hundreds of others that might be named, and equally barbarous, it can easily be seen that white men may well feel a dread at every step they take in Indian realms, after atrocities like these, that call so loudly and so justly for revenge, in a country where there are no laws to punish, but where the cruel savage takes vengeance in his own way—and white men fall, in the Indian's estimation, not as *murdered*, but *executed*, under the common law of their land.

—GEORGE CATLIN,
taken from the writings of Captain Bonneville,
Letters and Notes on the Manners, Customs,
and Conditions of the North American Indians

It is at this riotous point in history that our story begins.

Karen Kay

Please note: There is a glossary provided at the end of this book for unusual or uncommon words—also some definitions of commonly used Indian words.

Wide brown plains, distant, slender, flat-topped buttes; still more distant giant mountain, blue sided, sharp peaked, snow capped; odor of sage and smoke of campfire; thunder of ten thousand buffalo hoofs over the hard, dry ground; long drawn, melancholy howl of wolves breaking the silence of night, how I loved you all!

—JAMES WILLARD SCHULTZ, *My Life as an Indian*

Northw

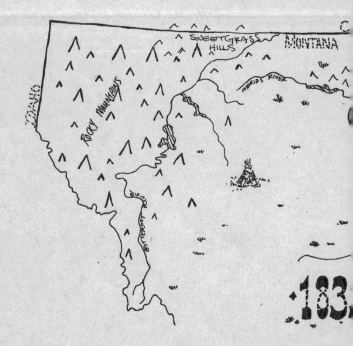

IDAHO

ROCKY MOUNTAINS

BITTEROOT R.

SWEETGRASS HILLS

MONTANA

MARIAS RIVER

·183

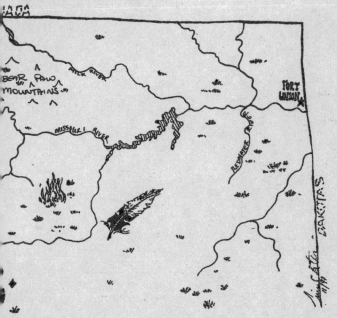

ST ◆
TERRITORY

CANADA

MILK RIVER

BEAR PAW
MOUNTAINS

FORT
LATION

MISSOURI RIVER

YELLOWTONE RIVER

DAKOTAS

Chapter 1

Northwest Territory
July, 1834

During the moon when the flowers blossom, Strikes The Bear's wife had been raped, abused and killed by the white men. Soon after, his sister had been taken to a white man's sleeping robes, supposedly in marriage, only to be discarded shortly thereafter.

It had to be these things, and these things alone, which accounted for Strikes The Bear's present behavior. No true warrior would treat a woman so badly. Not without direct provocation.

Night Thunder, hidden by many trees and bushes, sat considering, with the age-old logic which had been passed down to him since "time before mind," that Strikes The Bear had some cause for his anger. Still, this particular white woman had not caused the tragedy to Strikes The Bear's family. And Night Thunder had pledged to protect her; she was his responsibility. His to defend.

1

Night Thunder inspected the temporary warrior's camp, knowing with a sickening sensation what was to come.

The men stood in a circle around the fire, which burned ominously, its crackle and smoky, pine-scented odor offensive rather than pleasant. A drum beat steadily, slowly—a throbbing portent of what was to come. The woman had been placed in the center of the circle—fire to her back, Strikes The Bear in front. And in his hand, Strikes The Bear wielded a knife.

Voices were raised in song and in quiet murmurings, occasionally interrupted with a bellow from Strikes The Bear and a whimper from the woman.

Night Thunder observed that there were no guards posted to watch over the encampment. Either Strikes The Bear was overly certain of his safety, or the warriors, too aroused over the spectacle taking place before them, no longer cared.

Night Thunder suspected the latter and despaired.

How could he save her?

If these men had been of an enemy tribe, Night Thunder wouldn't have hesitated to act, despite the fact that they were fifteen and he was one. He would have already seized the opportunity for glory, rushing into the enemy camp and killing or being killed.

But such was not to be. These warriors were his own people, many of them his friends. True, they were *Kainah*, of the Blood tribe, while he was *Pikuni*—or as the white man called his people, the Piegan. Still, this made no difference. These warriors were Blackfeet, his relatives, his brothers. He could not fight them. Not and remain honourable to himself.

Yet he must save the woman.

How?

Custom dictated that a captured woman belonged to the one who had stolen her; that man being Strikes The Bear. It was not a law Night Thunder was willing or prepared to break.

Still, he had to do something.

He glanced at the woman now, noting in a single glance that her golden-brown hair, usually as bright and shiny as a full autumn moon, lay lackluster and disheveled around her face. Her eyes, which he knew to be as amber as those of a panther, mirrored her fear, though pride and perhaps resignation kept her silent. Her hands shook where they were tied together in front of her; her knees trembled, making her flimsy dress flutter as though it waved in a breeze.

Yet she had jutted her chin forward, had thrown back her head and had a look upon her face which could only be called defiant. And if those were tears which fell over her cheeks, she at least pretended to have no knowledge of them.

She had courage, this one. She might be young, perhaps no more than twenty winters, but Night Thunder knew very few women who would remain so stouthearted in similar circumstances. He added one more quality to his long, growing list of her attributes: her courageous spirit. Someday, he thought, she would make a man a fine wife.

Night Thunder drew his brows together in silent realization.

Wife? Was this a possible solution? If Night Thunder claimed her as his bride . . . ?

No, he couldn't.

But if he could make the others believe that he had married this woman, it would give him first rights to her. He could then save her without raising his hand against his brothers.

Could he do it? To do so would be the height of dishonesty. Surely Sun and the winds would carry the tale of his treachery into the Sand Hills, reaching the ears of his ancestors, bringing those who had gone before him great shame.

Yet the consequences if he did not act . . .

Strikes The Bear suddenly let out a growl and, gripping his knife as though prepared to use it, approached the woman.

Her scream split the air with a terrifying intensity as the knife tore through her dress, and in that instant Night Thunder ceased to wonder if and when he should act.

He would rescue her.

Now.

The Indian growled at her, striking out at her with his knife, the action plummeting Rebecca instantly and horribly into the present. As though in a dream, she'd been lost in the past. She wished she could have remained there; the present held too much pain, too much fear.

She wasn't certain how she had lived through the first few hours after her capture by these Indians, so strong had been that fear. Still, live she had.

She stared into her enemy's black-painted face,

trying to remember if she had ever seen a human being look more frightening. Nothing came to her. Nor did she register much else about the man, not even his nearly nude body. All she could focus on was his face and that knife he waved in front of her. Her stomach dropped and the scent of her own fear engulfed her. She needed no wise man to tell her what her future held.

Was this all she had left, then? Was she to join, at last, her dearly departed fiancé? Would she never see the shores of her parents' beloved homeland, Ireland? Would she die here never to have realized her dream? Would she never dance? This last thought, strangely enough, was more depressing than all the rest, even the idea of dying.

Odd, she considered, that here, before her imminent demise, she found herself bemoaning a ball she would never have, a party she would never attend. How her parents would have moaned her loss, had they been living—that their American-born daughter would not come to know her Irish heritage.

Her heart sank.

Perhaps in the hereafter, please God.

Well, if this was all that there was, then let the Indian get on with it. Taking what she speculated might be her last breath, she threw back her head, raised her chin, and voiced, "Is that the best you can do to frighten me, now?"

She knew her words were hollow, however, her bravery for naught. She would break down soon enough, more's the pity. But perhaps the Lord would let her keep her dignity, as least for a little while longer.

*   *   *

Propelling himself forward, out of the shadows, Night Thunder leaped into the *Kainah* encampment, making as much noise as he could, in order that he draw attention to himself.

"Night Thunder!"

He heard the woman scream out his name in the white man's tongue. Odd, he thought fleetingly, that her voice would sound so pleasant, even under such duress.

"Go back," she shouted at him. "There's naught you can do for me here. There are too many of them."

Night Thunder paid her little attention. He took note of Strikes The Bear, saw the man turn his head slightly. Night Thunder drew his arms together over his chest, preparing to meet the other Indian in silent battle. But all the other Indian did by way of greeting was grunt before he turned back toward the woman. He shouted, "*Omaopii*! Be quiet!" and at the same time, reached out toward her as though he might strike her.

"The devil bless you," she spat out, defiance coloring her voice, her composure, her bearing. And Night Thunder realized that though the white woman might not have understood Strikes The Bear's words, she had clearly grasped his actions.

Strikes The Bear shrieked all at once and sprang forward, slashing out at her again with his knife. Another piece of her dress fell to the ground. But the white woman held onto her pride, this time not uttering even a sound.

Night Thunder congratulated her silently for her fortitude. He cautioned himself, however, to show nothing: not admiration, not pride, not even his anger. "*Oki, nitakkaawa*, hello, my friends," he said at last to the warriors at large. Then, with what he hoped was a tinge of humor, he added, "Do we intend to start treating the white women as that man does ours?"

"*Miistapoot*, go away, my cousin." It was Strikes The Bear who spoke. "We do not wish to hear your talk if it is to say bad things about what we do."

"You think that I would say bad things about this?"

Strikes The Bear groaned slightly before he continued, "We all know how you cater to the white man, spending so much time in his forts and lodges. Many are the times when we have likened you to a dog seeking the white man's scraps. But you are alone in your regard for this woman. Most of us hate the white man for what he has done to us, to those dear to us. Look around you. Do you not see that each warrior here has suffered from the white man's crimes? We do not wish to hear your honeyed words about him."

Night Thunder listened patiently, as was the way of his people, and he paused only slightly before responding, "I come here before you with no pleasant talk for the white man on my tongue. But this woman, she is different."

"Go away. I will do as duty requires me. Can you deny that I have the right and the obligation to do to this white woman those things which were done to my wife? Is it not true that only in this way can my spirit, and my woman's, at last find peace?"

Night Thunder again paused, long enough to show respect for what Strikes The Bear had said. But after a few moments, Night Thunder began, "*Aa*, yes, my cousin has cause to speak and to do as he does, I think, and all our people weep with him in his grief." Night Thunder shifted his weight, the action giving emphasis to his next words. "But even as he scolds the white man for his ways and scorns his path, I see that my cousin adopts his customs, too. For is it not the sweet scent of the trader's nectar that I smell here in your camp? Is it not the stench of whisky on your breath that I inhale as you speak to me? I cannot help but wonder how a man can curse one part of a society while holding another dear."

Strikes The Bear howled and turned away from the woman. He took a few menacing steps toward Night Thunder before, motioning with his arms, he snarled, "*Miistapoot*! Go away!"

Night Thunder didn't flinch, nor did he raise an arm against his cousin. "I think you have had too much of the whisky, my cousin," he said. "It would be best if you slept through the night before you decided what to do with this woman."

"*Miistapoot*! I will hear none of what you say. No man can tell another man what to do."

Night Thunder nodded. "So the old men of our tribe tell us. But if you value your life and your few possessions, you will take great heed of my words."

Strikes The Bear hesitated. "You speak in riddles. Say what you mean."

"I mean that you must leave this woman alone."

These words seemed to cause Strikes The Bear

great humor, for he began to laugh, though there was little amusement in the sound of it. At last, though, Strikes The Bear said, "My cousin has taken leave of his senses, I think."

Night Thunder grinned. "Perhaps I have," he said, "or perhaps you should ensure that you learn all that you can about a woman before you decide to use her for your own purposes."

"A white woman? What value is a white woman to me? There seem to be so few of them that maybe if we kill them all, the white man will go away, since he will have no one in which to plant his seed."

This statement appeared to amuse the crowd, and Night Thunder smiled along with them. Shortly, however, he held up a hand, silencing all present as he said, "You speak with the foresight of a child, my cousin. Must I remind you of the teachings of the elders in the value of life?"

"Not a white man's life."

"Who said I speak of a white man's life?"

Strikes The Bear smirked. "Are your eyes so weak, my cousin, that you cannot see the color of this captive's skin?"

"Is your mind so cluttered," Night Thunder countered, "that you have failed to discover that she is not only white, she is *Siksika*? She is Blackfoot."

This statement stopped Strikes The Bear. And Night Thunder, quick to press his advantage said, "I hope that you are ready to give me many horses for the insult you bring to me."

With these words all sounds within the camp stopped. Everyone and everything suddenly stilled, and all attention swung to Night Thunder.

Strikes The Bear recovered before the rest. "*Miistapoot, nitakkaawa*, go away, my friend," he said, annoyed. "Your words make little sense. I have no quarrel with you. Leave here before I decide to begin one."

"You already have one."

"*Otam*, later we can talk of this."

"We talk of it now. This woman is *Siksika*, Blackfoot."

Strikes The Bear straightened up to his full height and glared at Night Thunder, a stare that would have sent lesser men scurrying away. Not only was Strikes The Bear a huge hulk of a man, resembling in size his namesake, he perpetually wore a scowl upon his face which gave him an evil cast. Most people, even the gallant men from the *Pikuni*, left him alone.

At last, the larger man spoke: "Why do you say this, my cousin?"

Night Thunder paused significantly. Then, slowly he uttered, "Because she is my wife."

Astonishment, utter and profound, filled the encampment, causing the silence to become ominous and oppressive.

"*Ohkiimaan*, wife?" Strikes The Bear spoke up, filling the void. He grinned, his smile becoming wider and wider until he laughed at length. "*Omaniit*," he said, "be truthful."

Night Thunder didn't even blink. "I am. This woman is my wife. You have brought me great insult. I expect you will have to give me many horses for what you are doing."

Strikes The Bear laughed. "*Ikkahsanii*, you joke.

We all know that Blue Raven Woman waits for you in a *Kainah* village in our homeland. Do you mean to dishonour her by taking another—a white woman—as your first wife?"

"*Saa*, no," Night Thunder answered without delay, though in truth, he desired more time to think. In his haste to save the white woman, he had forgotten about Blue Raven Woman.

"She will not be happy to learn that you have married another as your 'sits-beside-him' wife."

"She will honour our parents' wishes, as will I," Night Thunder asserted. "But we leave the point. This woman upon whom you seek to claim revenge is my wife and I assert all rights to her."

"*Saa*, no, I stole her. She is mine now to use as the whites used my wife."

Night Thunder allowed a moment to lapse before he spoke again. Then, calmly striding forward, he began, "*Aa*, yes, my cousin, it is right that you seek revenge, but would it not be better to wreak vengeance upon the men who did this terrible thing to you and your wife, than upon an innocent who knows not of it? Is it not true that if you do this thing to her, you will be making yourself into as treacherous a being as the white man? Is it this that you wish?"

Strikes The Bear screeched, then glared at Night Thunder. It was several moments before the other Indian answered, "You insult me, I think. It was *my* intention to *marry* this woman." A smile, more evil than humorous, split Strikes The Bear's face before he glanced back at the woman to say, "To have her take the place of my wife."

Night Thunder didn't flinch. "We all know that you lie."

Strikes The Bear growled.

Night Thunder ignored it and pressed on. "We all know what your intentions were before I walked into this camp. I will give you only one more chance to keep your honour before I am forced to challenge you. I am the husband of this woman. She is mine and you may not use her. Give her to me."

"*Saa*, no!" Strikes The Bear, holding up his knife, leapt before Night Thunder, and bending down at the knees, motioned Night Thunder forward. "If you want her, you must take her from me. But I warn you that if you kill me, which you will have to do in order to have her, my relatives will not rest until you, too, have departed for the Sand Hills."

Night Thunder had already bent forward, had already anticipated this fight. He said, "You are foolish, my cousin. Do you forget that your relatives are mine, too?"

That statement seemed to settle upon Strikes The Bear as no blow could have. Momentarily, Strikes The Bear straightened. "She cannot be your wife."

"She is."

"*Wai'syamattse*, prove it."

"I do not have to. My word is enough."

"*Aa*, yes, your word." Strikes The Bear's eyes gleamed with a peculiar glow. "You are quick to give your word to save this woman. A little too quick. If this be true, you should have no unwillingness to 'Swear by the Horn' that this woman is your wife."

Night Thunder stopped perfectly still, stunned. Though he had anticipated there would be punishment for any lie he told, he had not considered that Strikes The Bear might challenge him to this particular oath. Night Thunder hesitated.

To "Swear by the Horn" meant to pledge by the Honour of the Blackfoot Horn Society that what one said was truth. To lie meant certain death, and within very few moons.

Night Thunder quickly evaluated his choices. He could fight these men, but they were his brothers. It would mean killing his own kind; it might mean being killed. He could continue to lie; this, too, would incur his death and the destruction of his honour.

But wouldn't his lies also spare the woman's life . . . and that of his brothers?

Haiya, that was enough for him. Why did he hesitate?

With a spirit of loyalty and a sense of duty that would have put the most stouthearted patriot to shame, Night Thunder decided his future. "I will do it," he declared. "I will 'Swear by the Horn.' "

Strikes The Bear smirked. "Then let it be done."

Murmurings could be heard from the other Indians who had watched the entire proceedings. Preparations for the oath started, but an older, wiser man noted for his fairness and honesty broke away from the circle of warriors.

He stepped forward, pacing toward the two warriors who stood in the center of the circle. Slowly, and with what seemed great deliberation, he began, "*Saa*, no, the vow need not be done. Not here, not now." He strode up to Strikes The Bear. "We do not have all of the men from the Horn Society here that we might let our friend take this oath. All twenty-five members must be present before the oath can be clearly taken. I say our friend's willingness to do it is enough."

"*Haiya*," Strikes The Bear insisted. "I do not believe him."

The old man persisted, "It is enough."

Strikes The Bear hesitated, unwilling, as were most young Indian men, to challenge an elder's authority. He gave Night Thunder a malevolent glare, however, and continued, speaking to the crowd at large, "If she is truly his wife, surely he would not object to our demanding some proof."

"I have given you my word," Night Thunder protested. But the warriors seemed not to hear him, their murmurings supporting Strikes The Bear.

Night Thunder forced himself to appear aloof. Neither by face nor manner would he permit himself to betray his agitation. As strongly he was able, he said, "Did not all of you hear her call out to me as I entered your camp? Is that not proof enough?"

"That demonstrates nothing," spat out Strikes The Bear. "We all know that you have spent several moons within the white man's lodge. Because she knows who you are does not mean you are . . . special to her."

Though every muscle in his body tensed, Night Thunder forced himself to show no reaction.

Strikes The Bear continued, "Surely she would

not object to showing you some affection, here before us all, that we might know the truth of your words."

It took great control and strength of will for Night Thunder to keep from betraying his consternation. But after a few moments he managed to effect a smirk at his opponent before he said, "You know that she would not agree to express a fondness for me in so public a place as this. What would you have her do? Go against tradition? Both hers and ours?"

"It seems little enough to ask."

Night Thunder allowed himself no quarter as he glanced around the circle of warriors. Sweeping his arms toward all assembled, Night Thunder said, "This thing that Strikes The Bear asks is a great insult to me and to my wife. It would embarrass any woman, and a man, if she were to show her husband . . . feeling in front of so many eyes."

"*Haiya*!" Strikes The Bear glowered, speaking to all. "So there is the proof that he lies. He will not do as I ask because he knows that the woman will not come to him. By his own actions, we know that Night Thunder lies."

"*Saa*, no! Have I not already said I will 'Swear by the Horn'? Perhaps it is you who is the liar. Perhaps your intentions are not as honourable as you claim. Will you, then, also 'Swear by the Horn,' as you ask of me?"

"I do not have to. My honour is not in question."

"I say that it is."

Strikes The Bear started forward.

"*Ssikoo*! Enough!" The old man stepped between them, holding out his arms against the two men to keep them apart. "You sound as two old wives arguing over a piece of meat. Do you forget, brother," he addressed Strikes The Bear, "that our friend from the *Pikuni* has much medicine that he could wield against you? It would not be wise to go against him. I do not believe he would lie without fear of reprisal from the spirits of his ancestors. And if this woman truly is his wife, then we have committed a grave lapse in manners and we should do all we can to salvage her honour . . . and ours."

"Humph!" said Night Thunder.

"But surely you can understand Strikes The Bear's anger." The old man looked toward Night Thunder. "Not more than four moons have passed since his wife was killed. The desire for revenge burns in his heart. It is his right to seek judgment upon a white woman. The wise men say good for good and evil for evil." He paused. "But not if she is the property of Night Thunder."

Both men glared at the old man.

"There is a way to solve this. While it is true that Strikes The Bear was using this woman to seek his revenge, I believe him when he says his heart was pure and his intentions were to marry her soon after."

Night Thunder cautioned himself against objecting to what he was certain was a lie. Such an interruption would have been the height of discourtesy.

"The woman should therefore choose the man she wishes, with the warmth of her embrace. It is not too much to ask, given the circumstances." And to Night Thunder's grunt of displeasure, the old man added, "But it will be necessary only this once."

Night Thunder looked toward the woman, knowing that he might have already lost this battle. What the old man asked was little enough to request, yet too much. He could think of little reason why the woman would deem to honour him with her embrace. Perhaps this was to be his punishment, for was it not said that he who deals in lies will soon meet with all he deserves?

Night Thunder stood up to his full height. If he were to face ridicule or death because of what he had been forced to do, then he would face it bravely, with honour.

Still, he needed to tell the woman all that had transpired here, to translate for her what she was being asked to do.

Bringing to mind the language of the Long Knives or the Americans, Night Thunder began to talk to her, using gestures and sign language as he spoke. And if she denounced both him and Strikes The Bear as liars, then so be it . . .

Chapter 2

Surely Rebecca hadn't understood. Was Night Thunder asking her to kiss him? To show him a *wheen* bit of affection? Here, before all the others? Was this, then, an added insult on top of what she had been made to endure by these Indians?

She hadn't expected to look upon Night Thunder again. When she had been captured by the Indians, she had assumed Night Thunder would go back to his own people with nary a thought for her, believing as she had that the man would feel his obligation to her at end.

But she had been wrong.

Had it been only a few months previous that Night Thunder had pledged his word of honour to protect her?

"I will watch over Rebecca," he had told his friend and companion, White Eagle, *"so that your woman need not worry about her. I give you my word that so long as I breathe, Rebecca will remain safe."*

That White Eagle's woman had been the niece of a new breed of man that the Indians referred to as the Long Knives had made no difference to Night Thunder. White Eagle had needed help. Night Thunder had given it, no questions asked.

Rebecca remembered at the time being struck by the incongruity of it.

An Indian swearing his life to protect a white woman?

Yet he had.

She was suddenly glad she had spent the time necessary to ensure this man knew her language. Addressing Night Thunder, she said, "Do you want me to kiss you?"

Despite his stately demeanor, Night Thunder looked suddenly sheepish. And Rebecca could well understand why. Thus far in their relationship, Night Thunder had shown her nothing but the utmost respect, keeping a careful distance from her. Even during those times when the two of them had been alone, he had rarely spoken to her, Rebecca coming to understand that in his society, their association with one another—that of an unmarried woman with a man—would have been strictly taboo. Rebecca could only wonder at what else had been said among these Indians to cause Night Thunder to ask her for her embrace now.

"Why is it that you would be asking me this?" She put the question to him gently.

"I have told these people that you are my wife in order to save your life," he replied to her, his voice deep and strong, yet with a hint of chagrin. "They are demanding some . . . proof of our union. But I can say no more on it now. I can tell you only that you are being asked to choose one of us.

Either myself or my cousin who stands here beside me."

She glanced from one man to the other, her gaze coming back to settle upon Night Thunder. She held out her wrists. "If someone would untie me?" The old man stepped forward, the knife in his hand, cutting the rawhide bonds.

Several pairs of eyes watched her as she paced toward Night Thunder. She glanced up at him warily and raised her eyes to his. "Could you help me with this . . . kiss, now?"

She glimpsed no emotion on the man's countenance before he said, "This is a thing you must do on your own. I can only tell you what you have to do. You must choose either myself or my cousin."

"With all these people here watching?"

"It cannot be helped."

"And will this act truly make us man and wife within the eyes of your people?"

An embarrassed, almost bashful look stole over Night Thunder's face, though his voice was strong as he said, "Only if we consummate the union as a man and a woman who are truly married are bound to do."

She was certain her face filled with colour. She stammered, "And . . . and must we do this in front of . . . ?" Her hand swept out in front of her.

"No, just one kiss should be all that is required."

She sighed. "It is little enough that you ask in exchange for my life."

With this said, she came right up to Night Thunder and put her hand on his shoulder, reaching up on her toes to place a kiss on his cheek.

As soon as he received the kiss, Night Thunder stepped immediately back from her, and in his own language, said something to the others.

Chuckles were heard from around the circle surrounding them, and after some moments, Night Thunder said to her, "They say a kiss on the cheek is little enough proof."

She paused. "Then let them deny this," and she threw herself into Night Thunder's arms, placing her lips against his.

When her lips met Night Thunder's, something unexpectedly stirred to life within her. What was it? A warmth. Aye, surely, and yet more.

She felt her blood surge with newfound exhilaration. It made her want to curl in closer toward him, though she curbed the inclination to do so.

The faint scent of him engulfed her and she found it pleasing. He smelled of grass and smoke and prairie, yet more. . . . There was another, almost indefinable aroma about him, too, something very male, and very arousing.

And there was an almost soft texture to his skin, his lips. She wondered, how would the rest of his skin feel beneath her fingertips? She brought her hand up to trail her fingers down his arm, only half aware of what she did.

He moaned in response and his reaction, far from causing her to reevaluate her actions, made her lean in closer.

His lips were full upon hers, making her feel warm, protected. Making her aware of her femininity. She became conscious of her breasts pushing forward against her dress, suddenly sensitized, and that area of her body most private to her began to ache, as though that part of her had awakened to life, too. The whole effect caused her to utter a soft sound, deep in her throat.

Rebecca heard another groan from Night Thunder and then all at once his arms came around her, pulling her in so closely to him that she could feel the evidence of his masculinity against her belly.

She could barely think.

For the past two months, she had grown accustomed to the company of this man as he had watched over her, guarding her. She had observed him within this time, had become used to the look of him, the sound of his voice, his quiet humor. She had even come to admit a fair amount of respect for him.

But this? What was happening here between them was more than mere respect. This was . . . well, it was . . . *sexual.*

Ah, yes. Pure and simple. This kiss was communicating more than words could have, that she might . . . fancy him . . . and he her.

Had he felt this pull all these months? Had she? Surely not. Or were they both only realizing this now?

She barely heard the footfalls of the other men in the camp, as they moved away, uttering words she didn't understand. She was only aware of this one man whose arms held her securely, whose touch roamed even now up and down her spine, causing her to shiver.

Someone spoke from beside them, jarring Night Thunder's sensual exploration.

"Soka'piiwa," someone said. What did that mean?

His arms fell from around her, and she lowered her head, looking down at the ground. Without his arms around her, Rebecca felt suddenly embarrassed. She had meant to give him only a chaste little kiss. It should have been a simple affair. Yet the kiss they had just shared was anything but modest.

What did one say to a man who had affected her in such an unusual way? How did one act?

"Come," said Night Thunder, taking hold of her arm and causing a tingling up and down that arm where he touched it. "The others are convinced of our union and are erecting a *niitoyis*, a camp lodge, for us. It seems we are to be left alone for the night."

"A-alone?" A part of her gladdened at the idea of having no one else around her but this man; another wiser, more subdued part of her despaired.

"*Aa*, yes," he said. "Alone. But do not worry. I will not violate you, if it is that which concerns you. In the morning, I will take you back to the fort, as I should, and you will be no worse for your adventure here tonight."

"Aye," she acknowledged, nodding, "that is good." Although she wondered if, having experienced a kiss such as the one they had shared, things would ever be quite the same between them again.

She let Night Thunder lead her toward the outer circle of the camp, where, as he had promised, a lodge had been hastily constructed. She hesitated and Night Thunder stopped, turned around, and gazed at her. "If you take me back in the morning, won't the others in your camp begin to think that perhaps you lied to them? What will happen then?"

He shrugged as though the thought of such things were beneath him. Yet in his haunted eyes she glimpsed a hint that perhaps his true feelings were quite different.

"The others will find out, in due time," he said, "that all I have spoken of this night is not true. Then I must face what I must. But that time is distant from now. Now I must get you to safety. When that is done, I will seek to confront the wrath of my ancestors over what I have said and done this night."

"I see," she said, although she didn't, not at all. Ancestors? Did he mean dead people passing judgment, seeking revenge on the living? Had she heard him correctly? What strange manner of beliefs were these?

With any other man, she might have thought he'd gone daft to say such things. But not with Night Thunder. There was nothing about this man to suggest even a hint of weakness: in body, in spirit, or in mind. And so, she figured, if he believed such things, he must have good reason.

They had reached the tepee and Night Thunder pulled back the rawhide flap, entering the structure before her. And with little urging, she followed his example.

Since the tepee had been put together in a hurry, twigs and leaves still cluttered the floor and the tepee covering didn't quite fit with the lodge poles. Yet someone had set a fire to burning in the center, scattering a few robes across the ground, too.

Had this been done by the same men who had only moments ago been ready to destroy her? She was struck by the incongruity of it.

She glanced up at Night Thunder, who motioned her toward him.

"The fire throws shadows onto the tepee, illuminating our figures upon it," he told her. "Come, let me hold you, while the others might still be watching. Then we will put out this fire, or at least reduce it to embers, so that we can sleep in separate sleeping robes without the entire camp knowing what we do."

Rebecca rubbed her hands over her arms. She took a few steps toward him.

"Are you cold?"

She nodded.

He drew her into his arms. "Let me warm you," he said, and proceeded to run his hands up and down her arms, down over her spine.

It felt good. *He* felt good, and she trembled, but whether from cold, reaction to him, or the whole ordeal this evening, she couldn't be certain.

"You have been through much this night," he said, seemingly reading her thoughts. "Come," he said and sat down with her, still holding her in his arms.

It felt so natural, so right, to be held just like this by him. He ran his hands over her back, her arms, even her legs, through the layers of her skirt. But rather than his action being sexual, his touch felt soothing, and she relaxed. She lay her head against his chest and closed her eyes, not fully realizing until this moment how tired she was.

She opened her mouth to whisper a word of thanks for all he had done for her, for all he *was* doing for her, but the words never passed her lips. And the last thing she remembered was the strange melody of a song he sang as she drifted off to sleep.

Chapter 3

Night Thunder held her, even as she slept.

She felt so right in his arms, but how this could be he did not know. She was not truly right for him, could never be right for him. Still . . .

He glanced down at the young woman whom he knew by the name of Rebecca. Her golden-brown hair, as it spilled over his arm, felt soft and supple as she lay against him. Long eyelashes shadowed her cheeks, which were now blushed with the flush of warmth. Her face more resembled a heart than a circle—the Blackfoot beauty standard—and her lips were slightly thinner than those of the women of his tribe. Even so, her lips were parted slightly, beckoning him to savor again the exotic taste of her. Night Thunder felt himself shudder.

Looking away from her, he sighed. He did not need this complication in his life; nor, he expected, did she. It would be his responsibility, also, to put their relationship back to where it should be.

She moved slightly in his arms, sighing deeply

in her sleep, and unwillingly, Night Thunder returned his attention to her.

Her bone structure was small, delicate, and more slight than that of the women in his tribe, and he wondered how she would fare if she ever spent a winter in this place. The color of her skin was several shades lighter than his own, and it called to mind his first impression of the white man.

He had at first thought the white man, so unusually pale, a ghost; but as he had grown to realize that this person was flesh and blood, not an apparition, he had decided that the race as a whole appeared lackluster and sickish. More contact had made him develop, of course, accustomed to their look.

He had also pondered the lack of white women in this country, having seen only three in his entire life.

But this woman, the one in his arms—this woman was beautiful by anyone's standards, no matter their race.

Unusually pleasant, her sweet scent wafted up to his nostrils and he inhaled sharply, his body responding to her all out of his control.

That she was desirable was more than apparent. If he were to be completely honest with himself, he would have to admit to being attracted to her from his very first sight of her, white woman or not.

Yet in all the time that he had watched over her, guarding her within the white man's fort, he had not once compromised her honour, nor his.

Nor would he have ever done so now, if it hadn't been for . . .

He inhaled another quick breath.

Tomorrow he would return her to her own people, without arousing the suspicion of Strikes The Bear.

He had better forget about her, about that kiss. He had also better get some sleep so that his mind would not be cluttered on the morrow.

Laying Rebecca gently on the ground atop the bed robes, he paused for only a moment to look down at her before crawling to his own place within the tepee.

Settling down, he looked up toward the lodge poles where they met at the top of the tepee, the familiarity of the structure and the stars overhead setting his mind at ease.

He wondered for a moment at the spirits who had forced him to make a choice between two different sets of honour. No matter which path he had chosen this night, he would have lost his integrity.

He had long been of the opinion that nothing happened without purpose and he wondered briefly if *Napi*, if Old Man, were playing tricks on him.

It was the last thought he had before he drifted off to a fretful sleep.

Rebecca awoke to the sound of splashing.

Startled, she sent a quick glance across the embers of the fire, toward Night Thunder. He lay facing her, his gaze touching her softly.

"The warriors bathe before they go to hunt," he

explained quietly. "It is necessary to wash away the man scent each morning, if one wishes to be a successful provider for his family. It is why I believe the white man to be a bad hunter. An animal can smell him long before the white man spies the animal." He paused for a moment. "Tell me, why does the white man not bathe?"

She almost choked, so great was her surprise. How did one answer such a question? And what had prompted it? Prejudice? Surely not. At last she pulled herself together and answered, her voice barely over a whisper, "I reckon that the white man finds it unnecessary to bathe," she said. "Many people believe that bathing can cause a man to catch his death of cold."

Night Thunder laughed softly and shifted so that he lay on his back, arms folded behind his head. "Since before I had memories, or in the words of the white man, before the age of three, I have taken a bath in the stream each morning. It did not matter if the weather were warm or a blizzard. And never once have I caught a cold or known a man who has. Do you make a joke?"

"No."

Night Thunder continued to look amused. "I think the white man makes an excuse to remain dirty."

Rebecca grimaced. She'd never given much thought to bathing, but in light of Night Thunder's viewpoint, she could see why the Indian might see the white man as being a bit odd . . . and smelly. "Perhaps," she said, "you are right."

"Perhaps."

A long moment of silence passed. At last, however, Rebecca asked, "Night Thunder?"

She glanced over to him when she didn't hear a response. He still lay unmoving, hands behind his head, his gaze upward, toward the tepee poles.

"Night Thunder," she began again, "will it look bad for you now if you are in here with me, not out there with them, bathing, too?"

He grunted. "No one will expect me to do anything this morning. It would appear strange if I joined the others, rather than staying here with my . . . wife."

"Oh." It was all she said for quite a few moments. Then, "Night Thunder, why did you tell them I was your . . . wife in order to save me? Was there no other way?"

Night Thunder heaved a great sigh. When he spoke, he said his words slowly, as though brooding over each one. "I have many relatives in this camp. I could not fight them in order to protect you. And yet I had made a vow to do so. Within my camp, a slave belongs to the one who captured her; it is a law that I cannot break. But as I sat on the edge of camp last night, I realized if I claimed you as my wife, you would belong to me. In this way I could save you."

"I see," she said. "And did you tell true? Do you intend to . . . marry me?

"*Saa*, no."

Rebecca didn't know why his answer offended her. It was the response she had known she would receive; the one she herself wanted. Yet . . . "What kind of trouble will you bring to yourself, now, for the tales that you have told? I know there will be some."

Again he sighed and a long pause followed her question. At last, he replied, "There will come a day when I will have to confront the others in my village, and my ancestors, with what I have said, what I have done."

A strained silence followed his words. Rebecca sat worrying. Not about herself, but about a man— an Indian—who had abandoned his own honour to save her. She asked, "And what will happen to you, then?"

He looked over toward her, his glance sullen, though he said nothing.

"What?" she prompted.

He cut a glance to the lodge poles above him before he replied at last, "Why concern yourself about me when it is you who is in danger?"

"I . . . I can't help but have a wheen bit of worry about you. I . . . I have known you for several months, and I . . . well . . . you came to my defense."

"That is not the same."

"How is it different?"

"*I* am a man. I am expected to risk my life for the good of the tribe, for honour. But you, you are woman. What would happen to a tribe if a woman were to risk her life as must a man?"

She didn't answer all at once. At length, she voiced, "So you admit that you are risking your life for me, now?"

"Talk too much," he said. "Better a woman remains quiet."

Rebecca almost laughed. "If you will be bringing trouble upon yourself, why don't you marry me and make it a truth? After returning me to the fort, you could always say that my heart was low at the thought of leaving my own people. And this caused me to stay behind."

His eyes sought out hers across the fire's dying embers. She met his gaze and neither one said a word for several moments. Then he asked, "Would you be willing to give your body to me in that way?"

She coughed. "Give my body to you? As in when a man and woman . . . when they . . ."

He nodded.

And she gulped. "Performing a marriage ceremony is what I'm talking about, not—"

"To the Blackfeet," he interrupted, "there is only one way that a man and woman become truly married. They become united only after they are . . . joined in the flesh."

She gasped. "Oh," she said, catching her breath yet again. "I did not mean to be so bold as to—"

"I did not think so." He grinned at her before he shifted his position, his gaze once more becoming centered upon the lodge poles.

A new sort of tension stretched out between them, causing the silence in the lodge to become more pronounced.

At last she asked, "What will we do, then?"

He shrugged. "As I had intended. I will keep my promise to you and my friend. I will return you to the fort where you belong, and I will confront the lies that I have told this day in my own way. I knew the consequences of what I did."

"But—"

"It is not your concern. Perhaps you should get more sleep."

She became silent for so long, he wondered if she might have decided to go back to sleep. But then she said, "Thank you."

As they gazed at one another, she thought she glimpsed a particular warmth, there within the deep set of his eyes. Idly she wondered if there were an answering fervor within her own. She took a deep breath and asked a little too quickly, "When will it be proper for us to arise and start on our way back to the fort?"

He held her gaze for a little longer, his dark eyes sharp and assessing as they met hers, before he answered. "The others will prepare a feast for us. They will want to honour our marriage and will try to make you think more favorably toward them, especially because of what they tried to do to you. It would bring them dishonour if we were to leave before they are given a chance to make amends to you."

"It would? They would do that?"

"*Aa*, yes," he said. "It is the way of things. If one has harmed another, it is only right that he bring him gifts to try to make up for the damage he has done. And so my friends must do to you, or incur the wrath of my family. It is something none of them wants."

"They would not want to do something to anger your family?"

"*Saa*, no."

"Then your family must be . . . powerful?"

He shrugged. "There is much . . . medicine

which runs in my family. No one wants that power turned against them."

"Medicine? Power? Talking about magic, are you?"

"Magic?" he snorted. "What do you mean by magic?"

"I don't know," she said. "Tricks of the eye. Tricks to make a body believe that somethin' unusual, somethin' one doesn't see everyday, has occurred."

"Humph," he said. "Tricks? *Saa*, no. Within my family runs the ability to sense things that will happen in the future, to predict the weather, to heal the sick. These are no tricks." He snickered. "Leave it to the white man to believe that all things he cannot see with the eye are magic."

She drew in her breath. What was this? More prejudice? Rebecca felt taken aback. She had often heard the traders and others call the Indians as a whole a bunch of savages, rotten scoundrels, and many other, worse things. But not until now had she given such degrading statements any serious thought. Nor had it occurred to her that the Indian might also hold the white man in disregard. And although she longed to hear more about this . . . medicine of which he spoke, she held her tongue.

Silence reigned between them until at last Rebecca said, "To answer your earlier question, the white man does not bathe everyday, to tell God's truth, because he does not depend on the hunt for his food."

Night Thunder sent a glance in her direction. "He does not?"

Rebecca shook her head. "Pens his animals up,

he does, so that when the winter does come, there will be food."

"*Aa*, yes." It appeared to her that Night Thunder almost grinned. "That explains it."

Once again, silence stretched out between them. After a short while, however, she could stand the quiet no more.

With a deep breath, she asked, "Do you regret now the day that you gave your promise to your friend, saying to him that you would keep me safe until he and my mistress, Katrina, returned?"

"*Saa*, no," Night Thunder replied at once, rolling over and turning toward her, propping his head up on his hand. That this action pulled the covering of buffalo robe down toward his waist appeared to cause him no concern, if he even noticed. He asked, "Why would you think such a thing of me? Have I done something to give you reason to believe this?"

"No," she was quick to respond. "But I have brought trouble upon you." She sent a glance toward him. His chest lay bare and exposed to her view. And she *did* look.

A cascade of shock waves flew over her, shaking her reserve, and she almost groaned. She drew her own covering more fully around her, as though in defense.

But in truth, he appeared oblivious to her. She admired him for that discretion, and yet there was also within her a desire to make him notice her—really *notice* her as a woman.

She looked at him and gulped, drawing her blanket of buffalo robe even more fully toward her neck, ashamed that she would have such thoughts.

She said, "Truly, you have done nothing wrong. It is only that I am afeard of all the inconvenience that I have caused to you."

"Humph," he grunted. "It cannot to be helped. It is the way of things. Perhaps we should both get some more sleep."

"Yes," she said, "perhaps."

But neither one did. Though they both lay back down, each one seemed restless.

At last, Night Thunder was the one to break the silence. He said, a hint of intimacy in his voice, "I will never forget the first time that I saw you. Do you remember it?"

She hesitated. "Aye." she sent him a startled glance. "You won't?"

"*Saa*, no. It had been the night of the dance within my camp, as my people were crowded around that white man's fort where you and your friend were staying. We had finished a good trade with the white man that day and were celebrating with many dances."

"Aye," responded Rebecca, "my mistress, Katrina, had gone to your camp to speak with your friend, White Eagle. And I had followed her, afeard for her."

"You looked as scared as a jackrabbit that night."

"Did I?"

He nodded. "And I felt like a wolf on the hunt."

Rebecca chuckled, just a little. "A wolf?"

"*Aa*, yes. Do you not remember that I gave you the feather from my hair?"

"Aye," she said, "and I also recall that by doing so, you made me dance that dance . . ."

"Of the Sioux, *Sina-paskan*. It is a good dance, do you not think so?"

Again she gave a small laugh. "Aye, it is that, now. But neither Katrina nor I knew that it was a kiss you and your friend White Eagle would be wanting from us."

"See now why I felt much as a wolf that night?"

She grinned. "I do. But I gave you only a quick peck and ran quickly away. You must have thought I was a silly girl."

"*Saa*, no." He shifted his head to glance toward her. "I did not."

She drew a deep breath and made her gaze meet his. "What had you been thinking of me, then?"

He didn't answer for quite a while. If anything, his expression grew more serious, and he continued to look at her, his eyes darkening with a disturbing emotion.

"It is not important what I thought then."

"I think that it is."

"Do you?" he countered. "And what was your impression of me that first night?"

"I..." she hesitated. She couldn't very well tell him that at that time, she had thought him unusually handsome. What would he think of her? "I ... I thought that you were ... Indian."

He laughed. "We should get a little more sleep," he said, "before my brothers from the Blood tribe return with presents for us. We will need our wits about us, I think."

He turned over, his buffalo hide covering slipping farther down, admitting to her perusal the smooth length of his bare back.

A shudder fell over her spine at the sight of all

that handsome flesh and she gulped, the sound of it seeming loud against the silence.

"Aye," agreed Rebecca. "I believe you are correct." And she, too, turned her back on him.

But she couldn't help wondering. What *had* he thought of her?

She didn't know why, but she felt it important that she know. She would ask him again when they awakened, she decided. And this time, she wouldn't be put off by him directing the same question to her.

This she promised herself.

Chapter 4

A scratch on the tepee flap awakened them.

"*Ikkamssit*," Night Thunder's word had barely been over a whisper as he spoke to Rebecca, "be quick." He motioned her over toward him, telling her with gestures to lie next to him beneath his sleeping robe.

She didn't hesitate, either, and she hurriedly scooted toward him, more afeard of what would happen if she didn't than if she did.

"*Piit*," he called out, no sooner than she had settled herself down beside him. "Enter."

She pulled the robe over her head and kept it there, as Night Thunder spoke to whomever had entered their lodge.

She listened to the foreign conversation, comforted by the fact that the voice of the visitor did not belong to her previous captor.

She began to relax. Night Thunder, however, sat up, the robe falling down around his waist, barely enough to cover that part of him which declared him male. And Rebecca instantly became aware of one startling fact. Night Thunder sat beside her, naked. Utterly, completely naked.

She tried to look elsewhere, to think of something besides him.

She couldn't.

And despite there being little light beneath the robe, despite her inability to see as well as she might, there were some things one simply couldn't ignore. The sight of him surrounded her; the musky scent of him teased her. He smelled good . . . alluring.

She drew a deep breath, but instead of the action calming her, his scent tantalized her and she felt her stomach turn over.

But it wasn't pain she felt. It was . . . what? Excitement? No, it couldn't be. Yet . . .

She spun onto her stomach and turned her head away, any concern she had for their guest, what he might think of what she did, evaporating in her effort to hold onto her reserve.

She heard a chuckle, more foreign words, then the sound of the tepee flap opening and closing.

A quiet moment passed. Another.

"Come out now."

What was it she heard in his voice? Humor?

Still, she didn't move.

"Do you like it beneath there?"

What could she say? Rebecca had never felt more embarrassed in her life. Not only had she witnessed a naked man, she had responded to the sight of him as though she might like him to hold her.

She held her breath and without budging, without in the least moving her head, replied, "Why did you not tell me that you were naked?"

He paused and when he spoke, he said the words slowly, as though he were picking each one carefully, "There was not time. Besides, how else would you have me sleep?"

"In night clothing."

Night Thunder gave a short laugh. "Night clothing? What is this night clothing? Do you expect to make me believe that the white man wears clothing in which to sleep?"

"Aye."

Another chuckle. "Isn't is enough that the white man hides his body from Sun during the day? Does he also cower from Old Woman, the moon, at night?"

"Cowering has nothing to do with it. It would be only proper, I'm thinking, that since I am also within this lodge, you would sleep with some sort of clothing to cover yourself."

He gave her a low grunt that sounded more like disdain than acknowledgement. He said, "Sleeping in clothing is not something that I have known any of the men in our tribe to do. Why would you expect it of me?"

"Out of deference to me. Out of modesty."

"Humph!" She felt him scoot further under the sleeping robe. Scowling, she at last felt safe in turning her head toward him, and as she glanced at him, he gave her a lopsided grin. He said, "Sleep you in your clothes?"

"Of course."

"Do you not realize that they might smell bad and will look bad when you arise? Do you care?"

"Of course I care. But I couldn't take them off

. . . not here with you. I wouldn't . . . I only have this one dress to wear, now."

"Then do you not think you should take better care of it?"

She drew in a shocked breath. "I would not sleep unclothed."

He turned over onto his back, a smile upon his face. "That is your choice, then." He paused for a moment while he appeared to be thinking. After a time he said, "I would rather save my dignity for when I am around the others. What does it matter, after all? We are not sleeping within the same robes."

"Am I not here right now?"

He chuckled before he sat up, and throwing the robe off, stood to his feet. "Come, it is time to arise. The others have prepared a feast for us. Ceremony and dignity are a great part of the customs of my people. It would not be right if we do not join them and appreciate all they have done for us."

Rebecca knew she shouldn't be looking at him. She knew it was a sinful thing to do. Yet she couldn't help herself. How could she ignore all that hard flesh and masculinity? Especially when it was the sort of thing she had never had the chance to glimpse?

Well, she couldn't.

Not when the way he stood emphasized the strength of his legs, she realized, as her gaze roamed upward toward his thighs. The powerful muscles she spied there seemed to accentuate his buttocks, and how male he looked in front . . .

She inwardly groaned at what she was doing, what she was seeing, at that part of his body she was now scrutinizing. But she didn't glance away.

He reached down to pick up an article of clothing and her gaze followed him. His hands were brown, she noted, firm and strong, although his skin appeared to be smooth rather than rough-edged. His fingers were long, his nails seemingly white against the darker shade of his skin. Without being able to stop herself, she remembered how those hands had felt against her last night as they had massaged her, his touch soothing her, sending her to sleep.

But she certainly wasn't feeling sleepy now.

He drew on his breechcloth and she knew that this action should have ended her perusal of his body. It didn't, however.

He stood before her, handsome beyond belief, and her gaze went to his bare chest ... his well-muscled and powerful bare chest. ... She wondered what those muscles would feel like beneath her touch, what would be the texture of his skin? Hard and tough, or soft? She felt her fingers itch, as though if she didn't control them, they would reach out and discover all that luxury themselves.

She did control herself nonetheless, and she drew her hands together in front of her, almost wishing they were tied.

She wasn't finished with her inspection, however.

Long, straight black hair fell down over his shoulders almost to his waist, reminding her that this was no civilized man. The top of it was tied back with a strip of buckskin which gave him an incredibly handsome appeal. His face had been browned by the sun, his lips full, his cheekbones high, his face almost a perfect oval, his nose long and straight. He would have been considered handsome in anyone's culture, she came to realize, even if he did wear earrings: round shell-like earrings.

But the jewelry detracted not the least from his masculine appeal. He was a warrior, proud and dangerous looking. And she was certain that there was not a white man alive who would want to meet this red man upon the trail, unless it was in friendship.

It was then that her eyes met his, dark brown— almost black and—they were watching her.

She hurriedly gazed away, embarrassed. He clearly had seen her scrutinizing him. What must he think of her?

How could she have been so bold?

Yet he said nothing, nor did he appear amused by her overt appraisal.

"Are you ready to leave the lodge?" he asked, and she breathed a sigh of relief. For a moment Rebecca was glad that this man was not of the civilized world, that instead of calling attention to her brazenness, he seemed willing to gloss over what could only be a temporary departure from manners.

"I . . ." she glanced down at the wrinkles in her dress, trying to remember a time when she had gone before others looking as mussed as she did now. She could not recall any such experience. Perhaps there was something to be said for not sleeping in one's clothing. Still, it couldn't be helped now. She said, "I suppose that I am." She rose to her feet.

If he were truly embarrassed by her tousled look, he displayed no such reaction. He said, "Follow me and keep close. You do not have to say anything, but . . . you might smile a little. The others may expect to see you showing a little happiness after our night together."

She nodded, and he threw open the flap of the tepee and stepped outside. Rebecca had no choice but to follow.

The cool breeze of the morning greeted her as she stepped outside the tepee lodge. She inhaled quickly, the air heavy with the scent of smoke, of meat roasting, of pine trees and prairie grass. It smelled freshly sweet, clear and bracing. The invigorating scent even seemed to give her courage and she squared back her shoulders.

The earth felt solid beneath her footfalls as she trailed after Night Thunder, the grass soft for being so dry. She looked around quickly, taking note of her surroundings, something she hadn't really done last night.

Above her and to the east, deep colors of pink, red, and blue spread out low to the horizon. To the west, snow-capped mountains rose dark and purple in the distance, their peaks a sharp contrast to the silver of an early morning sky. The spot where they had camped was sheltered in a grove of pine trees and cottonwoods, their tops looming over her. Ahead of her, Night Thunder strode forward to meet his comrades, his stride sure, unhesitant, as though he were every day in the habit of facing danger.

Perhaps he was.

She followed him at a more sedate distance. There was something unnerving about being the only woman in a camp full of warriors who had been on the warpath, even when those men no longer exhibited antagonism toward her.

There was no drumming in the camp this morning, though from somewhere not too distant, a low baritone voice sang an unusual melody, the rhythm of the words seeming to keep step with Night Thunder's movements.

Night Thunder joined his people; she held back, not able to force herself to go in among them. To tell God's truth, she suddenly wished, quite fervently, that she could shrink to perhaps a few inches tall, simply to disappear.

But such was not to be. Night Thunder had glanced back at her, motioning her to join him.

She gulped and forced herself to take one prolonged step after the other. Never had she known her footfalls could be so painfully sluggish. Even so, she wished she could move even slower. A warm wind suddenly swept into the camp, coming up from behind her, as though it, too, were conspiring against her, shoving her forward.

"*Oki*, come on," Night Thunder said, motioning to her. "There is no one here that intends you any further harm," he told her in English.

Wasn't there? She wasn't sure.

Still, somehow she made herself move, if only because Night Thunder expected her to. Never could she remember having to place her fate, her very life, into the hands of another being;

never could she remember feeling more apprehensive.

She came up beside Night Thunder and he looked down at her. Suddenly he smiled. It was all he did; he didn't place his arm around her, or hug her to him, as one might have expected him to if he were to instill her with confidence. But somehow his smile seemed enough.

She gave him back a shaky grin, then quickly gazed down at the ground again.

"*Nit-ik-oht-yaahs-i'taki k-ikkaa o'too-hs-yi.*" It was an older voice speaking, and Rebecca glanced up to see the aged man from last night staring at her, smiling.

"He tells you that he is glad you have arrived," Night Thunder translated.

Rebecca nodded, and in a quiet voice, she said, "Tell him thank you."

"*Iniiyi'taki*," Night Thunder said.

"*Ikimopii*," the older man said to her, gesturing toward her, making motions to have her sit.

"He asks you to have a seat of honour," again Night Thunder translated.

"Where?" Rebecca asked. "Here?"

Night Thunder nodded. "*Aa*, yes, sit here."

Rebecca sat down, placing her knees to the side as she came to the ground.

Night Thunder squatted down beside her. "You did that well," he said. "In our camp, the women sit with their knees placed, as you have done, while a man sits thusly." He gestured toward himself where he sat, typically cross-legged.

At any other time, Rebecca would have responded to a compliment such as this one with a smile. But she was too nervous; it was all she could do not to shake.

Food was taken from the fire and passed to each warrior, then to her last. She didn't care. She was too anxious to eat, too overwrought to feel hunger, though it had been almost a fortnight since she had last eaten. Perhaps longer.

"*Oowat*," said Night Thunder, "eat."

"I can't," she whispered.

"You must," he said. "It would be considered an insult if you did not, after the warriors have gone to much trouble to bring it to you, and it might cause bad feelings."

"Please, I . . . I don't think that I can."

"*Aa*, yes, you can."

She swallowed, the sound loud even to her ears. Somehow, though, she found the courage to lift her head and glance around at the circle of men. Although no one watched her impolitely, she knew instinctively that all here were aware of her every movement.

She picked up a piece of meat. "What is this?" she asked Night Thunder.

"It is buffalo. Our warriors searched long this morning until they came upon a calf and his mother, I am told. You are being honoured."

"Aye," she said, "so you have said to me."

"Do you doubt it?"

"Please understand, Night Thunder, I cannot help it."

A long pause followed her statement, Night Thunder apparently lost in thought.

At length, however, after some deliberation, he said, "Know that so long as I live, so long as I draw breath upon our mother the earth, no one here will harm you."

She glanced at him quickly, but not fast enough. He had already turned his head away so that all she caught was a fleeting impression of what had been there in his eyes. She found herself staring at the man's profile instead: strong, proud, his chin thrust slightly forward. She found him magnificent. He might be Indian, he might be someone she would never have thought a hero only a few weeks ago, but no mistake, this man emanated valour. Had he always? And if he had, how had it escaped her notice until now?

She reached out a hand to touch his arm, a gentle, soft caress. She knew to do so probably went against some Indian etiquette she had little knowledge of, but she couldn't help herself.

She saw his body go rigid, felt the muscles of his arm stiffen, yet he made no attempt to remove her hand. In truth, what he did startled her all the more.

Turning his head slightly, staring down at her, he slowly brought up his own hand to cover hers, his action silently sealing a pact between them.

He had once given a friend his word of honour to watch over her. It was clear he would not renege on that promise. She gulped. The very decency of such an action, the strength he radiated, left her wondering if she had ever known anyone with such qualities.

She didn't think so.

His integrity, the fortitude of his character, touched her beyond all thinking. And she felt tears well up behind her eyes. He instilled her with courage, this man.

She brought her gaze up once more, her look sweeping around the camp circle, and again, though no eyes were watching her, an air of expectancy hung over the men.

Would it hurt her to eat this meat, a sort of peace offering?

All of a sudden it struck her. These men were trying to show her in their own way that though they might have erred, they were sorry.

Their actions touched her. Most men of her acquaintance, even knowing they had lapsed from good conduct, would defend themselves as though they were beyond reproach. But not these men.

Which took the greater strength of will? To defend oneself, even when one was fully aware of having done wrong? Or, so knowing, to try to make things right? Which was the more civilized action?

She knew which it was and she felt almost numb with the knowledge. These people were supposed to be the savage ones. Hadn't she heard that and been told that more times than she cared to think?

It was not a correct impression, however, she became suddenly aware. It was not correct at all.

It might appear silly, perhaps, but eating this piece of meat would symbolize her acceptance of their efforts to appease her. Was it too much to ask?

She sighed. It was difficult to acknowledge the

integrity of these people after all that had happened to her.

She inhaled deeply once again and looked at the meat in her hand, which appeared as appetizing as a piece of shoe leather. Still, she put the food in her mouth, her own pride taking a steep blow as she did so.

She chewed, slowly at first, but then, as her stomach seemed to come alive, she ate with more vigor.

"Hmmm," she said after a while, having taken several bites. "This is good." And tentatively, shyly, she gave the party at large a brief smile, before glancing once again toward the ground. It was the best she could do.

Almost at once, she could feel the anxiety of the crowd begin to dissipate. And slowly a murmur of voices could be heard within the group as those around her relaxed.

It had been a hard thing to do, to begin to eat a meal with these people. But now that she had done it, she felt better for it.

At least, if they had been sorry, she had been forgiving.

Perhaps these people were not the villains she'd been told. Yet if they were not, why had they treated her so poorly at first? Did they have a good reason? She would have to ask Night Thunder about it as soon as she was able.

"*Aàkahkayo'pa.*" The older gentleman from the previous evening spoke to Night Thunder.

Night Thunder nodded.

"*Aakitapaoo'pa ookoowa kiistowaawa,*" the old man said.

It was more a feeling than anything that caused her to become alert. Though he exhibited nothing outwardly to indicate he was uncomfortable, she was certain she sensed that something had been said to upset Night Thunder.

So she asked, "What did he say?"

Night Thunder didn't answer her. Instead he said to the elderly man, "*Nitsawaahkayi.*"

"*Saa?*"

"*Saa.*"

"*Maak?*"

It was Night Thunder's turn to respond, yet he remained silent.

"What are you talking about?" Rebecca whispered.

It took a moment, but at length Night Thunder answered, "He asks me if I had intended taking you to my village."

"And you said?"

"No."

"And?"

"He asks me now why it is not my intention to take you to my home, to my people."

Rebecca caught her breath in a long, drawn-out hiss.

Night Thunder continued, speaking to the old man, "*Nit-aakita-poohpi-nnaan nitaakii miistsoyis.*"

The other man shook his head. "*Maak-saw-wa: hkayi sstaa-waatsiksi? Akaawayami'takiwa?*"

"*Saa.*"

"*Maak?*"

"Night Thunder, what is it the both of you are saying?"

"He asks if you will not go home with me because you have taken too much offense at what was done to you."

"Well, he does have a point, does he not?"

"If that is so, my brothers here will not leave until they feel their obligation to you is at an end."

Rebecca gasped. "They won't? What can I do?"

"I do not know. I am thinking."

All at once the huge man who had first captured her leaped to his feet. And despite the fact that he had washed the paint from his face, the warrior still frightened Rebecca. He appeared contorted with rage, and it seemed all he could do to hold himself back, his body trembling with unexpressed rancor.

The elder of the tribe finally recognized him to speak.

"*Saayi-wa!*" the dangerous man yelled, his tone harsh, his words clipped.

"Night Thunder, what did he say?"

Night Thunder said nothing, not to her, nor to his challenger, though her hero rose to his feet.

At length, Night Thunder answered her, "He thinks the reason you won't go to my home is because I lied."

"No!" Rebecca, too, sprung to her feet.

"*Aaksikamotaahpihkaapitsiiywa!*" The big man fairly spat the words.

"*Saa!*" This from Night Thunder.

"*Iikamotaahpihkaapitsiiyiwa!*"

"What does he say?"

"He says we are both cowardly, seeking our own safety in dangerous situations. He says we both lie."

"*Saa!*" It was Rebecca speaking, having quickly learned this word meant "no."

"Stay behind me," Night Thunder chastised, "and do not ask me any more questions. I will protect you."

"But I—"

"I have spoken."

Night Thunder crossed his arms over his chest, his attention centering once again upon his opponent. He spoke, the sound of his words ruthless. "*Nitohkiimaan-saw-waahkayi maatini'stotowa hpoaawa!*"

A hush fell over the assembled warriors.

"What did you say?" This from Rebecca.

He turned toward her only slightly. "Did I not tell you to be quiet?"

"Please, I must know."

Night Thunder grunted and frowned at her. "Stay behind me. Your talk is not helping me," he warned, his voice scolding. "Do you not see that my cousin is angry?"

"Aye, Night Thunder, I do," she said, unable to keep her peace. "But I must know what is being said."

"Fine," he said. "I will say this only once and then you are to remain silent. Do you understand?"

"Aye."

"I told them that my wife did not desire to visit my home because she is uncertain that those of us here will show her the respect she deserves."

Rebecca drew in her breath. "Is that wise? Will that make them angrier?"

"Did I not ask you to say nothing more?"

"I . . ." She paused, frowning. Was that how she felt?

The argument continued between her protector and the giant of an Indian. But Rebecca wasn't listening anymore.

Hadn't she just reached the conclusion that these Indians did not appear harmful? Hadn't she realized that perhaps they were not as savage as she had once believed? Hadn't she felt some sympathy with them?

Was it only the one man that frightened her?

She said, all at once interrupting their argument, "It's not the way I'm feeling toward them all." Night Thunder paid her no attention. She shook his shoulder and tried again, "I'm not feeling this way toward all of these warriors. Only . . . ," she pointed toward the big Indian, ". . . *him*."

"*Sskoo. Aahkapiisa!*" The big Indian glowered, continuing to talk. "*Saayiwa! Ikkam-oosi aaksikamo-taahpihkaapitsiiyiwa!*"

Rebecca did not understand what was said, but the antagonism of the other Indian caused her to catch her breath.

"*Nitaasowatsii-wa,*" the big Indian said, and pointed at her.

"*Poina-a'pssi-wa. Itstsii-ohkiimi-wa,*" Night Thunder answered.

"What?" she leaned in upon Night Thunder's arm. "What are you both saying?"

"Be quiet. I do not want to have to tell you again—"

"Night Thunder, I will not—"

"Hush. I must think . . ."

"No, I—"

"He is threatening to take you as his wife by force," Night Thunder responded irritably. "He says it is obvious that I lie and it does not matter if you desire him or not."

"No," Rebecca said.

"I told him that you are my wife and that he is a nuisance."

"Night Thunder, perhaps we should . . ." She couldn't finish the thought. She'd been about to suggest that maybe they should simply accompany the Indians until the bad feelings were gone. If it were not for this one Indian, she might be able to endure a month or two with them. It seemed a possible solution—good for everyone but *her*. *She* would be in constant danger from the big Indian.

But hadn't Night Thunder put himself in jeopardy when he'd rescued her? Wasn't he still in danger? Was it too much to ask of her to return the favor?

What should she do? "Night Thunder," she began, taking in a deep breath, "if we went with them, would that put their minds at ease?"

He grunted and shook his head before sending her a sidelong glance. "Perhaps," he answered, "but it is not certain. Stay out of this. I will protect you."

"*Ikamotaahpihkaapitsiiyi! Sayi!*" This from the evil one.

"Night Thunder, I . . ." She gulped. It would mean a sacrifice on her part, but this man had saved her life. Shouldn't she be trying to do something as gallant for him? It seemed the right thing to do. Still, she couldn't bring herself to say the words . . .

"*Ikamotaahpikhkaapitsiiyi! Sayi!*"

She gasped. The evil Indian had stepped forward.

Night Thunder bent down at the knees. "Get behind me," he ordered her again. But this time, he brought his arm around her waist, effectively placing her where he desired.

The bigger Indian jumped forward, Night Thunder did the same.

And Rebecca sprang into action. Running the short distance to Night Thunder and pulling him back toward her, she pleaded, "Don't do this. If it will end the fight, then I think we should go with them."

"*Saa*, no," he groaned, not taking his gaze from the other Indian. "I said that I will take you back to the fort. And I will. Do I look like a woman that I would be afraid of a fight? I would honour my word."

"*Sayi!*" The big Indian hurled forward another step.

Night Thunder met it.

Rebecca gasped, and once again closing the short distance to Night Thunder, came up to his side. She said, "I don't think that now is the time to be heroic—"

"Get behind me, stay there, and be quiet."

"*Iitsskaat!*" The other Indian suddenly produced a knife.

No! Another thought struck her with sudden clarity. Night Thunder could die. Here. Now. Could she have the guilt of his death on her conscience for the rest of her life? Could she risk having the bigger Indian make good his threat to take her as his "wife" by force?

"Night Thunder," she began again, "please don't be doing this. Perhaps it would be better if we went ahead and accompanied them. Truly. You can still keep your promise and take me back to the fort. But we could do that later." There was more she wanted to say, but she didn't dare.

Briefly, Night Thunder looked away from his opponent and stared down at her. "Do you know what it is that you would be agreeing to if you do this?"

"I . . . I think so."

"*Omaopaat!*" The big Indian threatened.

But Night Thunder ignored him, turning his frustration upon her. "Do you?" Night Thunder asked her. "Do you realize that my brothers from the Blood tribe will wish to accompany us, to show us their goodwill?"

"Aye, well . . ."

"Do you know that there will be no more camp lodges erected for us when we travel?

"There won't be?"

"*Omaopaat!*" The other Indian jumped forward yet another pace.

But still Night Thunder neglected him. "*Saa*, no," snapped Night Thunder. "And do you know what that will mean?"

She gulped. "Aye," she said, "I think so."

"Consider it well, then, for we would be obliged to share a sleeping robe when we rest . . . during the day or night."

She sucked in her breath, the sound resembling a hiss. She actually hadn't considered *that*. She groaned. But truth be told, it didn't matter. She could envision no alternative. Not with the other Indian so antagonistic toward both of them.

"*Ksiststsoohsit!*" The evil one vaulted another step forward.

Night Thunder responded in kind.

She had to act quickly. His life, and perhaps hers, depended upon it. With all speed, she closed the gap between them and reached out to place her hand again upon Night Thunder's shoulder, saying, "I have considered it."

"Humph!" he glanced down at her, his gaze off his antagonizer and searing into hers. He didn't speak for several moments. In truth, he didn't move at all, or so it seemed. "Are you certain of this?" he asked her, his tone little more than a growl.

Words failed her. She tried to answer, but she couldn't. And as he stood beside her, not moving, not speaking, time seemed to stand still, until at last she nodded.

"*Saiksisaa!*" Again the big Indian lunged forward.

"I will not wear sleeping clothes," he stated to her, still disregarding the other Indian. "The others would laugh at me if I did this."

She heaved in her breath, stoutheartedly nodding as she said, "I understand. And though I object, I see no other way to avoid a fight."

"*Oki!*" The other Indian signaled Night Thunder forward.

Night Thunder, turned his anger upon Rebecca. "I will not have you act as a man for me, that you make me avoid a fight. Nor will I cower away from my duty as though I were an old woman."

"And what will happen to me if you lose that fight?"

"I will *not* lose."

"I hope not, but . . ."

"*Oki!*" The big Indian still urged Night Thunder on.

She watched her defender shift his glance to stare over toward the big Indian. Then, after some moments, he switched his examination onto her.

"You may come to regret it."

"I know."

"I will not listen to you complain."

"I will try not to."

He scowled at her. She knew he stood contemplating her words, and time seemed to pass much too slowly for her peace of mind. But at last Night Thunder hesitated no more and he let out a great sigh. "We will do it," he said, his hand coming down in the gestures of the sign language as he spoke. "I do not like it, but we will do it."

She let out her breath and watched as Night Thunder bent down to pick up his buffalo robe, signing toward the big Indian and toward the other men and saying to the crowd at large, as he straightened, "*Kiistonnoon-aakahkayi.*"

The whole group began to mutter, all appearing satisfied, all except the evil one who continued to glare at Night Thunder, at her. But then, muttering something to himself, the big Indian turned and strode away.

Was that it, then? Had the whole thing been handled as easily as that? Rebecca suppressed the sudden urge to swoon and, grasping at Night

Thunder's arm, she asked, "What was it that you said to them?"

He sighed. "I told them that all of us will go home. It appears that your future, and mine, my reluctant captive, will be as one for a time."

"Aye," she said, and letting out her breath, she realized much to her chagrin, that she was not experiencing the fear she had expected at the thought of spending more time in this man's company.

It couldn't be excitement she was feeling, could it?

Chapter 5

Glancing at Night Thunder as he trod ahead of her gave Rebecca an odd feeling.

Tall, straight, with wide shoulders and slim hips, Night Thunder had to be one of the handsomest men of her acquaintance. With his black hair falling down his back, emphasizing the slenderness of his muscular body, she couldn't be blamed if her gaze kept centering in upon him, could she? She had once estimated his age to be about twenty-seven years. Now she wondered. Though physically he might appear to be young, he exuded the emotions and wisdom of one much older and more experienced.

He wore a breechcloth and leggings that fit his legs so tightly, she could almost see the expanse of each muscle. Long fringe that looked to be part buckskin and part scalplocks, hung down the sides of his leggings, falling straight to the ground. And above his moccasins his leggings split, making a sort of rectangular panel over each ankle. His moccasins were black, making her wonder if this was perhaps how the Blackfeet had obtained their name. His gait was certain, sure, even when he was negotiating an expanse of difficult terrain.

He wore no shirt, like most of his companions. She supposed that was due to the hot summer weather. His lack of a shirt gave her more than an ample view of his back, the muscles defined for her inspection. He had several different small bags attached to the tanned belt that held up his breechcloth, as well as a beaded sheaf that encased his knife.

He wore an armband, decorated with beadwork and a certain type of fur she had trouble identifying. And across his back slashed his quiver full of arrows, his bow over one arm.

There were two feathers in his hair, tied with buckskin to a lock in back and hanging straight down. The feathers did not look like eagle feathers, although she couldn't be certain. They looked more to be the feathers one would see from an owl.

Not that she was studying him all that closely, she tried to tell herself. It was only that he afforded her a singular view, the only thing she had to look at as he took the lead.

She sighed, deciding she was fooling no one but herself, and determinedly glanced away from him.

They had been traveling in a northerly direction for a few days now, their party conspicuously lacking horses. At first they had wandered only during the night, but more recently, perhaps because they were closer to their own territory, they journeyed during the hours when the sun was full in the sky.

"Night Thunder? Why is it that we have no

horses?'' she asked, taking a few quick steps to catch up with him.

He didn't break stride or turn to look at her, and she feared he was not going to answer her. Then he said, ''This is a war party which set out to avenge the death of Strikes The Bear's wife.''

''Strikes The Bear?''

''The one who captured you.''

''Oh.'' She quickened her pace to keep up with him. It threw her out of breath, but she didn't slow down. She was too intent on having a conversation with this man. All day long their party had been traveling over dry, arid, seemingly endless prairie. And though the country they traversed provided a beautiful view and would seem to inspire conversation, no one appeared inclined to talk. It was a situation she intended to remedy.

''And capturing me, was that the way they were intending to seek revenge?''

''*Aa*.''

''But her death had nothing to do with me.''

''*Saa*, no, it did not,'' Night Thunder answered, ''but you are white and a woman, and Strikes The Bear's heart was grieved. It seemed to him that you provided the best means of retaliation, I think.''

''But that is not fair, is it?''

''Fair? What means 'fair'?''

''Fair means to be just, evenhanded, unprejudiced. It means to treat others as one would want to be treated.''

''*Aa*,'' he said, ''fair. That is a good word.'' He paused. ''And is it 'fair,' do you think, to kill many hundreds of Indians—men, women, and children—

for no other reason than sport?" His tongue slipped over the last word. "That is the way the white man described it when our chiefs protested the white man's murder of a whole tribe of people last spring."

"Sport? Surely you jest."

He didn't answer.

She tried again. "What you are telling me cannot be true. No man kills another man in sport. It isn't done. It is too incredible. Murdering innocent women and children? Truly, I find that hard to believe."

"I do not lie to you."

"No, I wouldn't think you would, but there is something wrong here. If this truly happened, there must have been some reason, mustn't there?"

He didn't respond. Several moments passed and all she heard was the wind rustling over the prairie, as well as their own footfalls. She picked up the conversation, saying, "The white man does not kill indiscriminately. His religion forbids it. And that's the truth, as firm as the Rock of Cashel."

Night Thunder stopped and turned around so suddenly and without warning that she bumped straight into him. And though she was more than aware of the contact made by his bare skin against her own, he seemed unaffected by her. He said, "There was no reason for the murders. The people those white men killed we call the fish people because their men are not warriors. They live by taking the fish from the lakes and rivers. They had no weapons to wield against the guns of the white

man. They had not the means to defend their
women and children. It was murder."

She did not know what to say, what to do. Night
Thunder rarely lost his temper with her such as
this, speaking to her in such a decisive manner.
She was uncertain she liked being on the receiving
end of it.

He had never shown her anything but the utmost respect. But then, she'd never said or done
anything to cause him to take exception to her, had
she? She was supposed to defend her own people,
wasn't she?

But if what Night Thunder said was true?
"I . . ." she began, the words coming more difficult
to her than she would have thought possible. "I'm
sorry. It is a terrible thing of which you speak. If
it is true, then those people, no matter their race,
are bad people. Maybe the white man had relatives that were killed by Indians. I have heard of
some men going on a vengeance against Indians
because of that. Mayhap that's why he . . ."

Night Thunder gave her a triumphant smile
over his shoulder. "You think that the white man
was justified in his murders? Perhaps also, then,
Strikes The Bear was justified in the same way for
what he was doing to you?"

"What? How can you suggest such a thing?"

Night Thunder merely snorted at her and
turned away, striding back toward their party.

She hurriedly followed him. "Night Thunder,"
she said, touching him on the shoulder as she
caught up with him, "how can you talk to me like
that?"

He shrugged. "I do not agree that Strikes The

Bear is right for what he did to you. You too are innocent," he said, though he didn't turn toward her as he spoke. "I only try to make you see that perhaps he had reason for what he tried to do. Perhaps."

She swallowed hard. "What did the white man do to Strikes The Bear's wife?" she asked, although she wasn't certain she wanted to know.

Night Thunder strode on ahead of her without answering her for so long, she began to feel their conversation had abruptly ended. She slowed her pace, not seeing any purpose in rushing to keep up with him, when all at once he began to speak, as though she were still trailing him. "The white man tortured her. He stripped her, maimed her, and then took her as a man sometimes takes a woman in anger before he killed her. There were several white men who did it. Not one alone."

Rebecca didn't speak. What, after all, could she say? The thought did come to her, however: if she had been in Strikes The Bear's place, would she not have felt the need to seek revenge?

No, never. She was too God-fearing a woman. Still . . . she gulped and took a moment before she was able to voice, "I . . . I'm sorry. But it had nothing to do with me."

"Likewise those fish people had nothing to do with what might have happened to the white man—if that was the white man's reason."

Rebecca became silent. She didn't *want* to understand. She didn't *want* to feel any more sympathy for these people than she already felt. Yet sympathize she did, and an understanding of sorts began to form within her mind, a comprehension of why the big Indian might have done what he had.

It didn't make her like the other Indian, but she didn't feel so . . . angry. She asked, after a time, "Where is Strikes The Bear? I have not seen him since the feast the warriors gave us."

"He scouts ahead of us."

"Why?"

"He has done that in the past."

"But I thought you said he was the leader of this party."

Night Thunder sent her a scowl.

"Did you have something to do with this?"

"I might have."

"Did you ask the others to have him scout ahead because you knew I would be uncomfortable?"

"Perhaps."

Which brought another question to mind. "Then he will not always be spending the evenings with us?"

"Not always. His eyes will watch us closely, though, I think. We need to be careful at night, so that we do not bring questions about our marriage to the minds of the others."

"But if Strikes The Bear is not here to watch us . . ."

"He has many friends who travel with us."

"Oh," she sighed, her hopes suddenly deflated. Then, deciding to change the subject, she asked, "Why does a war party have no horses?"

He gestured around him before he said, "Because it is easier to travel this way when in the territory of our enemies, the Assiniboin. But soon we will be in our own country and we will then travel with more ease."

"Ah," she said, "good. Will that mean we'll soon be getting horses, then?"

"*Saa*, no," he responded. "The capturing of horses," he went on to explain, "is done by making a raid upon an enemy. And that involves too much danger. This party is more concerned with getting the two of us to my home safely."

"I see," she said, and she did, although she wished the "home" of which he spoke were the fort.

That these men considered it their duty to accompany her and her "husband" seemed a terribly chivalrous act. It made it hard, too, to envision a way of returning to the fort any time soon.

Still, Rebecca tried to envision a plan that would take her back there, though none came readily to mind.

Perhaps her mistress, Katrina, would offer a solution. When Katrina returned to the fort, might she send someone to find out what had become of her maid? Rebecca could only hope so.

It was a thought which gave Rebecca hope, although the idea of meeting anyone in her current state of dress was less than appealing.

She glanced down at herself. Her apparel, a homemade item of trade cloth and ribbon, had never been a thing of beauty; but with its corals and browns, it had been pleasing enough. Now, ripped and torn, snagged on the bottom from the dried grasses and sharp vines they had traversed, it looked more duggins than dress, and she wondered how long it would hold up under the duress of their travel.

Her slippers, too, would soon be unserviceable and her hose contained more holes and rips than her dress.

But she wouldn't complain. It could be worse, she thought with a shudder, recalling the evil, big Indian who had captured her. What would he have done to her?

"Night Thunder." Again she quickened her pace to catch up with him. "Where were you the day I was captured by these Indians?"

He took so long answering that she touched him on the shoulder.

"Night Thunder?" she asked again.

He turned his head slightly to gaze down at her fingers where she had placed them upon him, and she wasn't certain, but it felt as though he shuddered. At last he said, "The fort was low on meat. I had been asked to hunt."

"Oh," she said. "I see. Did you not see the war party?" She drew back her hand as she spoke.

"I went west, they came from the north."

"It was silly of me, I reckon, to have gone out onto the prairie alone. But I had done it so many times in the past that I had felt no danger. You were always with me, though, were you not? Perhaps I felt too safe."

He shrugged, picking up his pace, and she had to practically run to keep up with him.

She said, "Came out of nowhere, they did, right enough. Before I left from the fort, I thought I could see in all directions. But I did not see these Indians."

"No white man would have. Do not blame yourself."

"I cannot help it. If I had not been out gathering wildflowers and fruit, it would not have happened."

"Perhaps. But no more of this. It is an unwise man who constantly looks into the past to condemn himself. You breathe life today, and it is what you do now that will see you through to tomorrow."

"I cannot help it. It was terrible."

"*Aa.*"

"His face was painted black."

"It is the way of the warrior."

"And smelled awful, he did."

"The anxiety of a warrior can often be smelled."

"I was so frightened."

He nodded.

"I thought I was going to die."

"You are too pretty to kill. Maybe Strikes The Bear spoke truth when he said he only wanted to frighten you before he took you for his wife."

"Slave, you mean. And no, I do not believe that to be truth. He is telling lies, I think."

"*Aa,*" he said.

They both became quiet for a few moments, and then she asked, "Did you mean it?"

"What?"

"Do *you* truly think I'm pretty?"

He chuckled slightly, and she was struck by the enticing quality of the sound. It wasn't often that she heard him laugh.

He said, "You are no different from women everywhere, I think."

"I am uncertain that you flatter me. But come now, you have not answered my question."

He gave her a curious look. "What is wrong with the white man that you are not told of your beauty every day of your life? You should already be certain of it."

"Then you do think me pretty?"

"You need not ask."

"But I am asking. Do you?"

"*Aa*, yes," he said with a sigh, "I do."

Such a simple word, *aa*. But it was at this moment the nicest of compliments. She smiled and glanced up at the blue of the sky, feeling strangely at peace as she said, "Thank you, Night Thunder. I will not be forgetting your kindness. Not for a very long time indeed."

"It's noontime. Are we not going to stop to eat?"

"Eat?"

"Aye," she said. " 'Tis that thing people do at this time of day to still the hunger in their stomachs."

"*Saa*, we will not eat. It is an unwise man who satisfies his hunger when the sun is at its zenith."

"Unwise? How can this be?"

"Have you never noticed what happens when a man eats to his fill at this hour? When a man rises, that is when he should eat. He goes out and hunts. He feels good. Strong. Powerful. He kills much game, provides for his family. The sun rises and if he has not consumed enough at the start of the day and he decides to satisfy his hunger, he eats until he can eat no more. Then he feels suddenly tired. He can't keep his eyes open. He falls asleep and maybe he is in enemy territory. The enemy finds him and kills him, or if he is lucky, he simply fails to hunt enough game, returning home to the frowns of his wife and children. There he lies and tells those close to him that there is little game to be found. No, you eat at this time of day if you dare; the Indian does not."

Rebecca digested all he said in silence. Hadn't she often observed in herself and in others a sort of lethargy which set in after the noonday meal? Perhaps there was a bit of wisdom in what Night Thunder said. "Then we will keep traveling throughout the day without the least amount of food?"

"*Aa*," he answered her, "tomorrow you must take care to eat more in the morning and to eat well."

"Aye," she said, "that I will."

The day was a warm one, the air clear, fresh, invigorating. Scents of wild sage and buffalo grass filled the air while the occasional squawk of a hawk could be heard from high above them. She looked upward, her hand shielding her eyes from the brightened sun. The hawk circled once, twice, his movements reminding her of a miniature ballet.

She smiled. It was an odd feeling, this sensation of contentment which began to sweep over her. What had caused her change of viewpoint? The environment? The plains? Or was it simply the presence of this man, Night Thunder, beside her? No matter, she began to understand why it is said of the adventurer that once he begins, he will never again be content with a more sedate life.

They set up camp that evening on a high butte overlooking the prairie. With no fire lit, they ate a supper of dried meat and stale bread. It seemed an unusual place to make camp, Rebecca thought. Gazing down from her spectacular view, she could see a deep valley far below them, the coulee seeming to beckon her with a lazy shelter beneath its shady willows and cottonwoods. There were groves of these huge trees, all standing tall beside a clear stream of pure running water.

She mentioned her thoughts to Night Thunder.

"Humph," he responded "our scouts spotted a Cree war party today. They are not too close to us, but we do not want to put ourselves into a position that would be hard to defend. If we were to camp in the valley down there, an enemy could more easily surround us and render an escape impossible. Here on this butte, it is safer; we can spot the approach of an enemy and have a better chance of getting beyond his reach, if he were even to see us. But because we light no fire, and the party is distant from us, the chances of that happening are not very good."

She had simply nodded to him and had glanced again into the coulee and the surrounding plains. She had once heard that the plains should be likened to a place of desolation. But seeing this place, she disagreed. Life teemed here, everywhere. Over to the left and in the distance grazed several buffalo; over to the south several antelope romped; on a distant bluff a wolf and its mate moved; and in the valley stood a herd of elk. She had never witnessed such abundance.

Material gain might be the only thing missing here. But if one had little use for the riches of the world, this place stood as a sort of haven for freedom, for the wandering soul. Perhaps it was the environment which began to disabuse her of the idea that fear and apprehension reigned the plains.

The evening passed quickly into night, the sun setting with a foray of pinks and golds, casting a reddish glow over the brown plains, making it appear as though the land and hills were nothing more than a reflector for the magnificence in the sky. Stars began to appear one by one; first in the west and soon more overhead.

It was dark by the time Night Thunder set out their sleeping robes, reminding Rebecca of what was yet to come. She had hoped to somehow avoid it, but she became more and more aware, as she watched him, that eluding their sleeping arrangements would be impossible.

She stood by nervously, watching him set up their place on the ground, far away from the others. Was she really going to have to sleep next to him again—throughout the entire night? She wasn't sure she could do it and still keep hold of her dignity.

If she were to be honest with herself, losing her dignity was not all that she feared. She wasn't certain she could sleep next to the man without becoming . . . aroused. She blushed at the thought.

The man made her feel all soft and warm inside. And something else . . .

He set the buffalo robe on the ground, and giving her a speculative glance, he commented unnecessarily, "This is where we will sleep."

Rebecca nodded.

"You will sleep in your dress, then?"

Another nod.

"It will be mussed."

"I know, but . . ."

"*Annisa*," he said, "all right," and gestured toward the robe. "You will lie down first."

"No, I . . . I think I would rather lie down after you."

He shrugged and began to undress, a gleam in his eye. With great preamble and a slow smile, he took the bow off his shoulder, setting it down beside the robe. Then, looking over to her and ensuring her gaze was carefully glued to his, he released his quiver of arrows; they, too, fell to the ground.

With precise care, he removed his sheath and knife next and bent down, placing the items carefully beside his robe; it was the only time he looked away from her.

She stuttered, "Wh-why do you set your weapons beside you, thusly?"

He looked over at her, a half smile curving his lips. He said, "In case an enemy attacks during the night, I will need to grab my weapons quickly. I place them as I do every night so that I might take possession of them rapidly if I have the need."

"Even when you are in your own camp you do this?"

He nodded. "*Aa*, even then."

He straightened up, and with a teasing glimpse

at her, removed his moccasins, first one, then the other. His hands came to his waist then, and with a ridiculous smile upon his face, his fingers began to fiddle with a string of rawhide at his belt.

She should be the one to look away; she knew it. Yet she couldn't.

He gave her a cocky grin before releasing first one tie on the belt, then the other. Rebecca gasped, yet she didn't glance elsewhere.

With a soft *thump*, his leggings fell to the ground. Bending, he set the articles of clothing neatly to the side.

She swallowed nervously.

He straightened up and looked at her as a cat might observe a piece of string. She became more than aware that the only thing remaining on him at the moment was his breechcloth and that belt upon which it rested.

His hand went to the belt.

She held her breath. All she seemed capable of doing was watching, waiting.

He grinned at her and gestured toward the buffalo robe. He said, "Take your position first, I will follow."

"M-must we?"

"It is expected. We are being watched."

It was only then that she remembered the others in their party. Glancing around, she saw that though every single warrior who was sitting nearby was silently attending to some matter close to hand, none appeared to be watching them unduly. But Rebecca knew their politeness was only superficial.

She muttered, "Surely you don't think that I

would undress in front of them . . . in front of you."

"I do not ask you to do any of that."

"Good," she said. "See that you never do."

He grinned broadly, and she thought it odd that he seemed in such good spirits. He said, "There will come a day when I will rejoice to hear you take back those words and beg me to undress you."

She gasped. "How dare you! I thought that you were . . . that I was . . . that . . . we are not truly married and you should not feel you can take liberties and say such things to me—"

He held up a hand, the simple action silencing her. "Is it always your way that you talk too much?"

"I—"

"But," he said, again silencing her, "you also speak truth. If you would like, I will scold myself for teasing you."

"Oh," she said, "is that all you are doing now? Teasing me?"

He grinned. "*Aa*, yes, so it is, young Rebecca. I only tease you. Now, hurry and get beneath the robes fully clothed if you must. I will follow you."

"But are you not going to remove your . . ." Her words fell away as she realized what she had been about to say.

He frowned. "I am disappointing you?"

"No."

He chuckled. "Too bad," he said. "I was beginning to enjoy the idea of having your eyes upon me here." He pointed to that private area of his

body and at the same time removed the breechcloth he wore.

Rebecca, gasping, decided to debate with him
no more. With hardly a thought, she jumped forward, and picking up the top buffalo robe, fled
beneath its folds.

Chapter 6

The problem arose in the middle of the night. Rebecca awoke to find herself cuddled up next to Night Thunder, his arms around her and her face against his bare chest. She tried to move; it was impossible, his arms had tightened around her.

She attempted to go back to sleep; she couldn't. The warmth of him, the sweet, musky scent of him made it impossible to think of anything but his state of undress. It prevented her from putting him from her mind.

And worse, she began to ache in secret places she dared never mention. Her breasts felt heavy, her nipples taut. Worse yet, down there, between her legs, she felt ... what? Stimulated? Wet? Heaven forbid.

Oh, truth be told, she wanted his kiss with a yearning need.

"Night Thunder," she whispered, attempting to break the spell he held over her. Pushing against him, she tried to gain some distance from him, if only a fraction of an inch.

He merely moaned, however, and drew her in closer toward him.

She sighed, venturing to back away from him once more, but it was impossible. She could not match his strength, which kept her held tightly to him.

What was she to do? She could feel his breath against the top of her head, soft and warm, feel the slight rise and fall of his chest. His legs had become entangled with hers, too, which certainly didn't aid her cause, and his hips pressed in closely against her stomach.

At least *he* wasn't in the manly way, she thought, surprising herself with her musings. But instead of the idea giving her comfort, as it should have, it only served to bring to mind a vision of that portion of his anatomy, the mental image of his nude body being quite a vivid one.

She squirmed restlessly. Unfortunately, she was more than aware of what it would take to quench that restlessness.

Again she sighed and tried to turn over, to present her back to him, but she failed once more.

"*Omaopii*," she heard him mutter in his sleep.

What did that mean?

"Be quiet," he uttered in English a few moments later. "Lie still."

She groaned and whispered back to him, "How can I, when you hold me too tightly? Relax your grip, Night Thunder."

He only snorted and pulled her in further toward him. "You will need the extra body heat," he muttered in a low voice. "It is a cold night. Besides," and here she heard a little humor enter

into his tone, "we want the others to think you
enjoy my closeness to you, is that not true?"

She could not deny what he said, but she didn't
want to let him know her true feelings, so she remained silent.

"If you like," he went on to whisper, "I can take
you down to the coulee beneath this butte and let
you bathe under the branches of the cottonwood
trees, a refreshing, cool bath. Would that help
you?"

"No," she said, "it most certainly would not."

She felt him shrug before he said, "Perhaps I
could do with a cold bath, too."

She froze. What did he mean by that remark?

Suddenly she felt a tautness where his body
touched hers—there at her tummy—and she suddenly understood exactly what he meant.

"Night Thunder, I thought we weren't going
to—"

"I cannot help it. I am not trying to be this way.
You are a beautiful female, and when you wiggle
like you are against me, I—"

"Sh-h-h."

"Why do you stop me from saying these things?
There is nothing wrong with how my body reacts
to yours. There is much that is right about it."

"It is *not* right. We are *not married*."

"A matter we could set straight at this very moment. Others think we are married; it would take
little on our part to make it a truth."

"But I thought you did not want to marry me."

"I do not believe I told you quite that. I do not
think it would be a good thing for either of us,
that is true. Marriage between us would be hard

for you because you are not Indian and are unused to the ways of my people, but it would be difficult for me, too. Difficult—not impossible."

"No, I don't see how it is possible at all."

"Consider it well, Rebecca. Do you feel how your body responds to mine, how mine desires yours? And this is only the first of several nights we will have to spend this way together . . . some people never have this readiness in a marriage, and yet we do not even try and it is there. Perhaps we should think of it."

"No, I . . . you could wear your breechcloth to bed."

"And do you think that would help?"

"Aye," she replied. "I do. Please, I'm sure of it."

"Then I will do it and we will see."

"Aye," she said, "please."

A few silent moments passed, an uncomfortable silence.

He broke it. "Do you want that bath?"

"Very much, yes," she answered.

He chuckled. "So, too, do I. Let us go to the coulee, now when there is no danger of a war party catching us and where the others cannot watch us, as well."

"Aye," she said, and together they made their way to the valley.

It was a clear night, though the moon shone with little light to guide their way.

A nighthawk squawked in the distance and the locusts filled the night with their own peculiar humming. A chinook had blown in, bringing with it a warm breeze to whisper over her skin.

A thousand, no, a million stars glittered overhead with a brilliance unseen and unheard of in the east. Rebecca gazed upward, amazed to see how close the stars appeared to be. She held up her arms as though she might reach them, and Night Thunder, seeing her action, gave her a cool grin.

He said, "My country is beautiful, is it not?"

She nodded. "It most certainly is."

They had come upon the stream, the clear water which ran there reflecting the shimmering stars overhead and the outline of the willow trees which ran along its bank. Had she ever seen anything more beautiful? She thought of her own beloved Ireland, yet never having witnessed its shores, she couldn't have said whether it would be worthy competition to this place or not.

She drew a deep breath, and looking down, dipped her big toe into the fast-moving water, screeching a little at the frostiness of the stream. She glanced back at Night Thunder where he stood behind her. "It's cold," she said.

"*Aa*, yes. That is what we want. What we need, the both of us."

"I see. Will you turn your back?"

"Must I?"

"Aye, you must."

She couldn't see his features plainly, yet when he spoke to her, there was a hint of humor in his tone. "You have seen me without my clothes. Why should I not witness the beauty of you, too?"

"Because that is different and you know it," she answered. "Turn your back, now."

Laughing slightly, he faced around, though he

said, "I will not always be able to stay with my back to you throughout your entire bath. I must stand on guard for you because there are animals that sometimes like to come to the water and drink in the evening. Some of them are dangerous."

"What sort of animals?"

"*Aa*, there are elk, some deer, maybe a bear or two, or a wolf. But the most dangerous animal of all is the man who is standing here watching you."

She gasped. "There is a man here?"

"*Aa*, yes, there is."

"Night Thunder, why aren't you—"

"And he is watching you very carefully."

"He is? Night Thunder, I—" she gasped, until it dawned on her exactly whom he meant.

"You tease me, I think," she said. "It is all right for that man—you—to be here, so long as you do not look at me."

"*Aa*," was all he said.

She made sure he was doing exactly as she had instructed, and seeing only his back turned toward her, she began to remove her clothes. She set them aside, at a distance not too far from shore, yet not too close. She didn't want her things to get wet. The night was cool, for all that there was a comfortable wind, and she wanted the clothing dry so that it might warm her after her bath.

She had removed her dress, her slippers, and her petticoat, and was down to only her chemise when he asked her, "Why are you not already married?"

She hesitated a moment. "I almost was once."

"Almost? What happened that you are not?"

She stared off in the distance, seeing without really taking note of the willow and cottonwood trees on the far shore of the stream. She said, "He was a sailor."

"A sailor?"

"Aye, a sailor. That is a person who makes his living by navigating boats on the water, taking things to and from other places. It is a good way to earn a living, but a dangerous one. We almost had enough money, enough goods set aside to buy our own place. It was only one last run he had to make at sea before our marriage. I never saw him again. He was drowned off the coast of North Carolina," she hesitated, amazed at the sob which threatened to tear at her throat, even after all this time. "Th-that's a place far away, in the east."

"Humph," he said. "The Water People took him, then?"

"The what?"

"The people who live beneath the water. One must be ever careful not to anger them, lest they take your life when you do nothing more than bathe or swim."

She nodded. "Aye, I suppose you could say that the water people took him."

"Then do not fret. It is said they live a good life underwater."

This time she couldn't help it. She sobbed. And before she could utter another sound, he had turned around, had taken the few short steps necessary to reach her, and had taken her in his arms.

"I should not have asked," he whispered against her hair. "I should have let you tell me about it when you felt that you could. I am sorry I caused you to think on this thing."

"It . . . it is nothing. Do not fret. You have done nothing that warrants an apology."

His chest moved as he chuckled, and he asked, "You think not?"

She didn't understand him. But soon, feeling the length of him as he stood so closely to her, she became more than aware of him and how little they each wore. She didn't move away, however. She knew she should if she were to protect her dignity, but she didn't want to; his embrace felt too good.

She could not think clearly and she found herself asking, "Oh, Night Thunder, do you feel it, too?"

"*Aa.*"

"And what do you feel?"

"How good you are in my arms," he answered. "How much I want to hold you. How much I want to do other things to you, with you."

She sighed. "How ever did this happen to us?"

He didn't answer. Instead, bending his head slightly, he kissed her—something, despite herself, that she'd been desiring him to do all evening.

She kissed him back, too. How could she not?

It was not a gentle kiss, although it started out that way. But it escalated—quickly. After all, they had already had a taste of one another. Instinctively, now, they knew what they wanted.

His hands came up to hold her face as he let his lips encompass and take over hers. She moaned. One of his hands caressed her cheek, the other moved down to her neck, while his lips foraged hers. Her arms slid around his shoulders, grabbed onto his neck.

His tongue swept into her mouth. And she melted. Saints be praised, she melted. Her fiancé had never kissed her this way. This was . . . *heaven.* She moaned again.

Or had he?

His lips moved down to a sensitive spot on her neck and she felt her knees buckle under her. But he held her up. She almost cried aloud from the pleasure of it.

His lips came back to hers and she felt a need to devour him, body and soul. She couldn't get enough of this, of him, and it was too much to consider where this was all leading. Instead, she settled in closer to him.

He groaned before he said, "Do we marry, then?"

She had trouble understanding him, though he spoke in English. She asked, as though she had never heard the word before, "Marry?"

"*Aa*, yes, do we marry?"

Though she understood the words, she still couldn't quite comprehend what he was asking her or why. Feeling dizzy with need, she asked, "Marry? Why would we marry?"

"Because I am about to love you, and in my village, when a man loves a woman in this way, either he marries her and makes her his sits-beside-him wife, or he ruins her. I do not wish to ruin you."

Marriage? Ruin? She tried to think clearly, but her mind was a blur. "Night Thunder . . . I . . . don't know what to say. I am not certain I meant to marry you. But it seems I'm not acting like myself at the moment . . ." She chanced to look up at him. "I would like you to kiss me again, though."

What was she saying, inviting him on like this? Yet she couldn't seem to help herself, not when they stood together as they were.

He stared down at her; she, back up at him. Moment followed long moment as they stood saying nothing, though the look in their eyes communicated what remained unsaid between them . . . respect, trust, desire, love . . . love? Where had that thought come from? She didn't love him, did she? She couldn't love him.

Still, if it wasn't a love of sorts that she felt, what was it? Admiration? Respect?

As he lowered his head toward her, they kissed again, hungrily, coming together and embracing one another as though their bodies were magnetic. He ran his hands up and down her back while hers traced the contours of his bare chest.

He shivered, breaking the kiss between them, and raising his head only slightly, he said, "I will make a good husband to you. I will be kind, I promise."

"Aye," she said, "I know that you would."

"Then let us make the vow between us now."

She swallowed, the sound of it noisy even to her ears. "I . . . I cannot."

"I do not understand. Why can you not?"

"I . . ." She cast her gaze down. "I cannot tell it to you."

"But you want me?"

"I—" She broke off.

He hesitated, and she could feel the heat of his glance radiating over the top of her head. "We belong together, I believe. We have known each other many months now as friends, but there is more between us, I think. Do you not see how we fit each other perfectly? I know that you must feel the same passion that I do. Do you not already feel it, the force between us here?" He put his hand to his heart, "when our lips touch?"

"I . . ."

"Do you deny it?"

"No, I . . . I cannot."

"Aa, then we will marry here and now."

"No, I cannot do that, either."

"Why? Do you not see that if we do not do the right thing here, at this very moment, you could be ruined? The feeling between us, it is too strong to be long ignored. Is there something else that I do not know?"

She balked at telling him the truth. Twice she opened her mouth to speak; twice she said nothing. She backed away from him, letting his arms fall from around her.

What could she tell him? That she could permit nothing more than a simple yearning for him? That she could never marry him, no matter the passion between them? That she was prejudiced?

She couldn't very well tell him about the dream she had envisioned all her life, as yet unfulfilled. She'd not tell him, the man who had saved her life, that she could not marry him because she hadn't yet attended a dance. That would sound petty, mean and fairly silly.

Yet wasn't it the truth? She couldn't give up her illusions.

She brought back to mind the balls her parents had thrown when she'd been a child, recalling the laughter, the gaiety. And she remembered her hope that someday, somehow, she would have all that. It might seem a foolish fantasy to another; for her it was real.

That her life had become a tangle of misfortune, that her parents' wealth had turned out to be barely enough to cover their debts, had all been hardships she'd had to face, alone. How could she explain that in the midst of all that pain, the agony, the only thing she'd had to cling to had been her dreams?

She chanced to look up at Night Thunder, who stared back at her steadily, patiently awaiting her response.

Finally, not knowing what to say, what to do, she began to tell him, "I am not Indian, you are not white. Our two ways are different. I would not fit into your world, nor am I certain I would want to. I cannot deny that we appear to have a . . . a feeling for one another, but it will pass with time, don't you think? I respect and admire you, but it can go no further than that."

"It already has gone further than—"

"No." She held up her hand, silencing him. "It has not. Not yet. If I were to marry you, soon I would be bearing your children, and if that happened, I could never again be a part of my own society."

"Is that so terrible? I vow that I will do all that I can to make your life pleasant."

"Aye," she said, and she smiled slightly before she continued. "But I would still be unhappy. For there is one thing you could never give me that I would be missing for all the rest of my days."

He didn't say a word, and his silence seemed to encourage her to continue. She looked up toward him quickly, giving him an erstwhile glance, "Do you promise not to laugh at me, if I tell this to you now?"

"I would not laugh."

She sent him a suspicious look, but when she saw that he appeared serious, she said, "A dance."

"A dance?"

She nodded. "When I was a little girl, I used to watch my parent's gaiety at the balls, at parties. I loved it, and my mother always promised me that someday I too would attend a ball. I can't remember how many times she told me that it would be there that I would meet my future husband and that we would live happily ever after."

Night Thunder stood staring at her for several moments before he asked, "And is this where you met that man you were to marry?"

She sighed. "Oh," she said, her gaze faraway, "you mean, my fiancé? No, I did not. But when he returned, we were planning to throw a ball that would announce our engagement. It never happened, though, because he was lost at sea, and then . . ."

Night Thunder's glance was warm, yet proud as he said, "I can give you this dance that you desire."

"No," she said, "not the kind I need. This ball is the sort where all the women wear their best gowns, where their hair is powdered until it appears almost white, where the young gents go to flirt with the young ladies and to pick out their future wives."

"Humph. We have many such dances in my village."

"No," she said, "they're not the same. With our dances, there is always an orchestra playing."

"What is this?"

"They are the very best musicians, playing the works of Mozart, Bach, and other composers, people who make music. Remember when you were at the fort and saw the people dancing, and some men were playing fiddles? It is something like that, only so much better. The people at balls dance to a waltz, a minuet, a quadrille. And above them the candelabra are all aglow, filling the dance hall with so much light, one would think it was day."

Night Thunder's chin had jutted forward, she noted, as he said, "And you think I cannot give this to you?"

"No," she commented, "I know you cannot." She stared down at the ground.

"And it is important to you, this dance?"

She nodded, shutting her eyes, not believing that she was about to ask this, but she couldn't seem to help herself as she inquired, "Could we have only an affair of the heart, perhaps?"

"What is this 'affair'?"

"It is when two people . . . make love to one another without the commitment of marriage."

She snatched a brief glimpse up at him, only to watch him raise his eyebrows. "You would have me ruin you? Willingly?"

"No, but I . . . but you saved my life, and I—"

"*Haiya*, you think that I would force myself on you because of this?"

"No, but—"

"Is it this that causes you to come into my arms?"

What should she say? Should she answer honestly? "No," she said, "it is only because I cannot marry you, but I seem to feel strongly about you and we have to share a sleeping robe, and . . ." she stared quickly away from him.

"Know this," he said, gently putting a finger beneath her chin and bringing her face around to his. "If we make love, it will be no affair. I would protect you. If we make love, you will be my wife in every way. The others already think it. All we need do to make it so is to do it."

"Oh," was all she could say.

She took a deep breath and stared up at this man's features, the starlight emphasizing his cheekbones, his straight nose, his full lips, his dark hair that strayed into his face in the slight breeze, and she was not at all hard pressed to admit that he appeared, at this moment, handsome beyond mere words. Truly, he would make some girl a wonderful husband.

She winced at the thought. She knew she could never marry this man, but the thought of him belonging to another, as he was certain to do if she did not take him, was less than appealing. At last, looking up at him, she asked, "And what about you? Do you truly *want* to marry me?"

"I have asked you. Do you doubt that I would honour you or my word? Surely you do not question that I want you."

"No," she said, "I have no qualms about that. I

know you would do your best. But do you love me?"

For an answer he took a few short steps forward and pulled her into his arms, where he proceeded to kiss her cheeks, her nose, her eyelids, even the crooked part in her hair. And she might have melted right then and there in his arms; she certainly wanted to. But she didn't. Not when even having a tryst with this man meant marriage to him.

She persisted, however, asking, "Well, do you?"

His look was that of a man deeply impassioned. "What is it that you ask me?"

"Do you love me?"

He sighed heavily. "I would honour you and protect you and keep you by me always." Suddenly he gave her a half-cocked grin as he asked, "And do you love me?"

She backed away from him. "You did not answer my question."

He followed her progress with a step or two forward as she took a few more paces backward. His arms reached out to try to hold her, and he said, "I answered it as honestly as I could. I will always admire you."

She avoided his arms and took a few more steps away from him. "It's not the same thing."

"What is not?"

"Honour. Admiration. It's not the same thing as love."

"I did not say that it was."

"Then you don't love me."

"I did not say that."

"Oh!" Was he trying to anger her? She stamped her foot. "You talk in circles. I know already what you have told me. I'm asking you to tell me what you haven't yet said."

He drew in a deep breath. "Perhaps you are right. Perhaps I am avoiding these words. Yet maybe you are not so wrong. I cannot tell you true because there is something else I should tell you, something you should know about me. It is not a woman's place to ask, nor a man's duty to confide. Yet though I do not understand why I feel that I should tell you this, I fear that I must."

Rebecca became suddenly still.

He continued, "There is another in my camp, a woman, who waits for me. For all of her life, for most of mine, we have been pledged to one another. Our parents made the pact that we must honour. Such is the way of things."

"Pledged?" she asked. "As in, vowed to marry?"

"*Aa*, yes," he said.

"Then you love her?"

"Perhaps. I do not know."

"You don't know?"

He shook his head. "We have always been promised to one another. But I have never kissed her as I kiss you. I have never felt with her the passions I feel with you."

"Why have you never kissed her?"

He jerked his head to the left, Rebecca observing the strange display that had to be a purely Native American gesture. "Because," he said, "the young, unmarried women in our village are closely guarded, and being alone with them is not permitted and—"

Rebecca snorted. "That is no excuse. If you'd wanted to kiss the girl, you would have done it."

"No, it is not that way. I . . ." He glanced down at the ground, then up at her, his look sheepish. "Perhaps you are right."

She gazed away from him. "What would happen to her if you married me?"

"She would not like it."

"No, I don't reckon she would."

"It has always been planned that she would be my sits-beside-him wife."

"Your what?"

"My sits-beside-him wife. The woman who sits with her husband in council."

"Ah, your wife. She will not like it, then, if you marry another, and she might hate me."

"It could be, but still she would be bound to honour her pledge to me, and I to honor mine to her."

"But how can you, then, ask me to marry you, if you must keep your promise?"

"She would be my second wife."

Rebecca backed away from him. *His second wife?* She took another step behind her and stumbled, brushing away his hands as he made to help her. *His second wife.* Suddenly she felt silly and stupid. Why hadn't she remembered this aspect of Indian life? *Indian males took more than one wife.* It was a well-known fact.

"Let me ensure that I understand you correctly. You would plan to marry me . . . and her?"

"*Aa*, yes, but not right away. You and I would come to know one another first. It is only right."

"It is not right."

That statement had him bringing up his head.

"First," she said, "how can you ask me to marry you when you cannot even tell me that you love me? Yes, you would do your duty to me, but I cannot say that pleases me. Not when I would be wanting the warmth of affection from the one I'd be calling husband."

"I did not say that I do not love you."

She held up her hand between them. "Second," she said, "there is the matter of more than one wife. My society does not permit such things."

"Does not permit it? Your people would have a wife grow old before her time because her husband cannot afford to keep two or more wives to help her with the work?"

"No," she said. "Our society does not permit it because it is considered a sin."

"A sin?"

"Our God forbids it."

"*Haiya*," he said, pausing slightly, "so you are telling me that if I marry you, I can take no other?"

She nodded. "*Aa*, yes, that is right."

She glared at him stubbornly; he, back at her. They stood there for several more seconds, staring at one another: he amazed, she determined.

At last he said, "I am pledged to marry another."

"So you have told me."

"I cannot break my vow without bringing dishonour to myself and to my family."

"I understand that."

He scanned her face quickly, staring deeply down into her eyes, as he said, "I want you."

Her stomach dropped. There it was. Raw, impassioned emotion, clearly stated. And despite herself, her heart responded to him as though he had declared his undying love to her forever. At least, she admitted to herself, he'd had the courage to speak of his desires aloud.

"You want . . . m-me?" Her voice was barely a whisper.

He nodded.

"And you want her, too?"

"It is not the same thing. I *must* take her as a wife. It is different."

"Perhaps," she said, "but the result is still the same. The truth is that you belong to another, even if that marriage has not yet come to be."

"There is a difference."

"There is none."

He took a step toward her and said, "You want me, too."

She wished she could deny it. Oh, how she wanted to tell him it was not so, that he could go and throw himself off a cliff. But she couldn't. So she stared away from him, off into the darkness of the night. At last she said, "I could never marry a man who takes more than one wife. My God forbids it. So do not press me on this any further."

He was silent. So was she. He shifted his weight from one foot to another, his gaze locked with hers. She did the same.

"*Haiya,*" he said, then again, "*Haiya.*"

She remained unspeaking, supposing that he could find nothing more to dispute in what she'd said.

"*Haiya!*"

Rebecca glanced down at the ground.

"Tell me now, this is what you want, truly?"

"Aye," she said, nodding, "it must be. If not for

this, then because of my dreams of a dance, of my future husband."

He drew in a deep breath, letting it out in a sigh, before he said, "We will have to be careful, then, because the passion burns deeply within us and we will need to stay away from one another. I will not have this 'affair' with you, not when the others already believe us to be married. What would you have me do? Lie, with you here, with my own people, pretending to be man and wife, when I know that you would go back to your own kind as soon as I return you to the fort? I have told enough lies. No more. I will do my best to remain as far away from you as I can without drawing others' suspicion onto us. Yet there will be times when we will of necessity have to lie close together to make others believe we are married. It will not be easy for us, I think."

"No," she said, still afraid to look him directly in the eye. "I don't believe it will be."

"Humph. So be it. Come, little Rebecca, I think we had better have that swim. And perhaps we will be wise to take a cold bath each night. Maybe it will help us to remember our . . . differences."

"Aye," she said, but she didn't wait for him to say more on the subject or to escort her to the stream. Turning away from him, she fled into the cold depths of the water, savoring the sting of its icy currents as though it alone stood as a reminder of their dissimilarities.

She only hoped the waters would work a miracle.

Chapter 7

Though he tried to resist, Night Thunder studied Rebecca as she bathed within the dim glow of the starlight. He admired her spirit, the way she acted, the way she looked with her hair falling to her shoulders like so many rays of a golden sunset. Her figure was slight, perfect; her breasts high and pert; her waist small; her hips femininely curved; her legs long. And he could not forget the way she had felt in his arms—soft, slim, and warm. Her sweetened womanly scent lingered in the air and on his skin, as though it alone were intent on tantalizing him. He felt a stirring within his loins, but worse, he acknowledged a yearning within his heart.

Aa, his heart.

He gritted his teeth until his mouth ached. He could not have her. How many times, before he finally returned her to her people, would he have to remind himself of this?

Her skin had darkened while she had been held captive, he noted. It made her face and arms appear much darker than the rest of her body. She didn't remove all of her clothing to bathe, either, and he watched as she attempted awkwardly to cleanse herself through her clothing.

It was not an easy thing to observe, her bathing, not without his body—his very shadow, as his people called the life force within all men—responding to the sight of her. He must, however, quench the feeling. He turned his back on her, the only action he knew which might put her out of his mind.

But it was not to be. His ears had not been closed to the sound of her and he could heard her movements, the splashing of water, the soft gurgle of the creek's current; it made him imagine how she might look with the water falling over her delicate skin.

He gritted his teeth and wondered if she had spoken the truth. Did the white man's God truly forbid a man to take more than one wife? It seemed a ridiculous practice to Night Thunder, yet if he were to trust his own observations of Rebecca, he knew that she did not lie.

Still, he couldn't help wondering why this was so. Always within a village there were more women than men. Would the white man, then, grant the right to bear children to only a select few women? It seemed an unusually cruel thing to do.

It was true that sometimes a man took on a jealous wife, making his and the rest of his family's life a misery. But such incidents were few. Usually the first wife welcomed each new addition to the family, more than willing to share her workload with another—as well as her husband. Such had been the way of things within his tribe since "time before mind."

She had asked him if he loved her and he had purposely dodged her question. He hadn't known what to say, and yet as he had watched her, memorizing the way her golden hair fell around her shoulders, the way her amber-colored eyes lit up with passion, he'd debated what to tell her. It was then that he'd realized: he might already love her.

It had come as a revelation to him. All these months he had supposed he was merely attracted to Rebecca. She *was*, after all, pleasing to the eye, and of a pleasant disposition.

But he'd been growing closer and closer to her all the while, without even realizing it. At first he had admired her beauty, then he had recognized a kindred spirit in her and had admired her for it all the more. Now he had bridged the distance between them and had held her in his arms, had tasted her sweet nectar. And he wanted more. Much more.

But he could have none of that.

In truth, he wanted her to be the first thing he awoke to in the morning, the last thing he held before he fell asleep at night. He wanted her in his arms. He wanted to kiss her, to tell her of his desire for her whenever and wherever he pleased. He wanted to hold her through the night, to make love to her. And he wanted these things for many, many years to come.

Yet it could not be.

Not if she believed that she could be his one and only wife. He had made a pledge to another. He could not take back the vow. It would be the height of dishonour.

Yet had he ever loved Blue Raven Woman? He certainly had never felt with her as he did with Rebecca.

Of course, he could always force Rebecca to become his bride; he had the right since he had saved her. By all the laws of his tribe, she belonged to him, was his to do with as he pleased.

But he knew he would never force her into his lodge. If he were going to have her, he would have her with him willingly.

Which left him with a terrible problem. He wanted her, but he couldn't have her.

The more he thought about it, the more he began to despair. How could he keep her near, yet have her so far? He would have to hold her and sleep with her each evening while they remained traveling. It would be the height of delight, yet also an exercise of pure misery.

He could not even take the cold bath with her now, not even to still his passion. Not if she were anywhere within his vicinity. If he attempted it, he was certain that not even the freezing water would hide his desire from her.

There was nothing for it. He would have to put her from his mind . . . somehow.

But as he listened to the sounds of the water splashing, there against her body, envisioning the image of her, he couldn't begin to conceive of how he could stay away from her.

Taking a deep breath, and focusing his attention on the familiar scents of prairie grass and pure night air, he jerked his head to the left in a self-conscious gesture and sighed.

"That's a lovely butte, now, isn't it?"

Rebecca saw Night Thunder look briefly to where she was pointing. Their party had stopped earlier than usual to set up camp for the evening. "Will we be crossing that river that runs next to it?"

"*Aa*, yes."

"I see. What is the name of the river, so that I might remember it?"

Night Thunder made a gruff sound, deep in his throat, before answering, "We call it *Onuhkis*."

"*Onuhkis*," she smiled. "What does it mean?"

"Milk River."

"Milk River?" She glanced toward the river and frowned. "It doesn't have the appearance of milk."

He looked away from her. "It is not so named because of its likeness to milk."

"Why do you call it Milk River, then?"

He shrugged before he asked, "Are you certain you want to know?"

"I wouldn't ask, if I didn't, would I?"

His gaze came back to her as he caught and held her stare. And several moments passed before he voiced, "If I tell it to you, it is possible I might embarrass you. Be certain, then, that you are willing to hear this before you ask me to explain it to you."

"Speaking in riddles, are you, Night Thunder? I'd not ask you if I didn't want to know."

He shrugged as though to say, "So be it," and pointed toward the river. He said, "Do you see that butte that runs close to the river?"

She nodded. "Aye."

"Tell me, then, what does the butte look like to you?"

"Look like?" She stared at it. "I don't understand."

"Look and use your imagination."

"I don't see . . ."

"A part of a woman's body," he encouraged.

"A part of a . . . oh," she gasped, suddenly silent. A breast. It looked like a woman's breast. As he had predicted, embarrassment swept over her. With the sun setting behind the butte, the shape was clearly outlined against the sky.

Despite herself, Rebecca became suddenly conscious of Night Thunder, of herself, of her own breasts straining against the material of her dress.

"*Onuhkis* means milk in my language," Night Thunder was saying. "*Onuhkists* means breast.

"Oh," she said simply, flustered beyond belief.

"Say it," he said.

"Say what?"

"Say the words. *Onuhkis* and *Onuhkists*."

"I . . . I don't believe that—"

"It is important that you learn my language."

"But—"

"I think," he said, giving her a sly look, "that you are afraid. Or is it because yours are fuller than even the outline of that butte, that you did not recognize the look of it at once?"

Had she heard him correctly? Had the man actually asked her such a thing? She should slap him. She knew it, and had she been in civilized society, she might have done just that. But this was

not simply any man. This was Night Thunder, the
man who had rescued her, the man who had been
her friend for so many months. Still, he went too
far.

Picking up her skirt, she moved away from him,
saying at the same time, "I don't know how you
can be thinking that you have any right to speak
to me in this way, but I can assure you that my
... body parts are not yours to speculate upon,
and I would appreciate it if you would keep your
thoughts to yourself."

He simply smiled at her. "I think yours are better than the look of that butte. Firmer."

She gasped. "You have not even seen me—"

"At the river."

"At the river you were not supposed to be looking at me."

"I stood there that night, telling you that I
would. Say them."

"What?"

"Say the words, *Onuhkis* and *Onuhkists*."

"Why?"

"Because it is important that you learn my language. And because if you say them, I will stop
trying to embarrass you and bring color to your
cheeks."

She sent him a mock serious look. "You will?"

He nodded.

"All right," she conceded. "If I must, I will do
so. *Onuhkis*," she repeated once, then, "*Onuhkists*."

"Which means?"

"I don't think that I need to—"

"How do I know that you understand the difference between the two words?"

"Night Thunder, I think that—"

"If you say the meaning, I will stop tormenting you with the knowledge of how you look naked."

"Naked? That is not possible. You have not seen me naked."

His eyebrows shot upward. "Did you not know that the thing you wear beneath your clothes disappears against your skin when it is wet?"

She drew in a deep breath and frowned at him. "Why did you not tell me about this sooner than now?"

He sent her a mocking smile. "I am Indian," he said, "not stupid."

She almost smiled, but she held herself back from doing so. The man was bold beyond belief.

"Say them," he reiterated.

"All right, then. *Onuhkis* means milk, and *Onuhkists* means . . . br . . . brea . . . a woman's bosom."

"Humph," he grunted, then grinned at her. "I will teach you my language while we are on the trail, for you must learn to speak it well. You will wish to talk with others besides myself once we come to my village, will you not?"

"Aye," she said, "your village." It meant she would come face to face with his fiancée. She groaned. "What is the name of the girl you are going to marry?"

"Is it important, since you are not truly to become my wife?"

"I think that it is. You are going to be telling the people in your camp that I am your wife. I am thinking, then, that I have the right to know who else it is that you intend to marry."

He stared off toward the sunset for a moment, the humor leaving his eyes. Several moments passed in silence before he at last made to move away from her, having said nothing to enlighten her further.

"Night Thunder," she called to him, reaching out to touch his arm, staying him. "I think I have a right to know."

He stopped and glanced down at her hand where it brushed him, then back up at her face, before he responded, "Blue Raven Woman is her name." He frowned.

Rebecca gasped, not because of the woman's name; rather, because of the sudden tension she witnessed in Night Thunder's eyes. From her touch? Or because she had asked about his dearly beloved? She had no time to ponder the question, however. Night Thunder had already turned from her and was striding away, leaving Rebecca to wonder what it was she had said or done wrong.

Her fingers still tingled with a life of their own, she noticed.

Another set of complications to add to her long growing list of problems: she was fast becoming enamored with this man.

And Night Thunder? He was clearly sensitive about his intended, which meant what?

That he loved her?

Why, she wondered, as she turned to watch him leave, did she have to care?

Chapter 8

Night came swiftly. Rebecca sat around the small fire, a buffalo robe across her shoulders. Night Thunder reclined next to her, chipping monotonously at the point of a stone arrowhead. He seemed unaffected by her presence, entirely caught up in his work. Rebecca, however, could think of nothing more than the sleeping robe she would have to share with this man yet again tonight.

Except for an Indian sentry sitting lookout, all the other warriors had long since gone to sleep.

It was a quiet evening, save for the ever present sounds of the prairie. Off in the distance a coyote howled, answered by the wail of a wolf, while closer to them, a brook murmured in its haste to find a larger body of water, its rhythm seeming to keep time with the sighing wind rustling through the trees. These noises were somehow romantic. All were sounds she didn't need to hear.

To add to her discomfort, the ever present breeze had become so cold this evening that she shivered as she sat within the confines of the robe, knowing warmth and comfort sat only a few feet away from her if she could only bring herself to go willingly into Night Thunder's arms. But she couldn't. Not when he intended to have two or more wives.

The earth felt cold beneath her, reminding her all the more that without Night Thunder's body heat to warm her, she would get little sleep this night. Even the crisp scent of the air, in combination with the fragrances of dried grass, leaves, and sagebrush, conspired against her, bringing to her mind images of family and home; images of love.

Things she dared not remember. Not now.

Soon she would have to go to bed with this man. Soon she would have to feel the warm pressure of his body next to hers. And too soon, she knew, she would hear the call of his body to hers.

Idly she wondered why the knowledge that the man had a woman waiting for him in his camp didn't dampen her desire for him. It should, shouldn't it? Yet it hadn't. To tell the truth, his integrity in wishing to do the right thing by her, within the confines of the beliefs of his culture, caused the opposite effect: she admired him.

But she would never let him know it. To do so might mean more danger to her heart than she cared to contemplate.

She knew he was waiting for her to go to bed. Patiently, with no attempt to rush her, he waited. Yet she couldn't make herself say anything to him or force herself to move.

She felt petrified. But soon his silence began to irritate her.

"Why don't you go to bed?" she asked in a hoarse whisper.

He stopped his work, looking over to her before he said, "Because it would be bad manners for me to go to the sleeping robes and lie down before you."

She groaned. "Even if I want you to go?"

He nodded. "Even then."

She inhaled deeply. "I can't lie with you this night," she said at last. "When we began our journey, I thought I could do it so as to avoid a problem, but now I don't think that I can."

"Humph," he said, and nodded. "I thought as much. It is why I believe we should both go to bed fully clothed, as you once suggested."

"I don't think I can do it even then."

"I will not try to ... violate you, I vow this to you. Now that we understand one another, and our differences, we know that we can never come to be man and wife in truth. It would be wrong, then, of me to tempt you, and I will not do it. Will knowing this make it easier for you?"

Would it? She would still have the warmth of his body against hers, the scent of his skin to inhale with each breath, the feel of his arms beneath her head to cushion her. Plus, he would have to contend with the same things from her. Could he really ignore her so easily? Somehow, she didn't like the idea that he could.

"I'm not certain that I can sleep next to you. Maybe if I were so tired that I would have no choice but to fall asleep at once. Maybe then."

"*Haiya*," he said, "I can do no more than I have already offered this night. Perhaps tomorrow I should try to make you walk farther than today so that you will be too tired to think of anything else but sleep."

"Perhaps, but that doesn't help us tonight."

"Possibly you are right. But maybe we should walk now. Will that not tire you enough to sleep?"

"Perhaps."

He set down the arrowhead and said, "Let us do it."

Without another word, he arose immediately and set off ahead of her, his footsteps making little noise against the grasses. He didn't look back at her, either. Was he assuming, Indian-like, that she would follow him?

She did, too. Shaking the stiffness out of her legs and holding the buffalo robe firmly around her shoulders for warmth, she ran after him, her own pacing making enough noise for the two of them combined.

It was a beautiful night. The breeze was cool, but the moon shone above them as a tiny sliver of light, the stars twinkling like shimmering jewels set against a backdrop of black velvet. The prairie stretched out before her, seemingly to infinity. She felt a part of all this, somehow; a part of the magnitude of the universe. It was a good feeling, one that she could not remember having felt before this moment.

Would she have come to think this way if she hadn't been stolen away by these Indians? Not a pleasant thought, yet it remained as a possible truth. She thought of her old life, of the drudgery of the meager existence she'd known since her parents' death over five years ago.

Katrina, though, had offered to pay Rebecca's debts in exchange for her services as maid and her company on this trek into the wilderness. Only Katrina had offered relief.

· Rebecca owed a debt of gratitude to Katrina. Without her, Rebecca would have never had the opportunity to come to know this place, to know Night Thunder.

She glanced up, realizing that Night Thunder's path had changed, his footfalls leading them to the river where the water ran smooth and fast, gurgling in its hurry. They crossed over the water to the other side, then back again, the river being narrow enough to step over in parts. Willow trees dotted the bank on each side of the water, the smell of their leaves scenting the air. Rebecca let out a gasp as a white-tailed deer flitted in front of them, heading for the hill which hid the stream from the prairie. Huge cottonwoods, their bark worn thin from where buffalo had rubbed against them, stood as though they were solitary sentinels on duty. Off in the distance a herd of antelope poised near the river, their hoofs making a solid thud against the earth as they fought for position to drink at the stream.

Night Thunder led her to the hill, climbing up onto the plains, where she stood looking toward the heavens in awe, so grandiose loomed the starlit sky above her.

"Looking up like this," she said softly, "gives a person the feeling he is the only living being on earth, doesn't it?"

"*Aa*, yes, it is so. But we will go back into the

coulee as soon as we pass the antelope down there."

"I see," said Rebecca, gazing back at Night Thunder. "But tell me, why is it that we are skirting around them from up here?"

"To go among them now would startle them and make them stampede," he said. "If there were an enemy nearby, it would betray our presence to them. I do not believe there is an enemy here near us, but why should we take the chance?"

"Aye," she said.

He glanced over his shoulder at her and she caught her breath. Why did he have to look so handsome? And why did she have to notice things about him, like the way the moonlight shone on his hair, the way his skin glistened under it, the regal way in which he walked, in which he held himself, as though he had the grace of a panther? She glanced away hurriedly.

"All day long," she said, a little out of breath, "we've been avoiding or killing rattlesnakes that we run across in our path. Isn't it feasible that we could come across one?"

She could see his head nod as he agreed with her. "That is always possible," he said, "but do not fear. It is why I go ahead of you. So that if we do run into something which is harmful, it will get to me before you, giving you a chance to escape."

"And leave you alone?"

"I would hope that you would. Sometimes," he said, "it is necessary that the woman escapes to safety while the man stays to fight. Women are very important in our village, since without a mother, a child has little chance to survive."

"But without a man to provide for them," Rebecca argued, "a woman would find it hard to raise that child. Therefore, you are just as important to that child's future as the woman and should have as much consideration."

She could see him shrug slightly as he continued to tread ahead of her. "The tribe would always ensure that a woman has food and clothing if her man is killed," he said. "The woman and child would never go hungry, nor would they want for anything."

"Is that so?" she asked, not adding that in white society, the woman and child would have to provide for themselves in a world where only the men survived well; that the woman and child might not subsist at all.

He asked, "Is it not this way for the white man, too?"

Rebecca shrugged silently, knowing he wouldn't see the gesture, yet unwilling to condemn her own society.

"Besides," he continued, "I have rattlesnake medicine, if we find we have need of it."

"Rattlesnake medicine?"

"*Aa*, yes."

"You mean, medicine that will cure a bite?"

"*Aa*, yes."

"There is no such thing, one has to dig and suck the poison out."

Night Thunder laughed. "I will not argue the point with you. Just know that I have the medicine with me if we should have cause to use it. I have seen it cure snakebite."

"But there is only one way to—"

"Hush!" He suddenly halted and held up his hand for her silence. Rebecca almost ran into his back.

Suddenly, though, he straightened up and turned all around him, scanning his environment.

"What is wrong?"

"Sh-h-h."

"What is it?"

"A war party—four, maybe five or six."

"A war party? But I thought you said . . . I hear nothing."

"Do you know how to listen?"

"I . . . Couldn't it be the warriors from our own party?"

"Traveling at night? This is Blackfoot country, we have no need to journey during the time when Old Woman must shine, but our enemies do."

"Old Woman?"

"The favorite wife of the Sun. You call her the moon. Hush!" He held up his hand.

She gulped. "What can we do?"

"We must hide. I am not enough to stop them by myself, and there is no time to return to our camp. Quickly."

She hadn't noticed it, but off to the side of the stream, down in the coulee, there were several dead cottonwood trees: one on its side, another with part of its trunk cut or worn out. Was that tree hollow? Night Thunder hurried her toward it as though it were.

If it were hollow, she wondered, was it big enough to hide them? Even then, if it was, wasn't it also possible that something else might have taken refuge in it? Some animal, perhaps?

She had no time to ponder it. The tree had a large cavity, and Night Thunder gave the inside of it a cursory glance, placing her within it while he gazed out upon the countryside. Then, seeing her settled, and with one final scan of the horizon, Night Thunder slipped in beside her.

The tree was barely big enough for the two of them, and of necessity they stood together, chest to chest, legs to legs, stomach to stomach. If she hadn't known the feel of this man before, she certainly did now.

Immediately the scent of rotten wood assailed her and something small and indefinable crawled up her arm. She gave a slight jump.

Night Thunder's arms tightened around her and he gave her a silencing look. He murmured, "You must not speak out no matter what happens, do you understand?"

She nodded.

He pulled her more closely into his arms—so close, she could hear the rapid beating of his heart, feel the warming touch of his breath against her ear. All at once, another fragrance stormed her senses, too: his scent, clean, fresh, undeniably male, perfumed with the sweat from his skin.

This was too much, she realized, his presence too intoxicating, and it was more than she could do to remain still. She wiggled, but Night Thunder quickly brought her under control, his arms tightening around her as he gave her another warning look.

Finally she heard it, the sounds of people—men—moving across the prairie. Dimly at first, but then with more and more clarity, they came toward them.

How could Night Thunder have heard them before? Did he have some kind of sixth sense?

She listened to the men talking and her heartbeat sped up to an incredible pace. She put her head against Night Thunder's shoulder and hid her eyes, as though that action alone would shield her from harm. It was odd, too, because though she felt frightened, she also experienced a sense of safety: being secure, here with Night Thunder to protect her.

The enemy was close now. She held her breath, afraid that even her breathing would be heard.

Suddenly a moccasined foot came into view and she held back a gasp, barely. Night Thunder's arms pressed around her and he glanced down at her, warning her again to silence.

As she gazed up at Night Thunder, an Indian, painted fully in black and carrying spear, arrows, and knife, appeared in her view, his back toward them. She opened her mouth to scream, but at that same moment, Night Thunder's lips suddenly closed over hers, silencing her.

Perhaps it was because her senses were already heightened; perhaps, also, were Night Thunder's. Whatever the cause, a minor explosion occurred within her.

She felt like weeping. If she had found him irresistible before, she found him doubly enchanting now.

He pulled back from her, away from the kiss—for only a moment—as though she had bitten him. He stared at her, there in their private world of rotted tree trunk, and nesting animals. Though it was too dark to see, she knew that if she could, she would witness shock within his eyes. It had to be. She felt it as well.

The other Indian disappeared, almost as though she had dreamed him, and Night Thunder took her lips again with his, only this time his mouth plundered hers, much as man immemorial has done in claiming his bride. His tongue swept into her mouth, dipped, and tasted before he pulled back to trace the outline of her lips with the tip of his tongue . . . around and around, over and over, until neither of them could stand it and he fell again to ravaging her mouth.

Had she groaned? She knew she shouldn't. Yet she didn't seem able to help herself.

She could hear the talk of the enemy outside, but her fear evaporated as sensual excitement took hold of her. Night Thunder's mouth made love to her—stimulating, strenuous love—and her body, pressed in closely to his, ached.

In and out of her mouth, his tongue invaded her, over and over again, he tasting her, she savoring the sweet flavor of him. It was as though he would make up here and now for all he could not do for her physically, emotionally. She opened her mouth to the full insistence of his, too, and he took instant advantage of her acquiescence, his tongue raiding hers.

She felt the clear evidence of his desire against her stomach, though she knew he would do nothing about it. He was too much the gentleman to take advantage.

Still, she wiggled, his arms pulling her so closely

to him, she might have melted into him.

Minutes passed, or was it hours? She couldn't be certain. She only knew the presence of his lips, kissing her on and on, taking her deeper and deeper into the realm of desire.

She felt frustrated. She wanted more, much more. Dear Lord, she wanted him to make love to her.

She almost wept with the knowledge. She couldn't let him know, of course, and she mustn't encourage him. He was too foreign to her; foreign, aye, but so dear.

Suddenly, in this rustic, simple place, at this time, the realization came to her: she had deep, involved feelings for this man. Did she love him? Was that what this was?

Praise the Lord, it might be; she might actually love him.

She inwardly moaned. What was she to do about it, if it were true? They held such entirely different beliefs, came from completely different cultures—and, she groaned, he intended to have *two wives*.

He broke off the kiss at last and rubbed his cheek over hers, his lips pressing tiny kisses against her ear. He whispered, "Prepare yourself, for we will not live beyond this evening, I think."

"No."

"Sh-h-h. Speak not so loud."

"They have done nothing to us," she whispered urgently. "Maybe they do not know we are here."

"*Saa*, no. Know this, though they have not yet become aware of us, if we do not escape this evening and soon, they will find our trail. Because

Old Woman, the moon, is dim this night, they have not yet discovered us. But know this, too: come morning they will see our trail, and they will seek us out and kill us, if they can."

She sucked in her breath and whispered back, "Is there nothing we can do?"

He nodded briefly. "If they do not discover us, we can wait until they sleep and then try to slip away. Perhaps we could cover our trail well enough, or maybe we would obtain sufficient lead that we could find our own camp and get reinforcement against them. But we can do nothing now; we must wait."

Rebecca nodded.

He then murmured against her ear, "I want you."

Her stomach plunged, as though it might drop to her feet, but she could only nod an acknowledgment, her voice not working.

"I should not, but I do. Know this, too," he said, his breath warm against her. "Should we not see the morrow, know that I will take your image with me to the Sand Hills, where I will keep you alive within me always."

"You . . . you would?"

"*Aa*, yes. I have feelings for you, my reluctant captive. A deep, strong passion."

"Then, do you . . . you love me?"

He paused and it seemed he might answer, but at that same moment a rustling movement came from outside and he whispered, "Sh-h-h. I can say nothing more about it now."

But she wanted to know more—now.

"Night Thunder?"

"Sh-h-h."

"Night Thunder, I wouldn't want tomorrow to come with us departed from it, and you never to know what's in my heart, or me not to know what's in yours."

He remained silent, though his regard of her became intent.

She said, "I want you, too."

His expression didn't change, though when he spoke, his whisper was as soft as a caress as he said, "Do not say this if you do not truly mean it."

"I mean it."

His look at her was full of promise as he said, "I would have made you a good husband."

"I know you would have . . . if it weren't for . . ."

He seemed to know what she had been about to say, for he uttered, "I could not dishonour a pledge that was made by my parents before I was even of an age to come to my senses. Know that if I had the power to change my life, if it meant being able to keep you, I would do so."

"But you cannot?"

He shook his head. "Never."

"And you do not believe that we will come through this alive?"

"We are only two and they are six warriors. In a fight, I would die and you would be captured. Know this." He reached down and took her hand, placing it against his chest. "You have taken and I have given you my heart, all that I am. From now, until Sun no longer shines, you will be a part of me here."

"*Aa*," she said, the Blackfoot word coming easily to her, "aye, a part of you." Their gazes lingered over each other there in the dark, touching one another, each one promising the other an untold wealth of tenderness.

Then he kissed her. Tenderly at first, as soft a touch as love's first embrace, but soon with more urgency.

His tongue slipped into and out of her mouth as she listened to the sounds outside, their bodies rubbing against each other to the beat of a drum, the warriors outside beginning to pound on it. She closed her eyes, savoring the feel of him against her, and she realized that here and now, inside this hollow tree trunk, she had finally given her heart, her very soul, to the one man who had so many times proved himself her hero.

"Love me, Night Thunder," she murmured against his lips, letting him kiss her cheeks, her neck, her breasts. "Don't let tomorrow come without me ever knowing the sweetness of your full caress. Please, Dear God, leave me with something of you to remember."

For several heart-stopping moments Night Thunder did nothing more than stare down at her, and she began to worry that she had spoken out of turn. But then, all at once, passion erupted in him and he set up her up against the side of their hollowed-out tree trunk, pushing up her skirts at the same time as his lips took possession of hers.

He pulled her upward, wrapping her legs around his waist. "This is not the time and place to accustom you to the feel of me. Be certain it is what you want, for it will be hard on you, I think."

"I want this, Night Thunder."

It was all the encouragement he needed. His lips

sought out hers, while his fingers touched her legs, the insides of her thighs, her womanhood.

She gasped, the intimacy proving almost too much for her.

But he hadn't finished with her. His fingers found the core of her fervor, where she discovered she had become embarrassingly wet.

"Rebecca, sweet captive, your body is ready for me. Are you certain?"

"I want you, Night Thunder."

His eyes held hers, and he swallowed with what appeared to be some difficulty. But with no more words, he drew aside his breechcloth, his manhood, swollen and hard, suddenly released against her.

She couldn't see the whole of him, she could only feel him against that most private area, but it didn't matter. She could still rejoice in the power she felt she held over him.

"You must not scream," he cautioned her, "for it will hurt at first. But the pain should swiftly leave you. Promise?"

She nodded, and he entered her, not cautiously, as she felt he might have liked. There was no time for niceties. They had gone beyond all that. He wanted her. She wanted him. And danger had made them hungry.

His lips caught her gasp, his arms pulling her tightly against him, and he ceased all movement, letting her become accustomed to the feel of him.

But slowly, he began to move inside her. Lingeringly, cautiously at first, until neither of them could stand it any longer, and, as though by mutual agreement, they began to push against each other, he thrusting, she taking, both seeking the thrill of romance, in the age-old dance of love. She began to move with him as a feeling she could never find words to describe began to build within her, centering where their bodies were joined. Was it supposed to be this way?

He pulled his head slightly away from her, his breath raggedly urgent against her, his gaze steadily on her as he thrust into her over and over again.

Desire, passion burned there in the depths of his eyes . . . and love, too. Watching him, smiling at him, Rebecca struggled against him with more and more vigor, seeking a release she had no knowledge of, yet sought instinctively.

Then it came. It came with an explosion of the senses, it came without her knowledge of what to expect. It came because of her love for him. Aye, that was it, and she moaned against him with the secure knowledge. *Love.* She *did* love him.

His lips suddenly captured hers, absorbing the inadvertent sound of her rapture, and within seconds, she felt the bounds of his reserve falter and crash as he thrust even more urgently against her, though he made no sound.

He drove inside her over and over, his pleasure seemingly going on and on, as though it might never end. And she relished in his passion, in what she was certain was his love.

But at last he shuddered and brought his forehead against hers, as he whispered, "Our passion for one another has made this act more pleasurable than I have ever known it could be." He smiled before he added, "Know this, sweet cap-

tive. Always," he murmured the word in her ear,
"you will be in my heart. Always."

And with his body slightly swollen and so very
pleasantly joined with hers, she murmured, "Always."

Chapter 9

"**K**yai-yo, what was my father's decision?" The young Indian girl kept her sights carefully centered upon her lap, looking over the beaded work she had finished on a new set of moccasins. She noticed one blue bead out of place and focused her attention on it as she awaited a response.

"What could he say, *nitana*, my daughter? Know you the honour that binds him?"

The young Indian maiden's stomach dropped as the import of her mother's words hit her. She needed to hear the thing said, however, and so she asked, "What then? Did he send Singing Bull away?"

"He had to. You know that he had to."

The young girl fought to keep her composure. She knew her lower lip trembled and so she bit it, in order that she keep her dignity. She loved her parents, had wallowed in their affection and their understanding for all her life. She would not—could not—go against them. Not even when her heart demanded that she do just that.

She also could not rebel against tradition. Not without bringing great shame to her family.

But oh, how her heart hungered for the touch of this one who had approached her father for the honour of her hand.

Still . . .

Was this it, then? Was this thing to be as she had feared?

The girl tried to swallow, but her throat refused to work and it was all she could do to hold back a sob.

Her mother's arm went around her, the older woman's unspoken sympathy practically the girl's undoing, but the young woman held onto her pride and forced herself to display none of her inner struggle. She would never let her parents know the utter distress their decision forced upon her. Such would serve to make them feel guilty. After all, weren't they acting in the only honourable way? She couldn't ask her parents to be less than they were.

Later, when she was alone, she would confront her sorrow. Later, she would vent her grief. For now, she had to pretend that her father's decision hadn't deadened her spirit. For now, she had to be strong.

"*Nitsiitsistapi'taki*, I understand," she said.

"Do you truly?"

She could not bring herself to say more, not even to agree. All she could do was nod and hide her face, hoping that none of her emotions communicated themselves to her mother. "*Noohk*, please, my mother," she said, keeping her voice as steady as she was able. "I need to be alone."

Her mother nodded and let go of her shoulders as the younger woman arose and negotiated her way, as well as she was able, to the *niitoyis'*, the tepee's entrance, the sound of her moccasins against the buffalo hide rug making a dull, flat sound as she moved. Pulling back the entry flap, the girl stepped out into the day, the brightness and cheer of Sun seeming to mock her.

She kept her gaze downward, refusing to note where her feet took her, refusing to look at anyone.

She needed to be alone. She wanted the silence of the plains, the magic of the gurgling streams, the sighings of the wind. She needed these to enter into her spirit, to take away the hurt. But most of all, she had to regain her composure.

Her direction took her toward the stream and she wished she had remembered to bring her water hide so that she might fill it. At least she could have made herself useful.

But she could not go back into the village. Not now. Not until she had come to terms with what was to be.

She bolted across the creek, which was only knee deep, and struggled onto the other bank, scrambling up a ledge which would lead her out onto the prairie.

Once there she ran, as fast as her legs would take her. She ran until she was out of breath, ran until she could run no more. Then she let the tears come, as she sank down onto her knees, hiding her face in her hands, sobbing as though her heart might never be the same again.

Truly, it might never be.

Soon, the healing rays of Sun drew her spirit

upward, however, and she realized she floated free above the prairie, above her home. She felt herself fly and for the moment, she drew comfort from such a simple action, admiring the tremendous show of nature and thanking Sun that she was being allowed to see it.

A hawk soared by her, its squawk a gentle reminder that she had to leave this place and go to her home. Her parents would worry.

She glanced at the hawk, but for a moment she saw not the bird, but a woman. A woman with terribly pale skin, a woman with hair the gold color of autumn leaves and eyes tawny like those of a mountain lion. Giving a squawk, the hawk turned all at once and flew away, but as it left, the young girl could have sworn she saw the bird transform into something else yet again. A warrior. A warrior she knew and recognized.

Shock made the Indian maiden plummet instantly and suddenly back into her body, the impact of her return to it momentarily sending the young girl sprawling onto the ground. But she quickly picked herself up.

Who was this woman, what importance did she hold, and why had she turned into a warrior?

Had she, an Indian maiden, imagined this, or had she obtained a vision? She, a woman, receiving a message from Sun? Surely not. Only the wise men of the tribe were so gifted.

Yet she could not deny what had happened.

What did it mean?

Perhaps, after she made her way back to camp, she would tell her father and they could seek out a medicine man who could relate to them the significance of the vision. If it were a vision.

No one would believe her, she was certain. Others might even laugh at her.

Still, it was her duty to tell one and all of this vision if it were truly a message from the Sun.

Picking herself up and drying the tears from her eyes, she set out on wobbly legs, making her course one that would return her to the village. And as she glanced up at Sun, Blue Raven Woman sent a prayer of thanks for the wisdom shown her, vowing that she would do all she could to learn of this thing she had seen, that she might do honour to herself, to her family, and to Sun.

Night Thunder despaired as he glanced down at the sleeping woman in his arms.

She had fallen asleep standing up, still nestled in his embrace. He tightened his hold on her and grimaced.

How was he to save her, himself?

The enemy's singing had continued on and on throughout the night, as had the dancing. What sort of war party was this that these warriors celebrated through the night—in enemy territory? Night Thunder wasn't mistaken about their identity, was he? No, he couldn't be. He had seen the cut of their moccasins, had listened to their talk. They were not Blackfeet, nor from any allied tribe that he could fathom.

He didn't recognize their speech pattern, either, which was odd. He might not be able to utter the different languages of the plains, but he could usually distinguish one tribe from another by their words. This one he could not.

There was more. Why had no one from this war party come to challenge him? He was certain he and Rebecca had made more noise than they should have. He was positive, too, that these warriors should have heard the two of them, or at least have felt their presence. Why had the men not attacked?

Had he been on his own, he might have challenged these men. He might already have had the glory of waging battle. But he could not do that now—not with Rebecca with him. True, her life might be spared by this enemy, but he did not wish to put that particular assumption to the test.

Which brought him back full circle: why was he being left alone? Was it possible his and Rebecca's lovemaking hadn't been heard? It seemed improbable.

But more important, hadn't these warriors "felt" that they were being watched? As a hunter and a warrior, Night Thunder had been trained never to observe the enemy too closely, since it was well known that they could sense the attention of others upon them.

Were these warriors delaying the inevitable for some reason of their own? And if they were, how could he spare Rebecca? He glanced down at the sleeping woman in his arms.

Aa, Rebecca. He sighed.

She remained a mystery to him. She had been distant from him for so long that he found it incredible to envision that she might desire him. Yet she had kissed him, had loved him, with as much ferocity as he had loved her. Surely this must mean that she held some fancy for him.

She had also been a maiden. Surely, no young miss would give the gift of her virginity without strong affection, would she?

She had said that she held a loving place for him within her heart, but her utterance had been whispered in the heat of passion, said at a time when she had not known if she might live from this moment to the next. These were the sort of words one could come to regret within the light of day.

Would she? Would she rue their lovemaking? Especially when she discovered that he could not change his alliance with Blue Raven Woman?

He tilted his head and frowned. Why, he wondered, did it matter to him?

Yet it did.

Looking away from her, another thought occurred to him. What if they lived? What if the enemy truly had not seen or heard them? What would he do then? How could he make Rebecca understand that he loved her, though he must marry another woman? Especially when, by the laws of his tribe, he had now made Rebecca his wife, too?

He didn't want to think about it.

Rebecca stirred and wiggled against him, and had Night Thunder been anything but the trained warrior that he was, he would have groaned.

His body answered hers, his manhood stiffening as though to reassure her that he remained in readiness for her.

He should make love to her again.

The thought came to him unbidden.

He should make love to her, yet he must not. The enemy lurked outside. Both he and Rebecca had been spared the danger of discovery once; they would be fools to tempt fate yet again.

Still, with her so near to him . . .

"Night Thunder?" she whispered.

He brought his attention back to her. "I am here," he said unnecessarily, and pulled her body in toward him.

"Night Thunder, has it occurred to you that this enemy is not keeping their presence well hidden?"

"That is true."

"If they are in dangerous territory, shouldn't they be? That is, shouldn't they be trying to keep hidden?"

"*Aa*, yes, that is as it should be."

"Then, why?"

"I do not know. I have been wondering the same thing."

She stirred against him again, her stomach up against his stiffness.

"Night Thunder, you are—"

"Sh-h-h. We must not talk about it."

"Why not?"

"Is it not obvious? There is an enemy close by and we must remain silent."

"But we are talking now and—"

"Sh-h-h."

She wiggled against him and he let out a low growl.

"Be still," he said, even as his hands reached down to massage her buttocks.

"But you are—" He captured her lips, then, ravaging her mouth with his.

Haiya, this must be a madness with him. With the enemy so close to them, he could think of nothing but her and he lifted her up against him, even while he was certain the enemy would discover them.

He wanted to be gentle, but he was not. He parted her legs, wrapping them around him as he drove into her with all the finesse of a buffalo bull in heat, and he sent a prayer of thanks to Sun that Rebecca appeared to welcome him.

He covered her sighs with his lips, and as their movements began to keep time with the beating of the drum outside, Night Thunder lost himself to the wonder of her, to the incredible feeling of being one with this woman. Never had he felt the powerful draw of another female, never could he remember having had such glorious pleasure.

He could sense her nearing her climax, and as he felt her tiny muscles tighten up around him, he emptied his seed within her, praying that the sound of their lovemaking would not betray their presence.

Her breathing was as ragged as his, and he held her even more closely to him as he drifted back to earth, content for the moment in the knowledge that the wind blew against them, carrying his moans and her sighs away from the danger of the enemy.

He would not let her go, he realized. Now that he'd had her, he wanted her even more. What this would mean to her, to Blue Raven Woman, and even to himself, he dared not consider. At least for the moment.

He only knew he would keep Rebecca with him, somehow, in some way. And despite himself, despite his troubled thoughts, Night Thunder drifted off into an amazingly contented sleep.

The silvery rays of early morning trickled into the hollow tree, while outside, the lyrical call of the lark and the mourning dove proclaimed the start of a new day.

Night Thunder came instantly awake and glanced around him. Shock kept him silent; his stomach fell. He had slept through the night.

How could he have done it? Now there would be no chance of escape. He groaned inwardly, trying to remember a time when he had acted so irresponsibly. He couldn't recall one.

He nudged Rebecca awake, putting a finger to his lips to silence her.

The enemy hadn't yet found them. Perhaps there was still a chance . . .

He chided himself for his foolishness. There would be no chance once Sun was fully up.

But it was still early morning. Maybe if the enemy still slept? The warriors had danced and sung most of the night away. Surely he might find the men resting?

Cautiously he drew Rebecca out of his arms, and positioning her so that her back rested against the tree, he motioned toward her to remain where she was. Meanwhile, he crept back toward the opening of the tree.

He peered over his shoulder at the outside, slowly, making certain to create no sound.

He saw nothing.

He turned, and bending, crept out a little farther. He glanced out.

Nothing.

He slunk back into the protection of the tree. Where were the warriors? Had they already broken camp?

And if so, why had they not attacked and killed these two who had been hiding within a tree trunk? He was certain that he and Rebecca had left a trail. Why had the enemy not acted?

Night Thunder bent down on hands and knees and crawled forward, taking care to make no sound.

Nothing.

He stood up and glanced around him in a full circle before stooping to examine the ground.

What was this? Not only could he see no warriors, he could detect no evidence of their having been there; not a blade of grass bent where they might have stepped, not even a broken twig.

Surely there would be some evidence. Had their fire not been here, in this place where he stood? Yet he could find no trace of it. Of course the warriors would have tried to erase all signs of a fire, but there still would have been some sign of it left behind, if only a warmer piece of ground. But as he covered the dirt all around him, he could find nothing.

What did this mean? Night Thunder could make no sense of it. Unless . . .

A cold chill ran down his spine. It couldn't be. Yet . . .

Spinning around, Night Thunder hurried back to Rebecca.

"*Oki*, come!" He reached a hand into the hollow

tree and took her elbow, propelling her forward and out. "Let us leave this place."

She followed him, albeit reluctantly. "But the war party . . . ?" she asked, her voice a whisper.

"Do not worry about them."

"They are not here?" Her voice was louder.

He shook his head.

"We are free to go?"

"*Aa*, would I ask you to come with me if we were not?"

"But I thought that—"

"Later I will tell you about it. We must leave this place now."

"Yes, of course, but—"

"*Now*." And with nothing more said to enlighten her, he ushered her from their hiding place, onto the prairie, setting their course to intersect with that of his fellow tribesmen.

He only hoped that the danger would not follow them.

Chapter 10

"**D**id I hear you correctly? Ghosts?"

"I do not know what this 'ghosts' is. I only tell you about the shadow of those who were once living."

"Ghosts," Rebecca repeated, saying it more to herself than to her companion. "I don't believe in ghosts."

"I do not ask you to believe," he replied over his shoulder, his intention clearly on keeping pace with the others from their party. Night Thunder had found their companions' trail easily this morning and had caught up with them, losing little time in doing so. "I am only explaining to you," he continued, "why there was no trace of the enemy warriors. A great fight must have taken place where we were encamped last night, and those who are still there must have been blinded or had body parts cut off in the fight, for they are unable to find their way to the Sand Hills."

"But I heard them, I saw them. One cannot see ghosts," Rebecca frowned. "And what do you mean, body parts cut off?"

Night Thunder didn't answer right away. Instead, he kept his stride on a par with the others, not even glancing over his shoulder to ensure she followed. When he finally did speak, she had to strain to hear him. "Most people cannot see those who are departed because they no longer have the physical body to identify them. But their shadow can be felt and experienced if one will only let himself be aware of them."

"But I wasn't trying to be 'aware' of them," she complained. "And I didn't *feel* them. I *saw* them."

"Perhaps it was because you were with me."

"With you, but—"

"Within my family runs the power to see into the future, to change the weather, even to call to the buffalo. And sometimes, there are those of us who can talk to the dead. It is something I have been trained to do."

Rebecca quickened her pace so that she kept stride with Night Thunder. "Trained? What do you mean, trained?"

"Perhaps this is not the right word. I have long been an . . . apprentice with our medicine man. It is something I have learned to do, to talk to the dead."

"I don't believe in such things. What are you, a mystic?"

"I do not know what this thing is, a 'mystic,' and I do not ask you to believe." He paused and seemed lost in thought, though he quickly picked up his pace. "Still there must be some reason why they chose me to see them, to hear them. Perhaps they are hoping that I can discover a way to free them from the spell of those they fought, so that their shadows might yet find the Sand Hills."

"Night Thunder, I—"

"I will have to think on it. Perhaps there is something I can do. Come here now and let us not talk of this again."

"But what did you mean by being blinded or having body parts cut off? What has that to do with them?"

He stopped and let the others move off away from him as he turned to face her. She froze. Despite the intimacy she had shared with this man last night, she felt herself cower from his imposing figure.

"It is a belief of my people that the way in which one departs this world is the same way he must spend the rest of eternity. And so there are those warriors who, after a fight, will blind an opponent or cut off a part of his body, that his enemy might have to go to the next world so burdened. There are those who, having departed this world with a missing body part, choose not to seek out the next life, but determine to stay in this one, hoping to find someone who might at last be able to reverse the spell."

Rebecca didn't utter a word in response to this bit of Indian lore, though she stared hard at the man who had only last night held her and made love to her. She frowned and silently fought a battle within herself to hold back her opinions about such things. It was not her place to pass judgment on the beliefs of another. Still, these things of which he spoke were so foreign to her, she found herself wondering about him, and perhaps even more about herself. Had she really given her heart to this man?

Somehow at this moment it didn't seem real, *he* didn't seem real.

"Come," he spoke to her, turning away from her at the same time. "We are too far behind the others."

Rebecca allowed him to tread on ahead of her while she stood still, lost in her own thoughts. Ghosts, or "shadows," as he called them, talking to him, calling to him, asking him to set them free from earthly haunts? Could one really be "trained" to talk to such spirits? She didn't believe in such things, she wouldn't believe. Yet didn't her own Irish heritage have similar tales? Aye.

Still, this was too much for her to grasp all at once, and she felt herself growing distant from Night Thunder, in more than just a physical sense.

The Indian's view of life made little sense to her. For instance, no one had made comment upon the fact that both she and Night Thunder had been gone the entire night, something she felt hard pressed to comprehend. In truth, it appeared that the Indians, as a people, rarely condemned one for things which seemed important to her, yet made much over what to her were trivial matters.

Perhaps she would never understand them.

With the flip of her hand, she shook back her hair and tipped her head to face toward the sun, welcoming the warm rays of the morning. She paused for a moment more, letting the sun settle in upon her as though it might wash away her thoughts. But too soon, she realized she could no longer see the Indians, and picking up her skirt, she hurried to catch up to Night Thunder and the others.

Though Blue Raven Woman knew she shouldn't, she met her brother's gaze from over the blaze of the campfire. Quickly she looked away.

Had he seen her?

Her brother would discipline her, she knew, if she did something to bring her family shame. But it wasn't this that caused her to look away. It was her own emotion she feared, not her brother.

Drawing her buckskin robe up to cover her face, Blue Raven Woman turned away from the evening's tribal gathering, feeling as though she were being engulfed by a sickening sensation of her spirit.

What could she, a lone woman, do? She loved the young warrior, and he loved her. But it could never be. She was promised to another.

It wasn't that she didn't love and respect Night Thunder, her betrothed; it was that Night Thunder seemed more brother to her than lover. Of course, she couldn't be certain, since she had never had a lover.

But she had known Night Thunder all her life, had grown up with him, played games with him as a child. He seemed a part of her family—not in the role of husband, but rather like a relative.

How could she marry him?

Yet, she must.

She had told her mother and her father of her vision, but as she had predicted, no one had believed that she, a young woman, without fasting, without doing the proper honour to Sun, had been granted a vision. Perhaps it was just as well. Surely the dream would only strengthen Night Thunder's cause. Yet she had wondered who was this golden-haired woman? What did the vision mean?

Still, it mattered little now.

Blue Raven Woman threw back the hide flap of her mother's *niitoyis*, tepee, and stepped a foot inside the lodge, ignoring the welcoming scents of sweet grass and smoke. Tears fell from her eyes and she knew she had to get away. She couldn't let her parents, her brother, find her like this.

Grasping hold of the water hide, she made her way back outside, her path taking her to the stream, which ran close by their encampment. Perhaps if she were lucky she would avoid her grandmother this night, too, since it was her grandmother's job to keep a close watch upon her, an unmarried maiden, in a village of virile men.

She didn't want to explain her feelings for the young warrior to her grandmother. A lecture, and a story of what had happened to other women who had been disloyal to their families, would be hers for her trouble.

Blue Raven Woman paused at the stream, her gaze seeking out Sun's favorite wife, Old Woman, the moon.

Somehow, she felt that Old Woman would understand her. Yet what could they do, she and Old Woman? Custom dictated she marry Night Thunder. It was binding upon her . . . and upon Night Thunder.

"You should not be out here at this time of night alone."

Blue Raven Woman jumped and dropped the skin that she used to collect water. This was not her grandmother's voice. This was male.

She made a grab for her knife, which she kept at her back. Perhaps she had been reckless to come here alone, especially at night. But she would keep her honour. She would not let this interloper seduce her.

The steel edge of her weapon glinted under the moonlight and Blue Raven Woman silently thanked her father for the gift of the white man's blade, which he had secured in last year's trade. "*Kyai-yo!*" she cried out. "Who goes there?"

"Do not be afraid. It is I, Singing Bull."

She sighed, while at the same time her heart lurched. But her voice was steady, giving no indication of her inner turmoil, as she said, "You should not be here. Others will talk if we are discovered, and I would shame my family; possibly I might even have to pay the penalty of being seen with you."

"No one has followed me, I am certain."

She turned away from him and picked up her water skin, though she didn't replace her knife in its sheaf. "You come here to me under the guise of starlight and there is no punishment for you if we are discovered, but there would be humiliation for me. Please, if you care for me, go away."

He didn't come closer to her, which she knew was good; yet at the same time she wanted him near to her, and the weight of the conflicting emotions made her feel unnaturally giddy.

"I will leave here as soon as I ensure that *Suyi Tupi*, the Water People, do you no harm."

"They would not dare to hurt me so close to our camp. Please, you must leave me."

"*Aa*, yes, I will." He paused as though he expected her to say something else, but when nothing was forthcoming, he carried on, saying, "I have only come here to ask you to wait for me."

"Wait for you?"

"*Aa*. I go to honour myself and bring home glory for you and your father, that he might think more kindly on me and upon my appeal for you."

"*Saa*! You do not intend to steal horses, do you? You might be killed."

He shrugged.

"Do you not realize that it matters not that you bring honour to the village? Your suit was not denied because of you or your family. I am to marry Night Thunder. It has always been so. It cannot be changed."

"Do you believe that?"

"I know it. I tried to tell you this once before— Night Thunder and I have been pledged to each other since we were children. Our parents made the oath and you know well that it cannot be set aside, no matter my feelings . . ." she glanced up at him hopefully, ". . . or yours."

He jerked his head to the left before he said, "Do you think your father would still ignore me if I bring him twenty, maybe thirty horses?"

"*Aa*. Have you lost control over your senses? Your lack of wealth is not the reason you were denied. No one disputes your prowess as a warrior. Wasn't it only last year that you brought home the glory of three Cree scalps, those who had tried to murder us in our sleep? No one doubts you."

She felt him look away from her and she glanced over her shoulder, wishing all at once that she hadn't. The moonlight played over the shadows of his features, making him appear as handsome as her idea of the Blackfoot legend, Scarface.

She observed Singing Bull shift his feet, and instinctively she knew something was wrong.

She arose and took one step toward him, "What is it?"

He didn't answer.

"What is it you do? There is more than horses you go to seek, is there not?" And when still he didn't answer, she knew it was true. She gasped. "You go to join the war party against the Assiniboin, do you not?"

He glanced away from her.

"It is not necessary."

"Perhaps," said Singing Bull, "and yet even if this is true, I do not want to live without you." His voice broke and she had to strain to hear this last part.

"*Saa*, you do not need to do this. There must be another way."

"I would rather die than watch you with Night Thunder." Singing Bull stood firm before her, though she heard a catch in his voice as he continued, "We could steal away this night, and when we return, we will be married. Your parents would have to accept it."

"They would only do so if you have the necessary payment of horses to give to my family to atone for the insult done to them. Do you have them?"

He didn't answer.

And she persisted, "And what of my brother? You know that he would have the right to discipline me."

"I can make him understand, I think. He respects me. And I would not let him mar you."

She remained silent. Oh, how she wanted to relent. But the consequences, if their marriage were not accepted, were far too great. Nor would it be easy to face the shame she would cause her family.

Singing Bull persisted, "Will you do it? After we become married, I will go and capture many horses and give them to your father. You know that I can do this."

More silence. She bowed her head and when she didn't answer at once, she saw Singing Bull shudder as though he had only now realized the impossibility of the truth. He uttered, "I ask too much of you, I think. I understand that. And it is as it should be. You will do as your father wishes and bring honour to your family and I will bring glory to myself and our tribe by driving the Assiniboin back to their homeland. So is the way of the people."

Staring up at him, her heart cried out to him, but what could she do? What he suggested was not possible. She closed her eyes and sighed, murmuring to herself, "Aa, it is the way of things." Bending, she picked up her water skin, replaced her knife in its sheaf at her back, and straightening up, she fled toward the shelter of her home; fled before she changed her mind and put honour and love of family second to the love of her life.

Chapter 11

The fire crackled and spit red-yellow sparks as it burnt the dry cottonwood and grasses that fed it.

Rebecca inhaled, and the sweet scent of buffalo grass reached out to engulf her. Fascinated, she stared over toward the man who sat opposite her, on the other side of the fire, the faint light from the flames throwing the man's high cheekbones into prominence. He had captured his black hair into neat braids at each side of his face, strips of red rawhide holding them in place. One separate braid fell down his back, she knew, though she couldn't see it.

She fidgeted, staring at his lips, as she recalled how it had felt to be held in his arms last night; how exciting his kiss had been, urging her on into a world of passion she'd only dreamed existed. Not even her fiancé had made her feel that way. It was a hard thing to admit.

Would Night Thunder expect more kisses from her tonight? More lovemaking? Or perhaps more important, would she give them to him?

The thought made her blush. She couldn't submit to him again. Last night had been different. Last night they hadn't thought to live through the night . . .

Realizing where her thoughts were going, she glanced away from Night Thunder, hoping he didn't possess the kind of "medicine," as he called it, to be able to tell what she was thinking.

She cleared her throat. Try as she might throughout this day, Rebecca had realized that she could not condemn Night Thunder for what had happened between them. Not believing they had any future, the two of them had simply followed their instincts. Besides, if she condemned him, wouldn't she have to denounce herself, as well? What she hadn't considered, and possibly what he hadn't, either, was what would happen if they lived. But again, they hadn't been thinking clearly.

She gazed back at him, sending him a fleeting glance.

Oh, dear, she gulped nervously. He was surveying her now in much the same way that she had been doing to him earlier. She fidgeted under his steady regard.

Was it her, or was his appearance tonight more exotic than usual? It was almost as though he had made an effort to make himself look more appealing to her. Had he?

She let her gaze travel over him, trying to determine what it was that was so different about him. Was it the shells that he wore? Shells which, fashioned as slim hair pipes and strung together with large trade beads, hung down each side of his face and onto his bare chest? Or was it the more rounded shell earrings which dangled from his ears? On a civilized man the effect would have looked ridiculous, perhaps even feminine. Night Thunder, however, appeared far from effeminate. He exuded more masculinity than any man of her acquaintance, civilized or savage.

Her gaze fell away from his face and she found it hard not to examine his bare chest, all the hard muscle and sinew, with no chest hair to mar its perfection. His shoulders were broad, his waist slim, tapering down to a flat stomach upon which rested the belt which held up his breechcloth.

His legs were long, his leggings tight, the bulge in his breechcloth more pronounced than . . .

Her stomach dropped.

She tried to think of something else; truly she did. Yet she couldn't stop herself from wondering how he would look without that breechcloth.

She almost moaned aloud at her thoughts, but she managed to keep the reaction to herself.

Still, she hadn't been able to see the full effect of him last evening when they had made love, had only felt the rigid solidness of him, and she couldn't help but speculate, how he would look when fully aroused. She had never before witnessed a naked man.

She almost gasped at the erotic meanderings of her thoughts, and biting her lip, she tried to keep herself from contemplating any more about it, about him. Yet she couldn't stop herself as she glanced once more toward that breechcloth, and she swallowed convulsively when it appeared that the swelling down there had grown even larger. Quickly, she glimpsed away from him, away from that part of him, and stared upward, toward the stars.

"Humph."

She heard him make the sound, but she ignored him. The man was dangerous—to her composure and the idea of how she should be conducting herself. She needed a moment in which to settle herself, and she took a deep breath, keeping her sights firmly away from him.

But his baritone voice split through the silence of the night, momentarily startling her as he asked, "Do you worry that I will make love to you again tonight?"

She gasped. The man was certainly direct.

"Or do you worry that I will not?"

Embarrassment consumed her, and she drew the buckskin robe she'd been given in toward her, trying to bury herself within its folds. Had her worst fear come true? she wondered. Had the man read her thoughts? Did he know that she wanted him?

She took her time answering him, although when she did speak, her words rang out clearly, carried toward him on the wind. "You should not ask me about such a thing," she said, her voice, she noted, lacking the hard edge she had hoped to instill in it.

But he didn't seem to notice. He grinned at her. "I would dare much, it would seem, with my *ohk-iimaan*."

"O-ki-m . . . what does that word that you said mean?"

He gave her a half smile, his look sheepish, as he replied, "Wife."

"Wife?" She gave him a quick look.

He nodded. "Wife. *Ohkiimaan*, wife."

She pulled at the robe as though she were trying to settle it better around her shoulders, and unconsciously she jutted out her chin. She said, "I am not your wife, make no mistake."

"Are you not?" he countered. "Do you forget that we have come together as man and wife? I do not wish to call you by the name my people give to a woman who comes to know a man intimately to whom she is not married. So tell me, if not wife to me, then what?"

"I..." she choked. What could she say? This was not a topic she wished to explore, talk about, or examine in too close a detail. She decided to change the subject. "What about Blue Raven Woman?" she asked.

He didn't respond immediately, and his silence made Rebecca stare up at him. She frowned. His smile, and the gentle teasing which had lit up his eyes only a few moments ago, had faded. She almost wished she hadn't asked. At last, however, he uttered, "*Aa*, yes, so that is what is bothering you. Say then what you mean."

She gulped. "I... I meant," she stuttered, "well, if you are married to me, then you wouldn't be able to—"

"I must make Blue Raven Woman my wife, too. Nothing about that has changed."

"Except that we... that I..." she hesitated. What had she been about to say? But he was right. It wasn't as though she hadn't known. She said, "Then I am not your wife. I could never marry a man who is already married, nor one who must marry another. I would bring on the wrath of my God. Besides, in my society, two people are not joined in marriage until they are declared man and wife by a person of the cloth."

He thrust out his chin. "What is this 'person of the cloth'?" he asked.

"A man of our church, a holy man."

"*Aa,*" said Night Thunder, "a holy man. Is it only in this way that a man and woman can be 'joined' in your tribe?"

She nodded.

And he grunted, while a dangerous glint lit up his eyes, causing Rebecca to shiver. "That explains much. Tell me, Rebecca, is it because of this that the white man will join with one of our women and leave them as though they mean nothing to him, when the white man returns to his own country?"

Rebecca sucked in her breath. "Has that happened?"

"Many have noticed that those men who take an Indian wife without the words of the Black Robe leave her. But those who bring a Black Robe to our village and take with them the words of this man treat our women as one would expect a husband to do. We have not understood why this is so. We have only seen that it is."

Rebecca stared at him, speechless. What could she say? If what he claimed were true . . . "Then it is a terrible thing that my people have done to yours."

He appeared to digest her words in silence. But then, all at once, he asked, "Is it this that you desire? Should I find a Black Robe that we might take his words? Would this make you feel that you are my wife?"

"N—no," she stammered, "I . . . it would not make any difference. The same problem still stands between us. My God does not allow a man more than one wife. And you are already committed."

"Is your memory so weak that you cannot recall the physical union that joins us as one?"

"Of course I remember. How could I not?"

"Then you wish to take the consequences?" His gaze seared into her own. "You could be with babe."

"Unlikely," she said all at once, although maybe a little too quickly.

"Perhaps you are right," he answered. "But have you thought what you would do if you have become in this way?"

"I'd have to return to my own people." *And move someplace where no one knew me*, she finished to herself.

"And cause my own people think that I could not capture enough horses or hunt enough meat to feed both you and the babe?"

"They would think that?"

"*Aa*, yes," he said, with a nod. "They would. Tell me," his eyes shone with a gleam of intelligence as his gaze burned into hers, "how would your people treat you, the mother of a child born without its father?"

"I . . . I . . ." Why did he ask her such tough questions?

"Vow to me," his voice brooked no relenting, "that the child from our union will be left with my people if one has been made between us."

"I cannot do that."

"Vow it."

"I will not."

"I would not have my child grow up not knowing his father, being made to think he is an oddity in your tribe because he is different."

"And do you think that I would have him growing up without his mother?"

Night Thunder seemed to absorb this, and then suddenly grinned. "*Aa*, yes," he said, "then you must take me as husband."

She sighed.

But his features remained determined. "Treat me then as your traders treat our women. Pretend you that you are married to me and you can enjoy all the rights of a sits-beside-him wife. But when I take you back to your people, you can leave me if you wish. I do not like it, but it could be done."

"You would allow me that?"

"A child would stay with me."

"No," she said, "I could not do that."

"Some white men have done this to our women and any children of their union, more times than I can count."

She glanced away.

"Come, now. Be my wife in truth and stay with me. Then you will do honour to yourself and to me."

"And Blue Raven Woman?"

His gaze bored into hers as he said, "My second wife. It cannot change."

But Rebecca was just as determined as he, and she said, "Neither can I."

He raised his chin. "Will your people allow you the honour of becoming one with a man, then, without marriage?"

She sent him an annoyed look.

"Will they allow you this, without ruin?"

When she didn't answer, he sighed. "Say to them that we are married, then, and know the truth of it in your heart."

She rose, pulling the robe around her shoulders. The devil take the man. Why did he have to keep going on and on about it? She gazed at him briefly, there within the firelight, hard pressed to remember a time when she had felt more frustrated with a person.

"I am going to bed, now," she said, and kicked dirt into the fire, pretending she was trying to put it out, when really what she needed was a good way to vent her futility. Before she left she added, "I cannot do as you ask. Just as you have honour you must follow, so too do I. Do not press me on it further."

Amazingly, he held his peace, though she knew in her heart that this was only the beginning of many such entreaties. She felt certain he would not rest until he had gotten what he wanted from her.

There was no other path for her. She would have to start planning her way home. She had to leave this place, leave him. It was the only way to hold on tightly to what she believed.

She only wished she didn't feel quite so dispirited about the prospect of it.

Chapter 12

Night Thunder stared at Rebecca as she slept next to him—her body cuddled up close to his; his responding to the nearness of hers. Although she rested, although he knew he could not take the sweet promise of her again, he still could not help remembering what she had felt like beneath his touch a few nights ago . . . how quickly she had responded to him, how he had rejoiced . . .

He frowned at his thoughts and brought his gaze upward, his glance studying the starlit sky, his mind troubled.

They had finally settled on a pattern these last few nights, she going to bed before he did, and he following when he was certain she was asleep. It had proved to be successful. Somewhat . . . But he worried.

What had he done that one night not so long ago? What had he done to her? To himself? It didn't matter that he had thought to die that night. Nor did it matter that she had consented. He was responsible for what had happened between them, and he knew he had placed her in a vulnerable position.

His problem now was that he still must honour his vow to protect her, yet he did not know how best to do that.

He could not break his promise to Blue Raven Woman. And yet if he did not do that, if he did not renounce that pledge, he would not be able to keep Rebecca with him, something which was fast becoming vital to him.

When he had made love to her, he had vowed to become a husband to her, to care for her and love her all the rest of his days. He had told her that he would give her all that he was, all that was in him to share. Yet it wasn't enough, and he knew it.

He had to change, to compromise, as so did she. He knew it, but how could he do it? Surely not by sacrificing his honour or that of his family.

And Rebecca: would she change her mind about Blue Raven Woman once she met her? He doubted it. It wasn't only Blue Raven Woman that stood between them, not in truth. It was Blue Raven Woman *and* the wide chasm between his beliefs and Rebecca's. It was *this* that he did not know how to bridge.

He could not ask Rebecca to cease thinking as she did. He could sooner capture a star from the heavens. Weren't all men—and for that matter, all women—free to believe as they saw fit?

He would also not ask her to be less than she was. Such would be the action of a fool. But he could not allow himself to become less either.

What, then, was the answer? To let her go? To

take her back to her people and pretend that she did not mean anything to him?

He did not know or understand the wisdom of what he must choose, and as he lay there pondering, he heard the faint sound of a drum. At first he drew in a deep breath, relishing the soothing beat of the rhythm.

But then it came to him . . . a drum? Far in the distance? Quickly, Night Thunder glanced toward the man who stood sentry over their camp, the man sitting unflinchingly and unaffected by the sound. And though the noise grew more distinct as voices, raised in song, joined it, no one in the camp awakened, no one appeared to hear it, even when the sound grew louder and louder.

He listened closely to the words of the singing, heaving out a great sigh when he recognized the speech pattern as what he and Rebecca had heard, a few nights previous. He groaned. The shadows of the dead. Had they come to haunt him again? Were they following him?

Rebecca turned over suddenly, her head seeking out Night Thunder's shoulder, her arm going over his chest. She stirred restlessly, but still she slept on. Would the call of the shadows awaken her?

As if she were attuned to his thoughts, he felt the flicker of her eyelashes against the bare skin of his arm.

It took only a few moments, then, before he heard her quiet voice. "I hear drums. Singing, too," she whispered.

"*Aa*," he acknowledged, "so do I."

She quickly glanced around their camp. "Why do the warriors still sleep?"

"Would you have them go out and do battle with the shadow of those who are dead? With those who they cannot see?"

She became quiet, seeming to think over his words. Suddenly she drew back her arm from where it rested on his chest, as though only now becoming aware of their intimate pose. Scooting away from him, she asked, "The ghosts are back?"

"*Aa*, yes."

"Do they follow us?"

He shrugged. "I do not know. I only can tell you that it is the shadows of the dead that we hear."

She glanced toward the Indian sentry. "Does he not hear all the noise?"

"*Saa*, no. It is few who can hear their words."

"But I can."

"*Aa*, yes, it is true."

"What does that mean?"

Another shrug. "I do not know what it means. But I do not think it is bad."

She glanced toward him, fear, clear and vivid, flashing within her eyes. "I am afraid."

He reached out toward her. "Do not be. If they meant harm, they would have done it when we were most vulnerable."

"That night?"

He nodded.

She scooted back to him, put her head once again upon his arm, and pulling up the sleeping robe over her shoulders, hid her face.

"I know I have been arguing a lot with you of late, but," a smile lit her voice, "I should tell you that I do appreciate you rescuing me. Have I told you this?"

"*Aa*, yes, but not in words," he said, humor in his tone. "Every night when you lie down next to me you tell me this."

"No," she said, "I do not mean that. Since our talk the other night, you have not pressed me any further to take you as husband. Nor have you made any more . . . attempts . . . I mean, you have not tried to . . ."

"Make love to you?" he supplied, saving her the embarrassment of saying the words.

He could hear her gulp. "Aye." she nodded.

The feel of her silky hair against his arm made him remember other things about her: the smooth texture of her bare body against him, the softness of her touch, the moistness of her response.

He felt himself stiffening in reaction to his thoughts, and he shifted, that she might not know the amount of effort it took him to act as a man should with a woman not his by marriage.

She asked, "Are you regretting, now, that you . . . that we—"

"I cannot regret something that made my heart happy."

"It made you happy?"

"*Aa*," he whispered.

"Then why do you not do more than . . ." She suddenly turned her back on him, scooting away. "Forgive me. I can't imagine what I was thinking. You must think me a hussy."

He followed her, his arm going over the indentation of her tiny waist. He brought his lips to her ear as he said, "I do not know what this 'hussy' is. But the two of us are not married, and I would not dishonour you any further than I already have.

It is not regret that I feel in my heart. Never regret."

The singing, the drums in the distance, became even louder, if that was possible, and Rebecca turned over so that she lay under him, his face practically touching hers. He breathed in the clean, pleasing scent of her, her feminine fragrance reaching out to him and embracing him.

He must hold himself back from her. He must, he must, he must . . .

But he couldn't help himself. Not here, not now. Not under the silvery glow from the beams of Old Woman. He kissed her, then, his sweet Rebecca, her lips soft and responsive beneath his.

Aa, pure medicine. She was as irresistible as the call of the great mystery, and it had been so long since he had tasted her.

She kissed him back, too, her response immediate, and she threw her arms around his neck, bringing him down more intimately toward her. His heart soared.

One of her breasts lay beneath the touch of his hand. She was fully clothed, but it didn't matter. His fingers traced the femininity of her, the image of her naked body not far from his immediate recall.

His tongue traced the outline of her lips as his breath mingled with hers and he heard her sigh. *Aa*, reluctant captive, he thought, the feelings between us are strong, powerful. How could he deny himself her sweet body?

He couldn't, and his mouth closed over hers as he kissed her with the depth of a man consumed. He tasted her, his tongue sweeping deeply into her mouth, thrusting and retreating, mimicking love-making.

Still, a part of him remained emotionally distant, as though to remind him of . . . what? It seemed so right that he love her. He wanted it; she did, too, if her reaction to him were any indication. He tried to remember, but the reasons why he shouldn't do what they both desired, the same arguments he had been pondering to himself all evening, fled, as lingering shadows flee the light of Sun. He couldn't think right now; he could only recall that he had promised he would be a good husband to her. *Aa*, yes. He would ensure it.

Husband? Promise?

Slowly he drew himself away from her, taking his weight onto his arms, his gaze seeking hers. In her eyes he glimpsed passion; in her arms, a certain refuge. Surely what he was contemplating doing wasn't wrong, was it? Didn't they both want it?

But wasn't it his duty to protect her? The argument waged on in his mind. And, he realized sadly, the person she needed protection from the most was, at this moment, him.

He threw himself away from her all at once, coming to lie on his back, trying to still the rapid beating of his heart and his ragged breathing.

He made himself remember: he could not marry her. He was already committed to another. Rebecca had already refused him. How could he have forgotten so quickly?

Her breathing was as disturbed as his, he noted with satisfaction; and her whisper was just as breathless as she asked, "Did you mean it, the other night, when you said that you loved me?"

He almost groaned. Women, he thought. Why could they not let a thing go? Didn't she know that he needed time to bring his body under control, not have more talk about it? Probably not, he answered his own question. She had been an innocent when he had taken her.

And though he felt not the least bit calm, he answered her sedately, "*Aa*, Rebecca, I have a great feeling for you, here, in my heart."

"As I do for you."

He groaned. He didn't need to hear that. Not now. Not when she lay so close to him. Not when he still breathed in the scent of her womanly response.

He sat up. He had to do something or he might . . . "Rise up now," he said in a low voice. "Rise up and let us go and talk to these shadows that follow us that we might determine why they are here."

He chanced a look down at her, thinking to see fear come over her because of his suggestion. Hadn't she been afraid of what she called "ghosts" several days previous, even a few moments ago? Yet he witnessed no concern now, finding himself staring instead at the glow of passion, still shining brightly within the amber depths of her eyes.

He shuddered. How was he supposed to maintain control when she appeared so desirable? When she had that look of hunger in her eye, the expression one might expect to find within that of a newly acquired wife?

She was *not* his wife, he reminded himself.

He leapt to his feet. He had to move. He had to do something before he lost all sense. He had promised himself to keep his honour with her. That meant he had to ensure she remained pure . . . and away from him.

Without another glimpse at her, he set a pace toward that place where the noise originated, more than aware that she followed him.

He came right up to the shadows of the warriors past. And perhaps more strongly than he might have if he hadn't been seeking a way to vent his frustration, he shouted at the gossamer figures, "Why do you come here?"

Not one of those shadows looked his way. Not one acknowledged him. Not even when he stepped into the line of their dancing, the flimsiness of their shadows passing through him. He didn't flinch from them, either, even as the coldness of their touch penetrated to the depths of his being.

But he did shout at them again, screaming, "Say now what it is that you want from me!"

No one stopped, no one looked at him, nothing changed, except perhaps that the countenance of one of the shadows . . . *aa*, yes, one of the shadows, perhaps a wise man, seemed to be glancing right at him.

Night Thunder tried again, this time directing his attention to the wise man. "Do you see that I am not afraid of you, old man? Do you see that I try to talk to you, even though you are not among the living? Do you see that I am here? Tell me then what it is you seek from me."

Though no words were spoken, the old man

waved his arm and an old woman appeared before them. Stepping forward, she surprised Night Thunder by what she carried on her arm: a dress made of snow-white antelope skin and decorated with hundreds of elk tushes, the kind that used to be made before the white man had brought the trade beads to this country. She held white leggings, heavily fringed and made of deerskin in one hand, while she clung to moccasins, sewn with fancy quills, in her other. Over her shoulder, the old woman had draped a summer robe, made of elk skin and without any hair, though dew-claws had been left on it.

The old woman's image walked toward Rebecca and, before Night Thunder's eyes, with a mere touch of the woman's hand, Rebecca became swathed in the beautiful clothes and robe.

What was this?

He recognized that type of clothing. It was ... wedding finery.

He grimaced. What did this mean? Rebecca wasn't one of his tribe, that she should be so honoured. To be dressed thusly on one's wedding day, to be given such an honour, had been always reserved for those fortunate few from among his tribe, those few who came from prestigious families. Why Rebecca? Why him?

The old gentleman's dewy image, the one who had caught Night Thunder's gaze, arose all at once and with what appeared more earthly feet than mist, came to stand before Night Thunder. And as though his image was a flesh body, not a ghostly one, he spoke in the ancient tongue of the Blackfeet. "Take her hand in yours."

After only a moment's pause, Night Thunder did exactly as he was bidden.

The shadowy vision then continued, "From this night forward, your paths will be as one. From this time until your earthly trail has ceased, know that each one of you will comfort the other. No longer will there be need of loneliness, for from this time until your breath upon our mother, the earth, has ended, you will have each other."

With these words, the drumming increased, the singing swelled, until all at once, Night Thunder's ears were full of the sound of it. Then, just as quickly as they had appeared, the shadows vanished. The camp, the drums, the singing, even the old, wise man—gone.

And in their place was nothing, not even the white dress, leggings, and moccasins which had so prettily adorned Rebecca.

Night Thunder didn't move. He didn't blink. Nor did he say a word. Silence descended upon them, until Rebecca, her voice quiet, at last asked, "What did that man say?"

"You heard?" he asked. "You saw?"

She nodded.

Night Thunder didn't pause, nor did he glance at her. "We have been honoured."

She shook his arm, then, as though to awaken him, and she asked, "Are you thinking I'm dull witted, now? I'm aware of that. I could tell from the way that he spoke. But what is the meaning of it all?"

Night Thunder didn't answer her question right away. Instead he said, "Do you know that the ceremonies of the dead are binding on the living?"

"Are they?" she asked.

He nodded.

"Please, Night Thunder, I suspect I'm not going to like this, but I don't understand your language and he was saying something that you understood, wasn't he?"

"We must mend that."

"What?"

"That you do not understand my language. We will soon be in the camp of my people and I would like you to be able to not only understand what is said to you, but to speak the language well."

"Aye," she said.

"Language," he continued on, as though she hadn't spoken, "is an important thing to an Indian. I do not know how it is in the white man's world, but in mine, one's status in the tribe depends upon a person's ability to speak well. For if a person cannot speak in his own tongue with complete correctness, he will never be allowed to talk before a counsel or in public, lest children begin to mimic him. A man who does not speak well is considered an outcast."

"Ah," she said, "I see. Then you are correct and I should learn your language. But tell me please, what just happened?"

It was only then that he dared to look down at her. Yet still he paused, reluctant to say what needed to be said.

"Night Thunder?" she prompted.

He grunted, the sound at last giving him the courage to say, "From this day forward, so long as we are alive upon this earth," he gulped, "we are married."

Chapter 13

❦

"**M**arried, did you say? As in man and wife?"

Rebecca was trying her best to recover. Her knees still shook and her body trembled, but she had to know. What did this mean? How would this impact on their lives?

She had been aware of what had taken place this night, even if she hadn't understood the words. She'd witnessed the old woman clothing her in what could only be wedding garb. She'd heard the words from the old man. And though it had been fantastical, it didn't take any great stretch of intelligence to reason it out. Still, she'd needed to ask, if only to reassure herself that she still remained among the living.

Night Thunder smiled slightly at her as he repeated, "Married as in man and wife? Do you know any other kind?"

The two of them hadn't moved from the spot where they had been so recently united. They stood, under the radiant beams of the moon, staring at one another, she studying him as though transfixed, he patiently staring back at her.

Night Thunder's long hair flowed forward, its strands caught in the breeze. A few locks of it swept over her hand, its fleeting touch as delicate as a whimsical caress. She wanted to reach out and touch it . . . him . . . Indeed, she opened her hand that she might feel the long fringe of his dark mane, her fingers extending out to grab it when . . . suddenly she pulled back her hand. What had she been about to do? She gulped before she said to him, quickly, "I . . . I cannot believe any of this . . . none of it."

He paused for a moment as though he, too, were caught up in the unspoken enchantment. Then, he asked, "Did you not see it? Did you not witness the old man and the old woman?"

She swallowed, hard. "I . . . I . . . you know that I did. But it was too strange for me to believe, it was too fantastical to . . ."

"You know that it—"

"What is happening to me? Not only am I seeing ghosts, am I now to commune with the spirits, as well?"

"It is a great thing that has happened to us."

"Is it?"

He nodded.

"I fear . . . I fear this could be as a curse, not something . . . good."

Night Thunder frowned. "What means this word, this 'curse?'"

"I . . . it is . . . taking something which should be cheerful and making it . . . bad . . . or making bad things happen to a person, or . . . it is—"

He reached out a hand to touch her face, his

fingers gently stroking her cheek, while his other arm came around her waist to draw her forward. Immediately, the fragrance of pure wholesome male, together with the perfumes of sage, of grass, and of moon-swept prairie assailed her. She breathed out deeply, closing her eyes, letting the scents, the wind, the very fiber of this man's soul sweep into her heart.

She realized all at once how hard it had been, how difficult it was going to be, to remain so constantly distant from this man. Was this, then, the way it was when a woman was in love? Was it wanting to be with the man she admired, to be held by him always?

When had this wilderness, this man, begun to bewitch her? When had she started to desire to stay here?

He spoke to her, then, interrupting her thoughts. "I know not this 'curse' that you speak of," his voice was low, his tone as loving as an embrace. "But understand this," he continued, "it is a rare thing when the dead bring themselves back to life, and few can experience the whole of it without ill effect. We have been honoured, I think. I do not believe it is bad. I see nothing bad here, I feel nothing bad, and yet we have stood this night among the dead."

She couldn't think, not when he touched her as he was, not when he spoke to her as though each word were a tender expression of love. She opened her mouth to say something, but no sound came forth.

He continued, "It is willed, I think, that we are to be together."

She moaned, at last finding her tongue as she asked, "Willed?"

"*Aa*, yes," he voiced. "It is a good thing. I think we are meant to be together, you and me. Perhaps there is reason for this, perhaps not. But I know in my heart that only good will come from it. I promise you this. Know you, Rebecca, we are now as one."

"Aye," she agreed, caught up in the rhythm, in the very captivation of this land, of him. "Aye," she said again.

She lifted her shoulders and frowned. Spellbound. That's how this man's nearness affected her. Spellbound and enticed; unable to function or think clearly when he was so close to her. "Please, at this moment it seems right, it seems good, but please, I need time to think."

"What is not right about it?" he asked. "That we are married? Do not the others think it of us already? Do we not seem to have the proper kind of feeling for one another?"

She opened her mouth to speak but couldn't. With the man holding her so intimately, she couldn't function correctly; she couldn't think.

"Do not worry," he comforted. "I think that you will be happy with my people. You will find that Blue Raven Woman is a good woman, I believe. You could come to like her, and it is she who could help you become acquainted with the customs of the people."

"No," Rebecca said, at last finding her voice.

He persisted, "Perhaps after I marry her, I can give her as a wife to another—a man of her choice—if you still object to having her in our household, but I think you might need her help."

Rebecca groaned. "If you marry her," she said, "you will not have me around to do any objecting." She tried to step out of his embrace, but Night Thunder held her securely.

He shook his head. Still she pushed at him, this time successfully maneuvering away from him.

She didn't manage to put more than a few inches between them, however, and she stared off into the windswept landscape of the night, trying to pull her thoughts together. The man was much too charming by far, and she was having considerable difficulty in ignoring him.

Taking a another deep breath, she voiced, "What happened here tonight was nothing more than fantasy. It was bizarre and unbelievable. The dead have no right to join the two of us in marriage. Only we two can make that commitment, and I . . ."

She heard him take a step toward her.

"Besides," she went on quickly, glancing at him and negotiating one step backward, "there is more. It is not only your duty to Blue Raven Woman that keeps us apart, I am afeard."

He grunted by way of answer.

She swallowed. "We could never marry because I am not, could not, become . . . Indian. I know it, and I think you know it, too. I could never tolerate the hardships that your women must endure. Nor could I marry into a group of people who treat their women so shabbily."

"How would you know how Indians treat their women? Has a person said something bad to you about this?"

Of course someone had said something bad. Practically her entire education in Indian culture had been based upon the cruelty of the Indians and their relegating their women to the role of slave.

But it was difficult to put her idea of it into words. Especially when she knew Night Thunder to be kind and considerate.

He took another step toward her and she had no choice but to stare up at him. She caught her breath. With the moonlight playing over his features, he appeared not as a savage, as she had been led to believe all Indians were, but as the man she knew him to be; a man who was wholesome, honourable, and desirable . . .

She breathed out with difficulty. Were the moon, the wind, the very forces of nature conspiring against her?

He asked again, when she didn't reply at once, "How do Indians treat a woman that you think is bad?"

She took a deep breath as if that might give her courage and began, "They . . . they handle her as though she were a . . . a slave, I think."

"Slave?"

"Aye," she peeped up at him again. A mistake. The man emanated masculine beauty and she found it increasingly hard to breathe. Still, she could not relent. She continued, "Do your men not feel that they own a woman when they marry her?"

He shrugged. "Among all people are those who treat others bad and with contempt. There are husbands who do bad things to their wives, as there are wives who nag at their husbands until their men cower from them. But such people are few. In my tribe, in yours, I think."

"You . . . did not answer my question."

Again he shrugged, but all he said was, "Does any man ever really own a woman?"

"I . . . you don't understand," she insisted. "Your women are made to cook and clean and sew and tan hides all day long. They are made to bear and tend to the children, carry water, look after their men. Hard labor."

He gave her a strange look. "Do you say that women in your world do not cook or look after their children? Do not they do all these things?"

"Some do not."

"Humph."

"Besides," she said, "I could never adapt to your way of life and I am not unhappy with my life as it is."

"Are you not?"

She opened her mouth to confirm her statement, but could not quite bring herself to say the words. She forced her lips closed. She couldn't lie to him. She might try to fool herself, but never him.

She stilled, then, wondering was it true? Though she hadn't been aware of being unhappy in her life, was it a fact that she had been, perhaps, dissatisfied?

She sensed a tingling sensation under her skin, knowing that color surely swept across her face. Momentarily, she felt glad that the moonlight might perhaps hide her reaction from this man's astute vision.

Still she wondered. Was it true? To tell God's

truth, she had never stepped off the day-to-day process of living long enough to examine her existence and what she felt about it, what she thought, at least until now.

Had she been disheartened? Grieved, even? For the last few years, she had made it a practice to endure, forced by necessity to shift from one capacity to another, barely able to stay ahead of her creditors. It had been one of the primary reasons she had been so willing to follow her young mistress, Katrina, into this wilderness. Katrina had paid Rebecca's debts with nary a question.

But would one call such a life as she had created for herself living?

At some length, Rebecca realized she was changing. Changing, yes, but that didn't mean she could become what Night Thunder wanted of her. She said, "In truth, most women in my society do all that you mention. It's only that I—"

"A sits-beside-him wife does not do any of the hard work of the household. A sits-beside-him wife directs all the other wives. If it is this that you wish, I can give it to you."

"I . . ." What could she say? The man could be so endearing at times. She said, "You are kind to me, Night Thunder, to say so, but there is more than that which keeps us apart." She swept her arms around her. "Do you see this? All this land, the moon, the stars, even the wind: it's yours. Yours to hunt in, yours to make war in, yours to envision and to hold your dreams. But it's not for me. I have dreams that have no place in your society. Dreams which are so dear to me that it would be as though I would be having to give up

a piece of myself if I were to part with them.
Dreams I cannot fulfill here."

He paused. "Do you speak of that dance? The
one where you were to meet the man you would
marry?"

"Aye," she said, glancing away from him, "the
dance. That and seeing with my own eyes the
beautiful shores of my mother's birthplace, Ireland."

His voice was soft as he said, "*Aa*, yes. I understand. A person must hold onto his dreams. But
know this, reluctant captive. I care for you. And
despite what you say, I will continue to hope that
you will find a way to be happy with me."

She whimpered and deliberately stared down at
the ground, away from him. "Please, Night Thunder," she pleaded softly, "if you truly do care
about me, you will not keep asking me to take you
as husband."

"Are you certain of that?"

"Aye."

He smiled at her. Reaching a finger out to place
under her chin, he brought her face toward his,
and said, "I do not think so. It is because I care
that I keep asking you to become my wife in truth.
Do you know this?"

She sighed. Of course she did. She perceived,
too, that if he could, he would make things different for her, for them. But he was as unable to alter
the way he was, as was she herself. And if she
were to be honest, she would admit that just as
she had asked him to allow her to have her
dreams, so too should she grant him his.

After all, how could she require him to relinquish his hopes, his aspirations, when she was objecting to him trying to make her over into something she was not? Didn't he deserve the same sort of consideration?

But she could never accept the kind of life that he offered her. Not ever.

And he could not give up his honour. She must grant him that.

Truly, there was no hope for them.

Yet, she did have feelings for him . . . deep, nurturing feelings.

He said, "Perhaps there will be a way for us that we do not see. It is what the dead are trying to tell us, I believe."

She moaned. How could she make him understand that these ghosts did not direct her life, that she did not believe in such things? That no earthbound spirits were more to her than her own hopes and desires?

He said, again, "We will find a way."

"Night Thunder, I—"

"Sh-h-h," he held a finger over her lips. "We must not think on it."

"But my life, I—"

The finger came back to her lips.

Still, she felt urged to say something, and she voiced, "Please, Night Thunder, do not misunderstand me. Though I have great feelings for you, I do not believe that I can find my dreams in your camp. My destiny does not belong there."

"What is this 'destiny'?" he asked.

"The future."

He considered this for a moment before he asked, "Are you certain of this?"

"I think that I..." She had meant to be emphatic, but somehow the words failed her. She tried again, "I think that I...I..." She couldn't bring herself to say it. Why? "I don't know," she admitted at last. "I have never seen your camp, I know nothing of it. So I cannot say, for true, what I will find there, but I will tell you that I was not unhappy in my old world. And there are things there that I would still like to do, places I would like to see."

"*Aa*," he said, his look at her tolerant. "I understand. But you say that you have great feelings for me?"

She nodded.

"Then let us not throw away what is here between us, not yet. Let us think on this."

She didn't answer.

"In your heart you know that we should remain together, do you not?"

She couldn't dispute him.

He smiled, then. "It is a good thing, not bad, that has happened between us here tonight, I think. But since our way of thinking is different, I would not have you do something that is not within the manner of your heart. And I would not knowingly hurt you."

She groaned.

While he continued, "Still, our path, even though it be hard, is to be as one, if only because what we feel for one another is so strong."

She shut her eyes. She knew she should say something about Blue Raven Woman, about his commitment to her, but she couldn't. What he said was too close to the truth, and it was not in her to refute him. Instead she sobbed, the unwilling whimper ending in a hiccup.

"*Omaopii*, hush, now." He took her in his arms. "No more until we have thought well on this."

She surrendered to his touch, melting into him as though she had been awaiting it all her life. Placing her face against his chest, she stuttered, "All . . . all right. No more. At least for now."

She could feel the hard muscles of his chest as she lay her cheek against him, hear the steady beat of his heart. It comforted her.

She would do as he had asked and think on it. She doubted that much would come of it, but she would try.

Perhaps, too, she would start to seek a way home. Although, the more and more she considered it, the less and less Fort Union began to appear as her home.

Where did she belong in this vast and unusual world? Ireland, a land she had never seen? America, the land she had been born to?

Was there truly a place for her?

She sighed. Her old life, at this moment, seemed as equally unappealing as the thought of Indian life. Nor was the homeland of her heritage, Ireland, holding out the welcome beckoning that it once had for her.

She didn't understand the change in her, nor could she appreciate why she was feeling the way she was. Perhaps she might never come to grips with it. But of one thing she was becoming more and more certain: she loved this man who held her. Despite who he was, despite who she was. She loved this man who had proved himself to be honourable, trustworthy and . . . a friend.

She peered skyward, toward the stars, and willed herself to think no more on it this night. Tomorrow would be soon enough to try to assimilate all that had happened here. Tomorrow she would force herself to start envisioning a way home, wherever that was.

Tomorrow . . .

Chapter 14

Blue Raven Woman heard the hoot of the owl, but she resolutely ignored the sound, turning over onto her side in her sleeping robe. It was Singing Bull calling to her, she knew. Hadn't she agreed to meet him tonight?

But she couldn't go. She could not risk her honour, no matter the urging of her heart.

Why had she agreed to meet him? Was it because he would leave soon on the warpath? Was it because she feared she would never see him alive again? Or was it because she could not deny forever the yearning of what was in her spirit?

Whatever the cause, to agree to meet with him had been a weakness, a weakness she had to restrain in herself from this moment forward.

Something touched her on the shoulder and she jumped.

A finger brushed over her lips, keeping her silent. She inhaled, recognizing the clean yet tantalizing scent of Singing Bull.

He had come to her. A part of her rejoiced. A part despaired.

He lay between the tepee covering and the inner tepee lining, a space which would allow for a single body. Blue Raven Woman turned her face toward the inner lining, lifting the soft rawhide slightly so that she might see him.

She let out a barely audible gasp. His face rested only inches from her own.

He smiled at her, a finger coming to his lips to silence her again.

If she were caught this way, her honour would be forfeited, no matter that she had not asked Singing Bull to come here. As it always was, she as a woman would bear the brunt of shame, while he as a man walked away unscathed.

Blue Raven Woman glanced around the tepee quickly, noting the sleeping bodies of her mother and father, those of her younger sister and brother. Luckily, her older brother was away, hunting with his more-than-friend. Her older brother would have caught her, she was certain.

Turning her head back toward Singing Bull and bringing one of her hands upward, she motioned toward him in the language of sign, "Why are you here?"

"You agreed to meet me," he signed back.

She inhaled deeply. "I changed my mind," she motioned silently. "Leave here at once, before you are discovered."

"Leave with me."

"I cannot."

"We will marry. Then there will be nothing more that anyone can do about it."

"You think that my brother would accept it? More likely he would cut off the end of my nose."

"I would not allow him to do that."

"You would be unable to prevent it. You know this. And if my brother did not, if he let me do this, his society, the *Mut'-siks*, the Braves, might do it in his place. Can you deny this?"

Singing Bull remained silent for a moment, his hands still. At last, however, he motioned, "We could leave and seek out my mother's sister who lives amongst the Gros Ventres. We could stay there until the bad feelings here are gone."

Blue Raven Woman lay her head back against her robe, the tepee lining falling at her side. She could do it. What he spoke of was true. Though she might not see her mother or her father again for many years, still, she could do it.

Singing Bull touched her on the shoulder and she lifted the buckskin lining to stare back at him. He motioned, "What say you? Do we do it?"

She hesitated.

She shouldn't have, because his hand slipped down beneath her robe, as though she had invited him. She drew in her breath in a hiss. She lay naked beneath the robe.

His hand cupped her breast and she almost cried aloud with the ecstasy of it. But that wasn't all he was doing. Slipping another arm under the tepee lining and over her body, he drew her closer to him, toward that inner lining of the lodge until she faced him. He slid the robe down her body, exposing her breasts; and where his hand had gone before, his lips now followed.

She withered beneath his touch and shut her eyes, willing herself one last time to pull away. But she couldn't, and though she told herself that she mustn't do this, it did no good. This was Singing Bull. This was the man she loved. She gloried in his touch, and her heart seemed to have more force of will tonight than her spirit.

His lips remained on her breast, while his fingers dipped lower, over her stomach, down farther toward that private place where no one had ever touched her, though that part of her ached for him to do so now.

Would he touch her there? She yearned for it, and yet she must make him stop . . . mustn't she?

Suddenly, he found the soft moistness of her and she barely held back a moan of ecstasy. She caught her breath as raw feeling overwhelmed her, and her mind ceased to function.

He rubbed her down there, his lips still nibbling on her breasts. Still stroking her gently, he slipped a finger inside her, and she thought that Mother Earth might open up and swallow her, so consumed was she with feeling.

He brought her upward in a passionate spiral, then, pushed her further and further, toward what, she did not know.

Then it happened: her body convulsed with so much pleasure, she thought she might die. But she didn't. Instead, she moved her hips toward him, straining for more. Such intense feeling she could never remember experiencing, and it went on and on, racking her body with a pleasure so strong, she thought she might cry out.

But she didn't. Such would be the height of foolishness.

She reached for him and he released his swollen member into her hand. She felt him shudder in reaction as she softly stroked him and she gloried in her power over him, feeling his pleasure as though it were her own.

He pulled her under the tepee lining, placing her between the lining and the outer buffalo-hide covering. Quickly he positioned himself on top of her.

But this action, far from bringing her again to the height of ecstasy, had the same effect as dousing her with cold water.

She grew stiff beneath his touch; she began to think.

She had not married this man, could not marry this man, and he was about to take her as a husband takes a wife—or as a man takes a dishonourable woman.

Dishonourable.

What had she done? What was she doing?

She pulled away from him all at once and scooted back under the inner lining, into the safety of her home.

She had almost let him take her—and without the benefit of becoming his wife. She would have shamed herself, her parents, her brother. She might even have had to pay the price for her wanton behavior, a thing that would mar her beauty and be a testimony to her dishonour for the rest of her life. Too, if she had let Singing Bull have his way with her now, wasn't it true that she would never be able to sponsor a dance to Sun when she grew older? Never be able to use its healing power to cure someone close to her—a husband, a son, perhaps even a daughter?

She began to weep.

Again Singing Bull touched her shoulder, but she brushed his hand away.

He tried to roll her over, too, to regain what he had lost, but she remained rigid beneath his touch, refusing to turn over and look at him or even speak to him in the language of sign.

He tried once more, again, but all to no effect.

Eventually she heard him sigh before he pulled up the buffalo-hide covering of her parents' dwelling, replacing the stones which had held the covering down. Quietly she heard him slip away into the night—without the bride whom he had sought.

But oh, what had she done?

With a hiccup, Blue Raven Woman tossed onto her stomach and cried to herself, until at last the forgetful calm of sleep claimed her.

"I have nothing to dry myself with," Rebecca complained. "No, do not turn around, only, please tell me what should I use to—Night Thunder!"

He had revolved around, despite her protest, and had begun to pace toward her. Startled, she threw her arms up in front of herself in an attempt to hide the fullness of her bosom. The attempt proved useless, however. She could tell by the cattish smirk on his face.

She said, "You promised that you would give me privacy this morning if I were to bathe."

"I said that I would *try* to give you privacy . . . there is a difference between *trying* to do something and a full vow."

"Is there? I am not so certain. Besides, I don't see that you have put a great deal of effort into

it," she complained. She glanced up at the handsome warrior who stood at some distance from
her, his countenance bearing the most innocuous
grin.

She had so looked forward to this bath, their
long journey almost at an end. This morning Night
Thunder had announced that they were only a half
day's ride from his village. Their entire party had
stopped here, close to this stream: the warriors to
employ themselves in preparing to enter the village, she and Night Thunder to plan what they
would do upon their arrival.

Night Thunder had offered to stand guard over
her while she bathed, and she, unable to deny herself, had taken him up on the proposal.

His voice interrupted her thoughts as he said, "I
try hard to give you this privacy you seem to desire. Very hard, I try." He grinned at her.

She made a face at him, all the while attempting
to scoot down further into the water. "Night
Thunder!"

He had already compromised the distance between them, was even now standing at the bank
of the stream. That the water only allowed her to
immerse herself thigh deep didn't help her cause.
Even squatting down, she remained exposed from
the belly up, arms over her bosom as a last defense.

"You promised," she attempted again.

"*Aa*, I did, and I tried to keep from looking at
you. I fought a great battle within myself to maintain this vow, too." He smiled at her again and
shrugged. "I lost."

Despite knowing that she should admonish him,

despite her own futile venture at modesty, she felt herself begin to smile, and she brought her hand up to cover her mouth that he might not know it.

"Come out now. I have a robe to wrap around you that you might not feel the chill of the early morning."

"All right," she said, "turn around and I will."

He grinned at her and stayed exactly where he was. He said, "I have the robe."

"Aye," she said, "I can see that. Now, please turn around so that you are not *facing* me, and back up a distance."

He did exactly as she had asked and rotated around, his back now to her. But instead of treading farther away from her, he came closer to the water and to her, the robe held in front of him and . . . unavailable to her.

She heaved a deep breath. "No, no," she said, "spin around and—"

"I have spun around, as you asked," he peered at her from over his shoulder.

"Aye," she said, "I can see that." She tried her best not to grin, but she couldn't help herself, and humor tinged her voice. "Turn your face around, too."

"*Aa*, you wish me to turn my head around, too?

"Aye."

"You must tell me all of these things that you wish, that I may do as you ask. Did I not say I would help you?" He turned his face back around, so that he could no longer see her.

"All right," she said, satisfied, "now, drop the robe so that I can pick it up."

He did so, but dropped the thing in front of him,

his body effectively providing her with a barrier to it. He stood with his hands on his hips, though now and again he peered at her from over his shoulder.

She groaned and said, "Now step over it."

"*Aa*," he said, "you want me to step over it. Of course."

He obliged her at once and the robe became momentarily accessible to her. But when she might have made a gallant effort to grab the thing from him, he sat down upon it.

"No, no," she admonished, "you're not doing it right."

Again he glanced at her from over his shoulder. "Am I not?" he asked innocently. "Come here and show me how to do it."

"No, Night Thunder, you're not getting the point."

"Am I not?"

"No."

"And what is this point?"

"You are supposed to be letting me bathe without watching me."

"*Aa*, I am glad you have seen to enlighten me about my duty. But am I not doing all that you ask me to do?"

She moaned. "Are you being deliberately obtuse?"

"Know I not what this means, 'obtuse.'"

"Stubborn, mulish, obstinate, willful, inflexible, childish . . ." She took a deep breath.

"What am I doing? Is the robe not here as you had asked? Have I not put it within your reach?

Why do you not come out here and take it from me?"

"You know why."

He chuckled.

"Now," she said, "stand up and *walk away from the water.*"

"*Aa*, yes, *away* from the water. You want me to go farther away, not closer. I think I have it now. You had only to say so and I would do it." He stood up and, true to his word, he paced farther away from her—taking the robe with him.

"Night Thunder," she stood up in the water, hands on her hips, "leave the robe."

"*Aa*, you want the robe, too," he dropped the robe, but turned completely around at the same time, a smug grin on his face. He gazed at her hungrily. "The robe is here," he pointed out unnecessarily.

"Aye," she dropped back into the water in an instant, hands over her bosom, although the attempt was too late. He had seen the whole of her nude body—which of course had been his purpose all along. Still, she couldn't help giggling at him.

She asked, "Are you going to cooperate with me or not?"

Eyebrows shooting up, he gazed at her, so innocently. "I am cooperating. Are you unhappy with what I am doing?"

"Aye, that I am."

"And yet I am trying to be helpful."

"Aye," she said, "you are trying."

"*Aa*," he rejoined, "did I not tell you that I would be 'trying'?"

She laughed. "I suppose you did," she admitted. "I reckon I did not understand exactly what you meant by 'trying.' "

He smiled at her. "Come out now before your skin turns as wrinkled as that of an old woman."

"I'm not going to manage to get you to look away when I get out of the water, am I?"

"Look away?" He shook his head. "*Saa*, no, why would I want to look elsewhere when something more beautiful than even the sky at sunset, is before me?"

"Flatterer."

"*Saa*, no. I speak only the truth."

She shook her head. "All right, then, if you're going to watch me, come closer."

He stepped right up to the bank of the stream, smiling at her and holding the robe out for her.

She said, "Now give me your hand that you might help me from here."

He grinned, but extended his hand toward her nonetheless.

With all her might, she exerted one gigantic pull, and with an enormous splash, into the water came the big, tough Indian warrior, robe and all. She giggled as she watched him surface after a few moments, surprise etched on his face.

But his amazement didn't last long. Throwing the robe to the shore, he cupped his hands and splashed her.

She retaliated.

He made a grab for her.

She shimmied away.

He fumbled with something beneath the water

and threw an article of clothing ashore. His breechcloth?

Oh, my.

He sent her another splash.

She leapt under the water and lunged toward his legs, pulling on them and dumping him back into the water.

He grabbed at her, and hauling her close to him, emerged, situating her body until she was pressed up close to his.

Immediately she became aware of the differences in their bodies, male and female.

Where hers was soft and rounded, his was contoured and solid. Where hers was delicate and dainty, his was all angles and hard.

She suddenly became aware of something quite rigid and substantial pressing against her belly. Heaven spare her, what was this happening to him, to her? A craving, suddenly urgent and consuming, burst through her body, hurling down her nerve channels, centering itself in that delicate spot between her legs. Her pulse leapt, her heart pounded, her breasts strained against him.

It would have been useless to deny that she wanted this man, wanted him to make love to her. The knowledge made her knees weak, and it took all her effort to stand. But she wouldn't give in to that weakness. She mustn't.

"Rebecca," he whispered to her, his hands cupping her buttocks, his voice suddenly urgent. "I want you."

She swallowed. Why did he have to be so direct? And why did his statement send a rush of eagerness through her?

He didn't stop at that single statement though, and he continued, "Let me love you as I should have done the first time."

"No," she answered at once, "you know that we mustn't . . . we can't . . ."

"*Aa*, yes, we can. Let me show you—"

"No, please, I . . ." She was fast losing her reserve. She had to do something, anything, to remember that this man was *not* her husband. Because like it or not, this man was fast becoming exactly that.

No, she could not allow that.

Perhaps it was pure lust that made her ask, perhaps. But she didn't think so, as she smiled up at him, and requested, a mocking note in her voice, "I would like to see you naked."

It seemed only fair. *He* had been pestering her all morning. It was her turn to get him back, after all. Although, if she were truthful, she might admit that she had been curious about it, about how he would look naked, ever since that one night when they had been caught together in a hollowed-out tree trunk . . . How did a man look when under the influence of . . . love?

Luckily, she wasn't quite so truthful, and so she stared at him as though she had every right to be asking him what she had, noting that he hadn't flinched, as she had thought he might. Nor had he laughed, as she had reckoned he would. Instead, he'd merely tsk-tsked and said, "*Aa*, such a bold creature is my wife," taunting her. He added, "I am naked now."

"I am not your wife, and . . ." Her teasing him did not seem to be having quite the effect she had intended. He seemed relaxed, while she . . .

Well, she would show him. Raising her chin, she asked, "Would you please step out of the water?"

"*Aa*, yes," he agreed, one of his hands reaching down to the small of her back, pulling her even closer to him. He continued, "Did I not tell you that I would do all that you ask of me if you let me attend to you this morning while you bathed?"

"As I remember correctly, you did," she returned.

"Then come, we will step out of the water and we can both have a look at one another."

"No, that is not what I asked. I would like *you* to parade before *me* . . ."

He shrugged his shoulders, as though such a thing were asked of him every day. "Have you never seen a man naked when he is aroused?"

"No, I haven't."

"Then I will do this for you, but you must promise me that if I do this, you will also agree to one thing that I might ask of you."

"I . . . I don't know that I—"

"It is not to entice you to make love to me."

"Oh?" Why was she disappointed? "Ah, and what is that?"

He peered down deeply into her eyes, his gaze as warm as a soft summer breeze, and said, "You will let me kiss you."

"Kiss me? That is all?"

He nodded.

"It is a deal, then."

He looked momentarily puzzled. "What is this deal?"

"It means that we have a bargain. We have a good . . . trade."

"*Aa*, yes," he said, "a good trade." Whereupon he proceeded to step out of the water.

She drew in her breath as he arose. First one thigh out of the water, then the other; one leg up on the shore, then the other, her gaze hungrily noting each shift of every muscle. Rivulets of water ran down his broad back, his narrow hips and buttocks, his muscular legs. She almost choked in reaction to the sight.

She blinked, once, twice. It had been a foolish entreaty, she could see that now. Instead of this display poking fun at him, as she had meant it to, seeing him this way only stimulated her, and she wondered if he could feel the heat of her scrutiny upon him.

She blushed fiercely at her thoughts, but still she had to ask, since she had come this far, "Would you turn around, please?"

He did so.

She froze, her eyes opening wide. How had this man fit within her?

Yet he had. She remembered it quite vividly.

Lust, pure and carnal, began to smolder within her as her gaze traveled all up and down him. And unaware of what she did, she held her breath.

His body, naturally darker than hers, boasted a healthy tan except for those places his breechcloth usually hid. Very few hair marred his perfection, except, of course, *there*, where nature had intended an inherent bushy protection to be.

She strained forward, and to her chagrin, she realized she had begun to think of this man more and more, everyday, as not only her protector but her husband. She might not like it, but there it was.

Why, she asked herself, did she not relax? Since he insisted on calling her wife, why did she not do as he had once suggested and agree to take him as husband, so long as she remained in the Indian encampment? With the view in mind to denounce him later, upon returning to the fort?

She cut a glance skyward and sighed. Because, she answered her own question, it was dishonest. That was why.

But my, to see him now. . . . Her gaze riveted back to him.

He said, his look at her tolerant, "Come out now and give me the kiss that you promised me." He stared down at his rigid form for a moment. "Now that you have brought me to life." When he stared back up at her, humor tinged his eyes.

She, in turn, could only gawk at him. She couldn't help it. Excitement, exhilaration, and soul-stirring urgency shot through her. Energy, sparking and flaring between them, blazed as though it were a wildfire. She tried to speak, but it became impossible when her stomach turned over, doing flip-flops. Still, she had to try.

She cleared her throat. As well as she was able, she said, "If it's a kiss you'll be wanting, you'll have to come in here and get—"

She never finished.

He forged into the water as if he had been awaiting such an invitation for years, or at least all morning.

He took her in his arms and she melted at first

touch. The fresh scents of the cool water, mixed with the clean and tangy aroma of his skin, assailed her, confusing her. She felt her resolve weaken.

She wanted him. She had wanted him for several days now, and their being constantly thrown together, yet having to remain so distant, was doing nothing more than intensifying her pleasure. Was this why people married? she wondered. Because they couldn't get enough of one another? Because they couldn't stand being apart? Or was there some other reason?

Surely morals, point of view, and culture had something to do with it. Didn't they?

Or did they? Wasn't it more important that two people tried to get along with one another? Compromised? Granted one another the right to be the persons that they were?

His hands were massaging her, all up and down her back, and Rebecca could no longer think with raw emotion, urgent and frenzied, racing up and down her spine. Every nerve ending strained for the caress of his fingers.

His lips closed over hers at last.

Ah, enchantment.

One of his hands came up to run over her cheek, her eyes, her neck. He drew back his lips, only slightly, to say, "Once you asked me if I loved you and I did not answer."

"I'm not asking you now," she whispered, their lips raining tiny kisses upon one another as they spoke.

"But I am answering you now."

She gulped. She didn't want to talk. She wanted . . .

"Know now, Rebecca, sweet captive, I do love you . . . here." He put her hand over his heart. "Know also that when we enter my village this day, I will have to make my way separate from yours many times. I will take up the habits of a warrior, you will go with the women. We will be often apart. Such is the custom of the village. But I would not take you there with you not knowing that if you decide to stay with me, my heart will be glad."

A part of her rejoiced. A part of her despaired. She frowned. "And if I decide I must leave?"

"I will always value the time which we had together. I would never regret it."

"But you would let me go?"

"From the first moment we have been together, it has been my duty to protect you. If you decide that the fort is the security that you desire, I will have to learn to accept it."

"But you would not like it?"

"I would not like it."

She shuddered.

"You are cold."

"No, I . . ." How could she tell him she was keeping herself back from touching him? From feeling the texture of his skin, the hard flesh of his muscles? How could she say that to him?

"Come," he invited, "it is warmer on the shore, and I—" It was his turn to draw in his breath, though his breathing was cut short.

Rebecca had begun to rub her hands up and

down his chest, just as he had so often done to her.

He grabbed her hands. "Do you know what you do to me?"

She nervously wet her lips. "I think so, if it's anything like what you do to me."

"Know if you continue, where it will end?"

She could barely believe it was herself speaking, when she said, "And where would that be?"

The intonation in her voice had been pure invitation, she knew it, and Night Thunder was not one to abstain, she was soon to discover.

"Sweet captive," he uttered, when her fingers came dangerously close to that area of his body so definitely male. "If you do not want to do this, then you must stop now."

She didn't utter a syllable, though the movement of her fingers, her hands, spoke far better for her than words could have.

He jerked his head to the left and she watched him shut his eyes as she continued her assault upon his chest. She knew she shouldn't; she would feel terrible about herself later in the day, but she couldn't help it. She loved this man, she wanted him. Why shouldn't she enjoy the love they shared, just this once? Especially when their time together was soon to come to an end . . .

She would have something of him to take with her, even if it was only the memory of their lovemaking.

She reached one of her hands up to his neck, his cheek, his ear, caressing him as he had so often done to her. And she was rewarded for her efforts by the hiss of his breath as he tried to breathe in.

"Unlike you, my friend," she said, so very softly, "I cannot see into the future, and I do not know what it might hold. But I fear that soon we will be pulled apart to travel our separate ways. But before I leave, before you take me back to the fort, I would have you know that . . . I would like to take the memory of your lovemaking with me. I would have you love me."

He stared at her for so long, he might have been stunned. But at last he nodded. "So it will be," he said.

"I must warn you, though, that if you take that other woman as wife to you while I am still within your village, I will leave you so quickly, and without your assistance, that you will not even remember that I had been there."

He shook his head. "Always, I would remember you."

She ran her hands over his back, down to his tight buttocks, and she placed her forehead against his chest as she said, "And I, too, will always remember you. No matter the future. Always, you will be in my heart."

"Our future," he said, bringing his lips down to her neck, nibbling there, while his fingers worked magic on her breasts, "will never be the same. It will be rough, I think, for us to remain together, but I believe we will be happy."

"Is that what you see?"

He nodded. "That is what I see."

"I am uncertain." She closed her eyes, her head rocking back and forth on his chest. "I have so much I want from life, you see, and the Indian village—that way of life—isn't what I had envisioned for me, and I—"

"Sh-h-h, let us not think about it now. Let us love one another. We may not have another chance once we are in camp."

It was only then that she realized he was still aroused and ready for her. And looking at him, she felt herself becoming more and more excited.

"Before, when we made love," he said, "I was as a man demented, seeking my own release. Now, let us take our time, let me truly love you, show you the pleasure that can be between a man and a woman."

"It was not as though I wasn't enjoying it that first time."

He gave her an odd look and said, "It can be so much better. Come," he led her to the shoreline. As though he knew every feature of this land, he took her to a softened green spot, a willow tree shading the place from anyone's ready vision.

She couldn't help one tiny protest, however, and she started, "But the others . . ."

"Will leave us alone. They will be a long time preparing themselves to enter the village. Do not worry."

"But what if they decide to come and find us?"

"They will respect our need to be alone, I promise this to you. You are safe here."

He lay her down then, and the soft grass immediately cushioned her backside, the grassy fragrance of it and the wildflowers adding to her already heightening senses.

"Night Thunder, I—"

"Sh-h-h. I am going to love you as I should have that first night."

"But we have not really come to terms with whether or not we are married, and I would not want to—"

"We have been joined by the forces of nature. Sun wills it, I think."

"But not my God."

"Our gods are not so different, I think," he said. "Though you may call Him something else than do my people. Spirits are everywhere, but there is but one Creator, I think. Let us not argue about this. You are free to believe as you wish. But know that you are my wife, in true. What you choose to do with that has yet to pass, but know that we are joined. There is nothing wrong in what we do."

She shuddered.

And as his lips found hers, he eased himself beside her, although far from making her feel relaxed, his kiss roused her.

She wanted more.

One of his hands discovered her breasts all over again and she moaned. Still, it wasn't enough. His lips followed the curve of her neck, downward, toward her swollen nipples, causing her to squirm beneath his mastery.

"You are beautiful," he muttered.

"I am not," she whispered, her voice husky.

"*Aa*, yes, you are," he said. "I think I would know."

He kissed her ears, then, her throat, her cheeks, her neck, and all the while his fingers massaged her softened mounds of flesh, urging her on toward a promised finale.

"Someday," he said, his gaze centered upon her bosom, "these will be filled with life-giving milk for our babies."

Babies? Aye, babies.

His statement should have had the same effect on her as that of a dash of cold water. Strangely, it did not. She would have hated to admit it, but the thought of having this man's baby stimulated her beyond belief. Perhaps it was because despite her misgivings about him, about society's right or wrong, she felt herself responding.

She put her hands on his chest, rubbing them up and down, and had the pleasure of hearing him groan.

"Do you like that?" she asked.

He gave her a nod. "*Hannia*. Very much." He stilled her hands, though, after a while, and said, "But please, a little of that is enough, lest I disappoint myself and you."

"I don't understand," she said, frowning.

He gave her a half-smile. "Always, I try to keep myself under control, but with you, I am much aroused. I do not want to be as a small boy and take my pleasure now. I would see that you have yours first."

"I still don't—"

"Someday you will. It is enough to know that I desire you very much."

She smiled at him. "You do?"

"*Aa*, yes," he said, "too much, perhaps."

He proceeded, then, to shower her face, her neck, her bosom again with kisses. His lips found the tip of her breasts, suckling them before moving downward toward her navel, his tongue and lips creating havoc within her.

Onward, downward, he made a path; down to her silken patch of hair. He glanced up at her quickly. "Indian women do not have curls here," he said.

"They don't?"

He shook his head.

"And how would you know?" she asked.

"I would know."

She ignored his response. "Have you stolen many a young girl's heart?"

"I would not seduce a young girl."

"Would you not? Then how did you come by your experience? Your fiancée, Blue Raven Woman?"

He shook his head. "She is a maiden."

"Then how?"

He didn't answer her right away. Instead, his fingers began rubbing that swollen, silken part of her body.

Slowly, seductively, he slipped a finger inside her femininity, and she thought she might die of the heady stimulation he created. Her stomach spun over several times and her fingers clutched at the grass beside her.

She opened her legs a little wider to him.

"There are some widows and a few second and third wives," he said, "whose husbands approve of them finding comfort elsewhere. It is not always the case, however, so one must be careful for there is heavy penalty for the woman if her husband does not approve. And one must never seduce a first wife, for she is the lifeblood of our tribe. It is she who can bring Sun to us in the Sun Dance."

All the while he spoke, he never ceased what he was doing with her, down there between her legs. She caught her breath as a warm glow enveloped her.

Suddenly, she felt something else, a wetness. She chanced to look down. His head was bent to her, his lips upon her. "Night Thunder, what are you doing?"

He didn't answer and she didn't press him. It felt too good to object.

She lay back and closed her eyes, letting the overpowering pleasure of what he was doing build up. She began to move with him, too, to open up to him.

He increased his demand on her and she knew, as he worked her up into a heated frenzy, that she would love this man for the rest of her life. Whether she was with him or not, whether he married again or not.

She would love him.

The man had integrated himself into her heart, into her life, and into her soul. Regardless of society, culture, or worldly goods, she realized she would care for this man, perhaps for eternity.

Ah, but she couldn't even think, the effort too much, as the pleasure built and built where his mouth employed magic. Onward and upward he took her, until she thought she would not be able to stand it, so good did it feel. She closed her eyes, suppressing the need to scream out her frustration, her gratification, as the heated tide of fulfillment raged within her. On and on it went, over and over she surrendered to it, until at last she couldn't hold back, and she whimpered and moaned, her tiny cries blocked by his kiss.

Upward, she floated on a wave of pleasure, a pleasure created by her, by him. She soared through the heavens then as though she were a winged creature. At length she settled back down to earth, her body bathed in a sheen of perspiration. She met his grin as their gazes sought out one another.

He didn't say a word to her, however. He didn't have to. His expression alone told of his satisfaction.

He was right, she capitulated. Just as he had said, there was much more to lovemaking than she had at first realized. She only hoped that he didn't intend to stop at this one, single act.

He soon disabused her of that idea, as he brought her again to one dizzying height after another, until at last, as though unable to help himself, he moved his body over hers, his dark eyes seeking out her own. She smiled up at him then, giving herself gladly to him, opening up for him as his body joined with hers.

Ah, she melted against him, the surrender sweet agony. This was what she had been waiting for, this final coupling, this act of love. And she wondered, as she began to move with him in the time-honored way of love, would it always be like this? Would he always look at her as he was now, admiring her? His gaze, as well as his body, thrilling her? Arousing her?

As though he knew her thoughts, he murmured, "Always." And he smiled at her, the smile of a man caught in the height of seduction, his body never once ceasing its demand upon hers.

She drew a strained breath, then, as the flames of pleasure built and zenithed again within her. But this time when she soared upward, caught in the ecstasy of fire, she brought him with her. She felt the rhythm of his release over and over as he spilled his seed within her, her body, her very being rejoicing in the heady sensation. Together, they floated high above the clouds, their very space entwined, as though each one were now an inseparable part of the other.

And perhaps they were.

They lay next to each other as they both settled down to earth, their limbs still linked together, their breathing rapid and intense, and their hands holding on to one another as though each one were afraid that if he should let go, he might lose the other.

Her mind drifted away, thinking of nothing, and yet much, and he said to her, "Know that I will not let you go."

She nodded, unable at this moment, and perhaps unwilling, to dispute him.

He continued, "Though I thought I would be able to do it, to take you back to the fort and watch you walk away from me, I know I cannot do it now. We will have to find another way, I believe. I want to keep you with me."

She closed her eyes and nodded, whispering under her breath, "Aye, my handsome warrior, I understand."

She left whatever else she might have said on the subject, unspoken, as did he. She didn't want to spoil the moment, nor, she believed, did he.

She would have to wait and see what the morrow would bring. Briefly she tried to envision how
Night Thunder might look in the white man's
clothing . . .

She groaned. Somehow, the image, the thought
of that, did not please her. Not at all.

Chapter 15

Their arrival in Night Thunder's village, that same day, seemed more an exercise in pomp and ceremony than in the simple act of returning home.

After her bath and before they had entered the camp, Rebecca had stood in awe as she'd watched these fearsome warriors tend to their toiletry. Each one of them had bathed and donned his finest clothes, had painted his face and adorned his hair—sometimes, to Rebecca's amusement, overly so. Even Night Thunder had dressed in the best that he had with him, going so far as to offer Rebecca his robe, that she, too, might enter his village wearing something of beauty.

His eyes had sparkled at her as he'd handed it to her, and he had said, "So that you might, every time you look at it, remember our morning together."

She'd been certain her cheeks had stained with color as he'd spoken and she had been glad that no one else had understood English.

She'd been about to refuse the gift, too, on principle, but under further consideration had capitulated. The garment was heavy and would provide her with warmth against the morning chill. It was a thing of loveliness, too, she realized, staring at the softly tanned hide, which had been ornamented and painted with stick figures, depicting, she supposed, Night Thunder's war adventures.

It would also hide her dress. Staring down at herself, she was sad to note that her gown, although never a thing of beauty, had long since performed its service and now hung on her like a lifeless fellow in duggins. She drew Night Thunder's robe around her that it might hide and perhaps outshine the weathered condition of her clothing.

Her undergarments, too, were practically unserviceable, and her slippers had been shed for moccasins, an extra pair brought by one of the warriors. She shuddered to think what the fashionable world might say about her state of dress. But she shrugged. No one here seemed to take offense.

Her hair, at least, was neat and orderly. Night Thunder had plaited it into two braids at the sides of her head, her handsome warrior explaining that this style was the most popular among all the married ladies within his camp.

Married . . .

He had even gone so far as to paint a red strip at the center of her part, a custom, he'd told her, which was considered beautiful among the Blackfeet.

But too soon their party was ready to enter the camp.

Earlier in the morning, a warrior from their midst had stolen into the tribal pony herd and had taken some mounts, bringing them back so that the warriors might ride proudly into the village. Even Rebecca had been given a pony from Night Thunder's vast herd, to honour her, she had discovered, that she might follow gladly behind him as they paraded.

Because their path had for so long followed a riverbed, Rebecca needed to look up to catch her first glimpse of the Indian encampment. Very soon the Indian village stood there before her, high above them on a broad, sunny plain.

She caught her breath. With the sun shining down upon it, the whole encampment appeared to shimmer under the August heat, and had it not been for the fresh scents of smoke and of food and the merry sounds of laughter, she would have thought she was staring at something mythical and fabled, not a village of substance and worth.

A hawk flew high above them, announcing their arrival as though it were a herald of old, while shimmers of excitement raced over her skin.

Their party made their way to higher ground and stopped for a moment, all looking over toward the Indian encampment. Smoke curled from the various lodges while dogs barked and children laughed. Sentries rode back and forth, from lookouts far in the distance, back toward the village. Women sat outside, tanning hides, cooking or just enjoying a good chat with one another, and men strode through the camp, amicably embracing some physical contest or sitting upon the ground attending to a needed chore. Even from this distance, she could feel the happiness and good cheer of the place. Feel it as though it were a part of her and she felt . . . stirred . . .

She had never thought to see an Indian encampment, not in this life, and certainly had never expected it to be quite the size of this. She voiced aloud to Night Thunder, "It's enormous."

"*Aa*, yes, that it is," he replied to her at once, his own gaze scanning the village, his look one of contentment and . . . pride? He had been riding a little ahead of her and, as she glanced toward him, she thought he must surely be the most beautiful specimen of man she had ever seen. And, she realized, he appeared happy: happy and untroubled as he looked out upon his home. A smile lit his face, while his voice was as soft as a tender embrace. He continued, "But there is not just one band of the Blackfeet gathered here on this day."

"No?"

"*Saa*, no. It is the beginning of the moon when we prepare food storage, or as your people say it, August. It is at this time every year when our people hold the Sun Dance. And all of the bands of the Blackfeet are here, the *Siksikauw*, the *Kainah*, the *Pikuni*. We all gather here every year to celebrate and to honour Sun. And we will remain here in this way for perhaps the full moon."

"I see," she said, and as she gazed out upon the sight, she couldn't help but admire it. From the hundreds of colorful lodges, which adorned the landscape, to the pony herd which grazed off to the side. It appeared a delightful symmetry of graceful tepees and sun-bleached ground, the village attaching itself to the earth as though it were as natural a part of the open plains as the land itself.

Painted tepees in colours of red, yellow, white, and blue stretched out upon the prairie for what must have been two or three miles. It was a sight that would have stirred the imagination of even the most stouthearted skeptic, and she knew why Night Thunder smiled when he looked out upon it.

In the center of it, she glimpsed especially painted tepees, arranged in an enormous circle, the very shape of it creating an immense, flat, campus-type center.

She asked, "Those tepees in the center, the ones pitched and forming a circle, why are they painted so differently than the rest?"

"*Aa*, yes," he responded, "look there in the center of the circle."

She did.

"Do you not see the skeleton of a lodge there?"

She nodded, and said, "Aye."

"That is the Sun Dance lodge," he went on to explain. "It is already erected and awaiting the dance to begin so that we can all do honour to *Natose,* Sun. Do you see that the circle, which is created by the lodges, is where we will dance?"

She did and she asked, "What kind of dance is it, now, that your people will be doing?"

"*Haiya*," he said, "you must wait and see. This is a time of rejoicing for the people. There will be much food, many games, lots of talk and joking. But here is where our boys will become warriors. Sun makes them strong. You will see."

She nodded. She knew that what he said must

be true. She could sense the excitement of the warriors who accompanied her, and she could only compare the anticipation of what she perceived with the same sort of expectation she had experienced as a child, at Christmas.

It must truly be a wonderful dance.

Soon their party was riding through the herd of ponies she had spied earlier. There were hundreds of these Indian ponies, the untamed animals having been turned loose upon the open prairies to graze. Some were hobbled, most, however, were not.

She began to smile at the antics of them, the animals kicking their hind legs in the air and prancing right up to their party, nipping the humans in the heels as they passed. She said to Night Thunder, "They almost appear as children, these ponies."

"They are happy to see us," he replied back to her. "Do you not see how they play, how they prance like they do with their tails erect and their heads thrown back? They are showing off for us, that we might take notice of them and train them to be war ponies or buffalo ponies. They are always as excited to be here together, as are we Indians."

"Aye, I can see that," she said, and fell silent.

Too soon, several Indian braves from the village spotted the returning party, and vaulting onto their prized mounts, came racing over the fields toward the new arrivals. The braves were yelling and screaming, too, at the top of their lungs. "*Hie, hie, hie,*" they yelped, and Rebecca's stomach plummeted at the sound, panic streaming through her.

But when Night Thunder glanced back toward her and grinned, as though to say, 'They are delighted to see us,' she knew that there was no immediate danger.

"*Po'kioot!*" the incoming braves were saying, and she realized, because of their hand motions, that they must be asking the warriors to follow them.

She felt the stare of the unfamiliar Indians upon her, as the young men brought their ponies to a stop, but Rebecca could not actually catch any of them looking at her. It was not the first time she had experienced a feeling of such scrutiny, without anyone actually staring at her, and she was beginning to wonder how the Indians did it.

No introductions were made between her and these warriors, however, and Rebecca decided to ignore them as best she could.

The young braves led their party into the camp, and at once the Indians, who had for so long accompanied her and Night Thunder, disassembled, the men obviously taking their leave to find their own lodges.

Rebecca stuck as closely as she could to Night Thunder, but she couldn't help noticing that the Indian women seemed not at all as discreet as the men: all stared at her openly, though Rebecca could not sense any particular animosity in their observation.

One woman, however, one very beautiful Indian woman, regarded her oddly—looking, Rebecca thought, as though she were witnessing a ghost.

The woman was beautiful. Was Night Thunder's fiancée so pretty?

Neither the thought nor her immediate reaction to it comforted her, and Rebecca hurriedly glanced away. Was this jealousy? she wondered. Was it jealousy when a woman wanted to hide her husband away from all other eyes, wanted to keep him with her so that no one else could have him?

He was not truly her husband, Rebecca reminded herself, and she threw back her head, glancing once more around her.

Children swarmed through the camp like wild little whirlwinds, and their gaiety, their very joviality provided her with a welcome sense of relief. Canines, half-wolf, half-dog, ran here and there, too, their howling adding to the sounds of the prairie's ever present wind, to the beating of the drums in the distance, to the murmur of voices and the happy laughter which seemed to surround everything here.

She became curious. Somehow she had thought that an Indian encampment would be a serious and frightening place, certainly not one of amusement and entertainment. The observation made her ache to ask Night Thunder more about this place, about these people, the children, and, in particular, that one woman who had looked at her so strangely. But she did not know how to begin to ask.

She was also uncertain of the etiquette involved in talking to a warrior in so public a place as this, and she hesitated to do anything that might throw disregard upon him.

At length, Night Thunder led her to a tepee in

the center of the encampment, and alighting from
his pony, dropped his buckskin reins and strode
toward the conical structure. Without saying a
word to her or even glancing in her direction, he
opened and entered the lodge, leaving Rebecca
outside to confront the curious stares of the Indians. But she needn't have worried; no one approached her or said a word to her, either.

The scent of roasting food and campfires teased
at her nostrils, and her stomach growled, reminding her that she hadn't yet had breakfast. There
was another smell in the air, too, a pleasant one,
and one with which she was fast becoming familiar—that of the sweet-herb aroma of sage and
sweet grass.

All around her came the sounds of camp life, of
laughter and good cheer, of the high-pitched
voices of children and the buzz of women's talk,
interrupted here and there by a hearty round of
giggles and laughter. And throughout the camp
came the sound of drums and singing.

Curious. Everyone appeared so happy.

She noted one elderly man, closer to her, engaged in painting what looked to be a war shield,
and entrenched around him were a group of
young boys, all of them listening in rapt attention
as the old man spoke.

It was odd, she thought, that the rumors she'd
heard of the Indians didn't include the description
of the fellowship and friendship which she was
witnessing here. Strange, since she had been in the
camp only a few moments and already she was
aware of it. How could another, reporting about
the Indians, have missed such a thing?

A woman approached her, the same pretty woman whom Rebecca had taken note of upon first entering the Indian encampment, the one who had looked at her so curiously.

"*Kyai-yo!*" the woman said to her, and Rebecca glanced down toward the girl. "*Ah'-ko-two-kr-tuk'-ah-an-on,*" the young woman tried again, but Rebecca shook her head, trying to communicate by body language alone that she did not understand.

The Indian woman touched Rebecca's leg where she sat astride her pony, and Rebecca flinched.

"*O'toyimm,*" the girl pointed to herself and smiled, extending her hand toward Rebecca.

Rebecca let out her breath. It was obvious the woman was trying to be affable, but still Rebecca hesitated, frowning. She had also heard too many stories about the deadliness of Indian "friends." Wasn't it Daniel Boone who had once said that one must never trust an Indian, even a congenial one?

Rebecca looked away.

"*Poka,*" the young woman tried again, and this time when Rebecca glanced back down, she was met with a hearty smile from the young Indian woman. Sighing, Rebecca capitulated. It was obvious the woman was not going to go away, and seeing the woman's hand still extended toward her, Rebecca decided it would not do her any harm to place her own into that of the other woman's grasp.

She did so.

And suddenly Night Thunder appeared at her side, though Rebecca had not been aware of him until the last moment, the man having stepped out from the tepee so silently. He looked pleased, too, and Rebecca could only wonder at it.

He said to the young woman, "*Nit-ik-oht-yaahs-i'taki k-ikaa-o'too'hs'yi*, I'm glad you have arrived."

"*O'toyimm. Ah'-ko-two-kr-tuk'-ah-an-on*," the Indian girl repeated, and Night Thunder nodded.

He said to Rebecca, "She tries to tell you that she has friendly feeling toward you. She had heard that there was a woman traveling with me and she is glad to see that we have arrived safely. She welcomes us home."

Rebecca raised her chin. She asked, "Why would she welcome you home, and why should she feel friendly toward me?"

Night Thunder's glance went from one woman to the next, looking as perplexed as any male might when confronted with something he didn't understand, and from two specimens of the female sex.

Why? Rebecca wondered.

He said, "She tries to make you feel comfortable. Do you not know who this is?"

Rebecca shook her head. "Should I?"

Again, he gazed from one woman to the next, his look more than a little mystified—sheepish, even.

What was going on here?

Rebecca had little time to wonder, however, for Night Thunder did not waste any time in telling her, his voice more than a little subdued, as he said, "This is a woman whom I want to you come to know."

Rebecca raised her chin, premonition perhaps steeling her nerves as she heard Night Thunder finish, "This is Blue Raven Woman."

Chapter 16

~~~∽∽OC∽~~~

S o, the other woman was beautiful.

Rebecca knew exactly why that particular piece of information upset her, and she didn't like it. Not at all.

She was jealous. That was all there was to it. Completely, utterly jealous.

She was not supposed to be here. She was not supposed to be in an Indian camp, sitting beside her husband's "betrothed," and she the "wife" of a man she could never actually marry. She smiled to herself at this last thought, thinking it would make little sense to the civilized world, yet it explained much here in the Indian encampment.

Rebecca sat inside a tepee on this bright day. The lodge had been given to her by Night Thunder's stepmother and aunts, and, she had been disheartened to learn, Blue Raven Woman's female relatives, with Blue Raven Woman herself helping Rebecca to erect it.

In truth, it was Blue Raven Woman who sat across from Rebecca this minute, chatting away at her happily in a tongue that Rebecca could barely understand. But it mattered little if she understood or not. She had no desire to learn what the other woman was saying.

In due time, if only to quiet the other woman, Rebecca said, "Night Thunder told me about you."

But when she was met with nothing but a blank stare from the Indian girl, Rebecca decided to try the phrase in the Blackfoot language which Night Thunder had been striving to reach her. "*N omoht-itsiniko-o; k-wa kiistoyi,*" she attempted.

Blue Raven woman giggled softly.

"What did I say? I wasn't speaking it wrong, was I?"

The Indian woman shook her head and responded, "*Soka'pssiwa.*"

Soka'pssiwa? What did that mean? "He is good?" Rebecca thought so.

She answered, "*Aa*, yes," and was rewarded with what could have been considered a heart-warming grin, if Rebecca were so inclined to give the other woman quarter. Rebecca wasn't.

They both fell back into silence, Rebecca stealing a look at the other woman, under the cover of her lashes. Slim and well proportioned, Blue Raven woman presented an image of all that might have been considered attractive about these people.

Two long braids, fashioned behind her ears, fell down each side of Blue Raven Woman's face and over her chest, the ends of them caught and held with beaded buckskin hair-ties. Pink shells hung from her ears and from around her neck. Her face and the part in her hair were both painted, and red dots, appearing like spots of rouge, brightened the young Indian's cheeks.

The woman's everyday dress was unusual, too, consisting of sun and clay–bleached buckskin, which had been dyed yellow, the top half of it ornamented with paint, beads, and quills. A leather belt, brightly beaded and quilled, was tied around her waist, and on her feet she wore moccasins, again painted yellow and slightly beaded. She smelled of clean buckskin and fresh herbs and gave the appearance of being so light, her feet barely touched the ground.

Good-natured, Blue Raven Woman never seemed strained to find something to smile about, either. To tell the truth, Rebecca had been astonished to discover the good-hearted cheer of most every woman she had so far met in camp, young and old. One would hardly know, from their constant and delightful prattle, that the rest of the world considered them slaves.

She thought they would most likely laugh if she were to tell them so. Not that she would. Besides, she didn't know the language well enough even to attempt what would have to be a lengthy conversation.

She had heard about another kind of Indian woman, however, in stories of how women had personally tortured prisoners, about how they would tear the clothing off one's back. Rebecca dreaded the day she would meet with such a one as that.

In the meantime, she seemed doomed to have to bear the company of a woman who didn't seem to comprehend that they were at best enemies.

The two of them had been working over a piece of soft buckskin, tanned so well that it felt more

NIGHT THUNDER'S BRIDE   227

like the touch of silk against her skin than that of
an animal hide. For most of the morning, they had
been fashioning the leather into some form of
clothing for Night Thunder, Rebecca supposed.

Not that she was being an extraordinary amount
of help. Rebecca was having trouble sewing whatever article they were making, as she was unfamiliar with the Indian's thread. Apparently, she
was learning, one had to soak the this string in
one's mouth in order to get it soft enough to work:
soak, that is, everything but the tip of it, which
was itself used much as she would have utilized
a needle.

Rebecca inhaled deeply and asked, in the Blackfoot tongue, "A'sipis . . . kayiiwa?" She hoped she
was asking what kind of thread they were using.

"Nitsstsinaa . . . sstsinaa," Blue Raven Woman responded, and pointed to her back.

Her back?

Rebecca shook her head. "I don't understand."

Blue Raven Woman glanced around her, in the
interior of the tepee, and spying something on the
floor, pointed to it. A buffalo robe?

Blue Raven Woman said, "Iinii."

Rebecca knew that word. It was "buffalo." She
repeated, "Iinii?"

Blue Raven Woman nodded.

What? They obtained their thread from buffalo?

"Mo'kakiikin." Again the young Indian woman
pointed to her backside, obviously attempting to
make herself understood. Then she formed the
necessary signs for thread.

Rebecca glanced down at the strand in her hand.
What was this stuff that she was soaking in her

mouth? She picked up the end of it, examining it. The thread was arid and brittle unless she put it in her mouth, at which time it turned soft and pliable. But it dried hard and became much more durable on clothing than cotton thread.

Rebecca looked at the material this way and that, sniffing at the substance, holding it out and away from her.

What the . . . then it came to her.

This was . . . this was buffalo sinew!

Rebecca dropped the piece of thread and, holding her stomach, stumbled to her feet. She felt sick.

"*Ikim?*" Rebecca asked Blue Raven Woman. "Water?" She made a drinking sign.

"*Aa,*" said the young woman and reaching around her, brought out a pouch holding the household water. She stood and offered it to Rebecca.

Rebecca took a sip of the liquid, but it didn't help. The pouch was made from some other part of the buffalo, and the water tasted worse than anything she had ever drunk. She choked.

She had to get out of this place.

But Blue Raven Woman only giggled at her, and reaching over toward her, started to pound her slightly on the back. Blue Raven Woman asked, "*Ohkoimmohsit?*"

Rebecca nodded, not understanding the words, but grasping what the woman was saying nonetheless. "Aye," she said, "I feel sick."

Again Blue Raven Woman chuckled, and Rebecca bristled. Was the other woman having fun at her expense? Was she trying to make Rebecca look silly?

Rebecca jutted out her chin. Well, she'd soon show her.

She threw back her head, glared at the other woman, and sat down again. Picking up the piece of sinew, after only a moment's hesitation, she shoved it back into her mouth. Her stomach threatened to be her undoing, but Rebecca did her best to ignore it, sending a vehement look up at the young Indian woman, who, still giggling, held her hand over her mouth.

That did it. Rebecca forced herself to collect up the bone awl she'd been using as a means to punch holes into the buckskin, and pulling another face at Blue Raven Woman, sewed up that seam she'd been working so hard over all morning.

Blue Raven Woman simply smiled.

The next series of days seemed to pass in much the same manner. Night Thunder was gone for most of the day while Rebecca was on her own, although Blue Raven Woman had become her constant companion, sitting with her, chatting to her, following her everywhere.

Rebecca never ventured too far from her new "home." Too afraid to roam through the camp, Rebecca rarely saw anything outside the tepee, except on those few occasions when she needed to fetch water, and even then she would undertake the task early in the morning, when she felt sure she would not encounter another human being, except, of course, Blue Raven Woman.

Amazingly, the young woman kept her well supplied with firewood, food, and water, which,

Rebecca learned, was a wife's duty to supply. Still, Rebecca could never bring herself to smile at the Indian girl nor acknowledge her unless given no choice.

Rebecca had been in the camp for about five days now, and except for an occasional visit from one of Night Thunder's sisters, Rebecca rarely saw other people. Of course, she could not bring herself to attend the tribe's dances, feeling as she did like an outsider. Frightened that she might commit some faux pas, she declined to watch the tribal games, which she learned were numerous. Nor could she socialize with a people whom she struggled to understand.

She was beginning to feel more and more like an outcast, although she had to admit, it seemed her own fault; no one treated her unjustly.

But people here rarely talked to her. That is, except for Blue Raven Woman.

The Indian girl sat across from her now, having arrived at Rebecca's lodge early this morning, bringing with her more work to be done, this time in the form of another piece of soft buckskin. Another shirt for Night Thunder, most likely, Rebecca thought.

Rebecca grimaced and stared down at her own clothing. The unsuitability of what she wore was becoming more and more noticeable. Sometime soon, she promised herself, when she returned to the fort, she would obtain some cloth and make herself a new dress. Sometime . . .

But for now Blue Raven Woman held up the piece of buckskin, and handing Rebecca the tools of their trade—and awl and sinew—they began to work over the clothing.

As usual, Blue Raven Woman kept up an amazingly cheerful monologue.

"*Niipoipoyit*," Blue Raven Woman said after a while, the article they were working over beginning to resemble a piece of clothing. She motioned to Rebecca to stand up.

Rebecca, seeing no reason not to do as asked, stood, the young Indian woman following her up.

"*Yaamikskaapiksi*." Blue Raven Woman gestured toward her to turn around.

Rebecca did.

Then the strangest thing happened. Blue Raven Woman came right up to her, and holding out the article they had just sewn together, began to fit the thing onto *her*.

Blue Raven Woman said, "*Soka'piiwa*, it is good."

It was only then that Rebecca began truly to understand. However, the knowledge left her dumbfounded.

This piece of clothing was for her. Astounding, but true. Blue Raven Woman had helped her, was helping her even now, to sew a dress. For her own possession.

Astonished, Rebecca spun around to face this woman, who had, for the past few days, dogged her every step. Rebecca looked upon this gentle being with "new eyes," as the Indians would say. And what she saw there she would remember for the rest of her life.

The young Indian woman looked back at her. The girl's dark eyes were clear and filled with such kindness and good-heartedness that Rebecca's throat constricted, so much so that she fought to hold onto her reserve.

Rebecca could little understand Blue Raven Woman's behavior.

So far Rebecca had taken away the Indian girl's fiancé, had relegated the woman to the position of second wife, had made her displeasure in the other woman's presence quite well felt. And yet as Rebecca continued to gaze at the other woman, she could find no trace of resentment or cruelty on the girl's countenance.

In truth, what she saw within Blue Raven Woman's regard touched some deep chord within her. Without willing it, her heart went out to this person.

Had she been wrong? Had she been mistaken to judge this woman? These people?

She had thought the Indians were stone-aged and simple, had been taught of their savagery, and had regarded them as little more than children. But now she was starting to realize that she had unknowingly passed judgment on an entire race of people without ever once trying to get to know them or understand them. And the truth was, the Indians were not savages, they were not cruel.

How had their true nature become so maligned?

Certainly, as with all peoples, there would be the exceptions, the troublemakers in a village, as with Strikes The Bear. Just as they were not the bulk of the citizenry within her own race, so too they were not the majority here.

Rebecca tried to say something kindly, for a change, to this woman for whom she had so far shown nothing but disdain, but she could not remember the right Blackfoot phrases. So she did the best she could with a simple smile.

Blue Raven Woman returned the gesture.

They stared at one another in this way until Rebecca felt she must attempt to say something, and placing her hand upon the young girl's shoulder, Rebecca began, "From this day forward, I will try my best to get along with you," she said. "From this day forward, I will try to be . . . kinder to you. But please understand, I cannot share Night Thunder with you. That I will never do. But I promise you this: I will, from here on out, treat you with the sort of consideration that you deserve."

Blue Raven woman grinned back at her as though she'd understood each and every word. Then, the Indian girl moved both her hands down her face, as if she were combing her hair, and immediately followed that by holding two fingers up to her lips and moving them forward, "*Insst.*"

Insst. What did the word mean? It had such a pretty ring to it.

"*Insst,*" Rebecca repeated, and was startled to note the Indian girl's face change, suddenly filling with emotion and . . . tears? From the simple action of Rebecca repeating that word?

What had she said?

She didn't know, and she couldn't ask, because just as quickly as she'd spoken, Blue Raven Woman turned, and on soft moccasined feet, fled the tepee so quickly, Rebecca could only stand and stare at the place where the woman had been.

She had taken the buckskin with her, too, and Rebecca knew with certainty that tomorrow, the young Indian woman would present Rebecca with a new dress—a gift of fellowship and generosity from someone who should have been an enemy.

But she wasn't. Nor had she ever been.

Rebecca felt the sting of tears at the back of her eyes.

It was all so very, very strange.

Chapter 17

✦✦ **I**t is a good thing that you did, Blue Raven Woman. This stranger will need a family of her own in our camp: somewhere she can go, away from *his* relatives. In his home, they are always so close to her, listening to her, and she will have to be on her guard. It cannot be an easy life for one so different from us. It is right that you made her a part of our family, *insst*, your sister. Here, she can speak freely, laugh and express herself, without fear."

Blue Raven Woman nodded at her mother and gazed off to the other side of the lodge. "She has kind eyes, that one. My new sister will make Night Thunder a good sits-beside-him woman."

"And did you take her the new moccasins that we made for her?" her mother asked.

"*Saa*, no," said the young woman. "I will take them to her tomorrow, when I will also offer her the new dress."

"*Aa*, yes," said the older woman. "*Soka'piiwa*, it is good."

The two fell into a companionable silence. In

235

due time, however, Blue Raven Woman said, "She is the one from my dream."

"*Kyai-yo!*" The elder woman quickly raised her hand over her mouth. "You speak true?"

"*Aa*, yes, my mother. I saw a hawk fly by me that day, which turned into a woman with eyes like those of a mountain lion and hair the color of yellow at sunset, and then the image just as quickly changed into the figure of Night Thunder."

"*Kyai-yo!* We did not believe you."

Blue Raven Woman shrugged. "I did not believe it myself. But here she is, and now I think it was a vision that Sun gave to me. What do you suppose it means?"

"I know not what it means. But I will ask your father and he will give a pony to our medicine man that he might interpret the dream."

Blue Raven Woman nodded. It was as it should be.

She felt suddenly at peace, knowing that as soon as she learned what it was Sun was telling her, she would do everything she could to live up to her duty, even if it meant that she would have to become a second wife.

But she couldn't help holding onto the hope that whatever her vision, she would not have to risk the love of her life, Singing Bull. Fervently she sent a prayer to Sun, promising that if he would shine upon her this one favor, she would gladly sacrifice a part of herself to him.

And as a special offering, to show her good intention, she broke off a bit of meat and left it on the family altar.

* * *

It had been a week since Night Thunder had
brought her to this camp: a week since she and the
handsome Indian had spent much time alone. A
week during which she'd had no one to talk to,
expect for the company of women. Rebecca remembered Night Thunder telling her that once in
the camp, he would be unable to spend much time
with her, but she hadn't realized how difficult the
reality of that would be. She had to admit, though,
that being forced to communicate with these people, was, perhaps, the best thing that could have
happened to her, at least as far as the language
was concerned. She was learning it well.

It had been a warm day so far. She sat outside
in her new Indian garb, which had been given to
her by Blue Raven Woman. Except for the colour
of her hair and the gold of her eyes, Rebecca
thought she might have appeared Indian.

Insst. Rebecca smiled when she thought now of
the other woman. It hadn't taken her long to learn
that Blue Raven Woman had bestowed upon her
the honour of being her sister—her, a strange,
white woman. Rebecca had to admit that she felt
touched by the gesture. Though still, she would
never be able to think of Blue Raven Woman as a
sister.

As a friend? Yes. The young woman was fast
becoming a friend. But as a sister? Never. Not
when Blue Raven Woman was still betrothed to
Night Thunder.

Rebecca sighed.

This day she had set up a tripod made of sticks,
as she had seen and been instructed to do by the

other women. She had several times attempted to light the fire underneath it, too, but couldn't seem to manage it. She was struggling over the chore when Blue Raven Woman approached her.

Blue Raven Woman immediately sat down beside her and within seconds had lit the fire and positioned a few slabs of meat to be held suspended from the sticks.

Rebecca smiled her thanks at the other woman, saying, "*Nitsiniiyi'taki*, I am grateful."

"*Soka'piiwa*, it is good, you are welcome."

"*Iik-iksistoyi-wa*, it is very hot."

Blue Raven Woman nodded.

They fell into silence, then, both of them watching the fire. In due time, however, Rebecca asked, as though she couldn't help herself, "*Aahsa k-omoht-o'too-hpa*, why do you come here? Why do you keep helping me even when I have been so rude to you?"

Blue Raven Woman shrugged and responded, "*Maano'too-wa*, you were new and did not know our ways. It has been my duty to make you feel welcome and to become your friend." She gave Rebecca a shy smile. "Now we are sisters."

Rebecca didn't dispute the other woman, although again she knew she could never experience that close a relationship to the Indian girl. She took a deep breath and attempted a smile. But it was difficult.

She persisted, "*Mao'k*, why would you want to help me? Wasn't I discourteous to you at first? Haven't I taken your place as a sits-beside-him wife to Night Thunder? Why do you not feel anger at me?"

Blue Raven Woman looked sad, all at once, but the look was so quickly gone from the young Indian's face that Rebecca couldn't be sure she had seen it. Blue Raven Woman said, "It was not your fault. Did you know that Night Thunder was to be my husband when you married him?"

Rebecca shook her head.

"Did you know our ways when you came into camp?"

Another shake.

"Then there was no reason for me to feel anger. Isn't it true that it is only angry men and women who make our lives a misery? And isn't it often just as true that the anger that they feel is not justified?"

Wasn't it?

Rebecca could only stare at this young woman, who not only appeared to be constantly cheerful, but suddenly seemed very wise, too.

"Besides," said Blue Raven Woman, "a second wife's life is always easier. Plus, your eyes were kind. Even when you were scolding me, I could see the thoughtfulness behind your words. Come," the Indian girl took Rebecca's hand, "let us go to my lodge, where we can talk more on this and speak freely."

"*Saa*, no, I couldn't. I . . ."

"Your husband's stepmother and his sisters are close by to you. Do you know that they hear every word you say?"

Were they? Did they?

"Come with me and enjoy the lodge of our mother, where you can be yourself and not have to worry constantly over what you do or say."

Blue Raven Woman sent Rebecca a cheeky grin all of a sudden and went on to enlighten her, "Come, and I will tell you about Night Thunder and his strange powers."

Rebecca gasped and sent a disbelieving look toward Blue Raven Woman. She said, after a moment, "I do not know what you mean."

Blue Raven Woman did not look impressed, however, and went on to say, "Have you not noticed that he has some strange abilities? That the spirits talk freely to him? That—"

Rebecca had held up her hand, silencing the girl. Then, glancing around as though she were about to reveal a secret, Rebecca said, "Then *you* know about that side of him."

Blue Raven Woman nodded. "Since he was little," she said, "he has always had the power to call upon the spirits, to talk to them and to the animals. It is why he is to be our next medicine man."

"He is?"

"*Aa*, yes. Come now with me?"

Rebecca hesitated a moment more. Though she hated the thought of leaving her new, safe "home," though she dreaded having to walk through the Indian camp where other eyes would follow her, after sweeping a quick glance around her, she did exactly as Blue Raven Woman asked. She went.

"*Oomi*, your husband is a very important man in our tribe," Blue Raven Woman said, as they sat within the lodge of Morning Child Woman, the mother of Blue Raven Woman. "Did Night Thunder not tell you this?

Rebecca shook her head.

"He would not," she said, "because a man of any worth is reluctant to boast of his deeds, and yet though he is young, Night Thunder has many."

Rebecca sent a startled glance up at Blue Raven Woman. What was it Night Thunder had once said, that "medicine" ran in his family? Did that make him important? But Blue Raven woman was right, Night Thunder was still so young. How could he . . . ?

Blue Raven Woman continued, "Night Thunder is *saaam*."

"*Tsa*—? What?"

"Night Thunder has much *saaam*, much medicine. Many are the important men in our tribe, but there is only one medicine man, and that one single man is sometimes more powerful than any other person in a tribe. It is he who decides on matters of importance, it is he who can talk to Sun, and it is he who can settle a dispute."

"*Nitsiitsistapi'taki*, I understand, I think. Do you tell me that Night Thunder is your *saaam*, then, your medicine man?"

Blue Raven Woman swept her hand to the right and front in a curve, at the same time saying, "*Saa*, no, but he has long been training to take the place of our medicine man, should something bad happen to that one."

"Ah, I think I'm beginning to understand. Night Thunder would be succeeding your own doctor, then?"

Blue Raven Woman nodded.

Another thought occurred to Rebecca, who was curious. Almost as an afterthought, she asked, "What training?"

"*Aa*, yes," Blue Raven Woman answered, "you would want to know of his training. Let me tell you." A calm seemed to settle over Blue Raven Woman as she continued, "From about the time he was fourteen winters, Night Thunder has been making trips with our medicine man in order that he come to know and become one with his power. A medicine man always chooses the boy who will succeed him, and so it is one of the highest honours a boy can receive, to be picked to follow the medicine ways."

"*Nitsiitsistapi'taki*, I see," Rebecca said, though she was uncertain that she truly did.

But Blue Raven Woman continued, "After the medicine man has chosen a boy to follow him, he will take that boy away for about six moons." She glanced up quickly. "Do you not have such people among your tribe?"

Rebecca could only shake her head and sweep her hand to the right as she had seen other Indians do when muttering something in the negative.

Blue Raven Woman shook her head, and asked, "How do your people stay well, then, and how do they banish an evil spell?"

"There are no evil spells among my people," said Rebecca in the Blackfoot language, using many gestures to help communicate. "And we have doctors of medicine, though that medicine is different than yours, I think."

"Humph," said Blue Raven Woman, before falling silent.

Rebecca prompted, "What happens when the medicine man takes the boy away?"

"*Aa*, yes," the Indian girl said, "they remain away for about six moons or months and the medicine man teaches the young boy to be master over his body. His spiritual side must become stronger than his body."

"Oh," said Rebecca, "and how is this done?"

"I do not know it all, but some of it is that the youth must go without food for many days at a time and must inflict upon himself some torture, and he must do this all voluntarily. He is never the same when he returns from this first trip with the medicine man. Always, the boy looks as though he has learned some deep secret."

Rebecca pondered these words for a moment before she uttered, "And perhaps he has."

Blue Raven Woman nodded.

"Is that all that there is to it, then?"

"*Saa*, no. After this the boy must learn that he cannot be strong in spirit and in heart if he is not also strong in body, and just as he has trained himself to know his own mind, so too must he condition his body. This lasts about three suns, and after this, his body is as strong as his heart, and his willpower is such that he can withstand even the greatest torture without what seems to be the least suffering. It is as though his body is no longer a thing to be considered and he ignores it. Making the body secondary to oneself is the first thing he must accomplish. Without this, he cannot influence others with his mind."

What strange ideas. Could a medicine man really do all these things? Rebecca asked, "But I thought you said a medicine man was a doctor. Aren't doctors supposed to cure disease and illness, not try to control men?"

"*Kyai-yo*, you do not understand, I think. A medicine man should not try to control others and force them, against their will, to do as another thinks right. This would not be good, since all men are free to follow the paths they have chosen. But a medicine man must be able to *influence* another with words and with the powers of his mind alone. And he must be able to drive the evil spirits from the body, too, when a person is ill. This requires a strong mind."

Rebecca contemplated this for a moment before she asked, "And is this how a medicine man cures the sick? By his mind alone?"

"*Saa*, no," said Blue Raven Woman, "there are herbs and plants that he uses, too. A medicine man, and some of the women in our village, also, know the right plants and roots that will heal, and this is also part of a medicine man's training."

Rebecca remembered Night Thunder's saying he had "rattlesnake medicine." Was there really such a thing? It seemed incredible.

Blue Raven Woman continued, "A medicine man also must be able to call upon the generosity of Sun to aid another in recovery. And this he must be able to do with his mind. So it is during this training that the boy will learn to talk to the spirits, if he cannot do that already, and from those spirits, he will discover what the future holds. This is so that our men will not go on raids where they might be killed. The medicine man does this for the good of the tribe."

Rebecca didn't even want to think about her own experiences with Night Thunder—how the spirits of the dead had talked to them both, how they had performed a particular ceremony. Really, there wasn't such a thing. Was there? Still . . .

"There is a tent for each part that the boy must learn," Blue Raven Woman was saying. "These tents represent one great sun, or one year. And there are seven tents in all, the last two tents being the ones where he learns 'bad medicine.' Here, he must learn to throw spells on other people, but he also learns that one must never use the dark side of medicine unless the need is great, for it will always diminish one's power.' '"

Rebecca sat stunned. "And Night Thunder has done all this?"

Blue Raven Woman nodded.

Rebecca could barely comprehend it. She said, "But it's all so silly."

"And yet I have seen many strange things."

"I don't believe it." But even as she said it, Rebecca knew it wasn't true. Not completely. Try as she might to convince herself, she could never deny what she had seen, nor what she had experienced. It would always remain with her, if only as a mystery unsolved.

She shook her head, as though that action would clear her mind, and changed the subject by asking, "I have been wondering about something. It might seem unimportant to you, but I have been wondering. I hope you will not object if I put this on you."

"*Kyai-yo*, are we not sisters? You may ask me anything."

Rebecca took a deep breath. "Do you mind becoming a second wife?"

Blue Raven Woman cast her gaze downward quickly. Had Rebecca seen a fleeting look of hurt, there in her eyes? Had it been only her imagination?

But Blue Raven Woman was proceeding to speak and Rebecca listened heartily as the other woman said, "I do not mind so much being a second wife. More things will be expected of you than of me, and my life will be a little easier because of that."

"Will it?"

"*Aa*, yes."

"*Soka'pii-wa*, that is good."

The two girls became silent, until at last Rebecca felt compelled to say, "It was the spirits of the dead that joined Night Thunder and myself in marriage."

Blue Raven Woman's eyes grew wide and her hand flew up to clasp over her mouth. Said she, "The spirits of the dead visited you?"

Rebecca nodded.

"And they married you?"

Another nod.

"Then your marriage to Night Thunder must be as Sun wills it. You have been honoured. And you, my sister, must have great medicine, too, for it is only a few people who can witness the talk of the

dead and walk away from it." She grinned. "I am
pleased that we are sisters."

Rebecca shifted uncomfortably. She wanted to
tell this woman that she didn't believe in that
"marriage." She wanted to tell her, too, that they
were not really sisters, not in truth. And she
wanted to let the Indian girl know that she would
never allow her "husband"—if she stayed here—
to marry another.

Yet she couldn't bring herself to do it. Not when
Blue Raven Woman had been so kind to her. Not
when Rebecca was starting to like and admire the
other woman. So she asked instead, "You must
love him greatly?" She had to know.

And Blue Raven Woman gasped.

Rebecca glanced quickly at the other woman,
but could detect nothing. Had she only imagined
that startled cry? She wondered at it, but when
Blue Raven Woman recovered herself so quickly
and said so earnestly, "*Aa*, yes, I do love him,"
Rebecca was left with no doubt of the truth of Blue
Raven's words.

Rebecca sighed.

What a mess. The both loved Night Thunder;
they both wanted him as a husband. Rebecca
frowned since, much to her chagrin, she discovered that she could not hate the other woman, not
anymore. Nor did she want to be the cause of pain
to the Indian girl.

Yet if she were to remain here with Night Thunder, as his wife, would she not be the cause of
unmerited and unwanted heartache?

It all seemed so complex.

Inhaling deeply and sending the other woman a

sad, yet quick smile, Rebecca rose to her feet. She had to get away, if only for a little while. Padding swiftly to the tepee's entrance, Rebecca pulled back the flap and, stooping over, took her leave.

Chapter 18

Drums beat out a steady rhythm. Bodies swayed to the pulse and throb of the tom-toms, while singers chanted the verse of a song hundreds of years old. Some of the dancers squatted down low, as though following on the trail of an animal; some jumped up madly, imitating their experiences on the warpath; others, older and wiser, merely kept step to the rhythm of the intoxicating beat.

The warriors had dressed in their Sun Dance best. And anyone, newcomer or old, would have stood impressed. Here were hues of white, red, and black; blue and yellow; white and blue, on this one's regalia, on that one's. Brightly painted beads and shells flashed under the sun, while jingles and bells, tied around feet and arms or dangling from the waist, clattered and jangled in time to the beat. Feet pounded upon the solid earth. Owl and eagle feathers fell from hair, from spears, from clothing, and from bows and arrows. And in the center of it all burned a fire, shooting out a shower of sparks into the audience, filling the lungs of spectators and dancers alike with its smoky, sooty fragrance.

Even Sun appeared to have paused in his endless arc across the sky, in honour of the celebration.

Around and around the circle the dancers sprang and leaped, their antics creating a haze of color for those who stood off to the side, watching the festivities on this hot and lazy autumn day.

Night Thunder relaxed on the sidelines, observing, without really seeing the celebration of the Dog Society dancers. He was distracted, watching Blue Raven Woman and Rebecca . . .

Haiyu, his Rebecca. This was the first dance his wife had attended. He knew. If only because he watched for her.

He would not go to her, however. It was not his place to do so, even though she bore the distinction of being his wife. Here, in camp, when under the eyes of the villagers, men kept with the men; women with the women. But it didn't prevent heated looks from passing from one group to the other.

Night Thunder felt his heart swell as he caught sight of Rebecca looking at him. Did she desire him as he did her?

He nodded to her in acknowledgement, and saw her quickly look away.

Still his heart surged. Under Blue Raven Woman's guidance, no doubt, Rebecca had dressed in the style of his people. Her golden hair had been parted and carefully braided at each side of her face, held there with beaded shell hair bows, while smooth pink shells dangled in a buckskin "chain" around her neck. Her dress, and even her moccasins, had been dyed blue all over and were patterned with porcupine quills and trade beads of white, blue, and red, their design resembling the first budding of the wild rose.

She looked beautiful and . . . content?

Was it possible? Was his Rebecca at last beginning to feel at home in his village? Did he stand a chance of influencing her to stay?

He grimaced.

What good would it do him if he could, and she did? It would change nothing. He would still be obligated to marry Blue Raven Woman, and when he did, Rebecca would leave him, no matter where they lived, no matter how comfortable she became here. He knew it. He must try to accept it.

It was an interesting thing to note. Whereas another might have felt justified in attempting to change his wife to suit him, not so this Indian. He was a man of honour, a man of strong belief, and he would hold dear Rebecca's convictions even if they differed from his own. After all, weren't all men, and all women, for that matter, free to believe as they chose? It was not his place to pass judgment on the opinions of another. It was his duty to protect all within his tribe, no matter their beliefs or practice.

He glanced away, his heart tormented.

He had many problems, not the least of which that he had yet to seek out Blue Raven Woman's father and make arrangements for his second marriage. His second marriage.

Custom dictated that he should have done this as soon as he had come into camp, but he had been avoiding it. What would he say to the man who had thought his daughter would become a sits-beside-him wife? Not that Night Thunder would of necessity have to explain himself; it was only that Night Thunder didn't know *what* to say.

And if he were to be truthful with the elder man, he would have to admit that he was seeking a way to avoid the marriage altogether. How could he say this to Blue Raven Woman's father?

It wasn't as if he didn't have feeling for Blue Raven Woman. Night Thunder would always admire her. But it went no further than that. His feelings toward her were more brotherly than husbandly.

Haiya, it was true. Blue Raven Woman could have easily been his sister.

"She is beautiful," someone whispered from behind him, speaking in a language as old as time itself.

Night Thunder stiffened. He had heard that voice only once before . . . the shadow of the dead.

"Go to her."

Night Thunder clenched his teeth in irritation. What did these spirits want from him? Why did they follow him? Did they not know that he could do little to help them?

With slight impatience, Night Thunder asked, without the use of words, "Why come you here, speaking to me?"

"Why should I not?" answered the voice. A long pause followed and then, again, "She is beautiful."

"*Tahkaa*, who?" Night Thunder didn't say the words aloud, he thought them.

"*Ohkiimaan*, your wife," the voice whispered again.

Night Thunder didn't look behind him, nor did he glance to the right or left to see if anyone else had heard the strange words. He knew no one else could hear, had long ago accepted that few people could commune with the dead. What did these shadows want from him? he wondered again.

He asked, still in thought only, "*Tsak*, which wife is it that you speak of?"

"Know you which one," whispered the voice. "Go to her, she, to whom you are married, for I tell you this with good intent in my heart, she will be your only wife."

"*Haiya*, that is not true, old man," Night Thunder conveyed silently. It was not an easy thing to do, communing with the spirits, for they imparted fear and dread as well as knowledge. However, forgetting for the moment that he seldom enjoyed speaking with the dead, he added, "Do you know of my vow to Blue Raven Woman?"

"*Aa*, yes."

"Then shadow, know that I am the next medicine man for my tribe. Know too that I must always put the good of the tribe before myself, before all earthly desires, even my own."

"Have I asked you not to do so?"

"Perhaps you have," Night Thunder thought, "perhaps not. But know, shadow, that I am committed to Blue Raven Woman my pledge."

"Your pledge?"

"My father's pledge to her father. But that does not matter. I care not who made the compact. It is already done. And it is my duty to fulfill the honour of my father's word."

"Is it?"

"You know something else I should do that is as honourable?"

"I might."

Night Thunder snorted. "Tell me of it, then, so that I too might understand."

With little hesitation, the shadow declared, "Love your wife."

"I do."

"Love her alone, for she will never be comfortable with another in her household."

"You think I do not know that? You think I am so deaf that I cannot hear? But if I do as you ask, if I put my honour aside as a thing to be ignored, if I refuse to acknowledge Blue Raven Woman as my next wife, you know that I would be as the liar who cannot keep his word, and I would never be able to serve my people in the manner in which Sun has directed me. I would have failed my people. I would have failed myself. You know these things, shadow?"

"*Aa*, yes."

"And so knowing, how can you ask me to go to one wife and ignore the other?"

"Only the one wife, now, you have."

"*Aa*, yes, but soon I must take the other. And when I do, I will return Rebecca to her people, for I know that she would be unhappy, then. Do not speak to me any more of this. You know that I must do this. You know, too, that my desires, my own happiness, are nothing to be considered in this matter." Night Thunder was glad that he spoke in thought only, for his throat felt choked with an emotion too closely resembling grief, and he did not want to acknowledge it. He continued, still strictly in ideas alone, "I must keep the honour of my father, of my tribe."

"*Saa*, no, not yet. You must wait."

"I cannot," he returned, although he paused. Perhaps it was because the shadow's idea so closely mirrored his own desire. Or perhaps it was because he was anxious to grasp onto something, anything, that would delay his having to take Rebecca back to the fort. He became curious, and he asked, "*Mao'k*, why? Why must I wait?"

"Some things you will discover on your own," said the spirit. "Come I here not to change you or the path of your life. Come I here to guide you."

Even in contemplation Night Thunder felt his frustration build up within him, and he thought, though none too gently, "Why do you haunt me?"

"Why think you?"

"What is it you want from me? Can you not see that I am not yet the medicine man of my people? I have not called upon your spirit that you should follow me and talk to me."

"And does a person always choose his conversations with the dead?"

The truth of the question, its delicate knowledge, stilled Night Thunder and he fell silent in reflection.

The apparition continued, "But look you there at the one who would have been your wife."

Night Thunder looked toward Blue Raven Woman.

"See you not where her eyes travel?"

Blue Raven Woman spoke to Rebecca. That was all.

But then, quickly, so fast that Night Thunder almost missed it, Blue Raven Woman shot a glance over toward . . . Night Thunder stared around the circle.

Who?

His scrutiny took in that one, a young man whose eyes were trained on . . . Rebecca. Night Thunder's chin jutted out and his gut twisted before he realized that it wasn't Rebecca the young brave watched . . . it was Blue Raven Woman.

What was going on there?

"They are in love. Good it is to see."

"Blue Raven Woman and Singing Bull?"

"*Aa*, yes," said the spirit, "she will make him a good wife if she were free."

"But she and I—"

"Parents, they make mistakes. Both your hearts belong elsewhere. Find you another way. It is right. Your wife could never permit your heart to be given to another. And you are both needed for your people. Find you another way."

"But the vow of my father, hers . . ."

"Think you that your people want you to be a slave?"

"Slave?"

"Is it not a slave who is committed to a promise which will hurt a great many people? Be you a slave?"

"*Saa*," Night Thunder hissed under his breath.

"Old ways must fall away for the new. And I tell you, from here on, until Wind no longer blows and Sun no longer rises, you are freed from a vow that never from your lips was given."

Night Thunder stood for several heart-stopping moments as motionless as if he were an animal, hounded and hunted by wolves. For so long had Night Thunder been committed to this vow, it took some time for the old man's words to settle in. Night Thunder was greatly baffled. At length, however, the old man's words began to have effect upon him. Still, he could not completely accept what for so long, had been a way of life.

"By what right do you break the vow?"

"By right of your father."

"My father?"

No answer came back to Night Thunder. Also, he could perceive no ethereal presence behind him, and he swung around to try to catch a glimpse of this one who kept haunting him. But the shadow that was the old man had gone. Nothing remained.

He didn't care.

Tender hope gave his heart strength, and enthusiasm soared within him. He swung back to face the dancers once more.

Did he dare to believe he could have Rebecca as his only wife?

Saa, no, he cautioned himself against becoming too zealous. His father had once told him . . . wait. His father had long been in the spiritual world . . .

All of a sudden, a mental image came to Night Thunder, a memory of his father as he had been before he had died, his father attempting to speak, to advise his son of something. Was it possible that his father had unfinished business? Was his father, even now, trying to send a message to his son, trying to communicate in the only way he could, what he had been unable to articulate in the flesh?

Night Thunder frowned. It could be true.

And if so, what was the meaning of it? What did it have to do with Rebecca?

Nothing, he answered his own question. It could have nothing to do with Rebecca.

Rebecca was white, not Blackfoot; she hadn't been here when his father had been alive. What could her presence here now possibly have to do with his tribe? With him?

As though in answer to his question, a feather fell at his feet—a golden eagle feather.

All at once, the entire proceedings of the dance stopped. The drums and singing, the dancers and dancing, everything ceased as one and all became aware of the feather lying on the ground in front of Night Thunder.

It was an omen. Such was bad medicine . . . or good . . . Still, nothing could be done until the proper rites had been recited over the feather, lest bad luck follow all who sang and danced.

A medicine man from among them advanced forward to perform the appropriate ceremony.

But before he bent to the ground, before he began the appeal to the spirits, the wise old man stared at Night Thunder. His eyes narrowed, and he said in a voice only Night Thunder could hear, "The spirits are with you, my boy. Determine, you must, what it is that they need from you, what it is they want. This feather," he said, pointing to it, "is for you. Say I a prayer over it, but it belongs to you."

The fact that the medicine man had just spoken in the old tongue of the elders, the fact that the man had obviously witnessed the presence of the spiritual world here this day, did not surprise

Night Thunder. He acknowledged the wise old man with a nod.

But before a ceremony could be done, before the medicine man knelt to the ground, a swift whirlwind caught up the feather and whisked it high into the air, throwing it to and fro, until it came to drift back down to the earth, landing before . . . Rebecca.

Perhaps it was only Night Thunder who could see the shadow of the old man place the feather on the ground before Rebecca. Perhaps.

The old medicine man, however, glanced at Night Thunder and said, "Why have you not said to me that your wife has much medicine?"

"I did not know it."

"Did you not? And yet she sees the spirit as only you and I can do."

Night Thunder jerked his head swiftly to the left.

"I will have to think long about this," said the old medicine man.

Night Thunder remained silent, although he acknowledged the wise old man with another nod.

The medicine man turned and strode toward the feather, toward Rebecca. Kneeling down in front of it, he said a prayer over it, for those here today, for Rebecca. But although the ritual demanded the safe return of the feather to its Indian owner, this one time the medicine man deviated from ceremony. Holding the feather out to Rebecca, the old man placed it into her hand.

Night Thunder saw Rebecca peer at those around her, at the faces of all those assembled here, and he knew at that moment that Rebecca belonged here with him. There was purpose—a reason—for her to be here.

His heart grew light, and the very essence of who and what he was took wing and soared. His being filled with a sense of eagerness he had not felt in a long time.

It didn't matter that he knew not for what purpose Rebecca had been given to him. It only mattered that she could remain here . . . with his people . . . with him.

With great certainty, too, he realized that he could no longer continue his plans to marry Blue Raven Woman.

His life had become entwined with that of Rebecca's. And if she objected to the other woman as a second wife, Night Thunder would have to find a way to end the old pledge, regardless of how others in his village might judge him.

Chapter 19

Afternoon turned to twilight, twilight to night. By the time Night Thunder entered their lodge that evening, Rebecca had returned to their home, had hung the golden feather from the tepee lining, in plain view.

Silently Night Thunder stood to his full height within the confines of the tepee, and after only a slight pause, came forward to stand before the golden feather. Delicately he ran his fingers over it.

He said to Rebecca, "You know that the medicine man has honoured you greatly by giving you this?"

Though the words of his language contained many harsh guttural sounds, Night Thunder had unconsciously imbued a soft inflection into his speech, his voice full of gentle consideration.

Rebecca appeared to respond to it, too, though she didn't speak. She simply nodded.

He asked, "You saw the shadow of the old man today?"

Another nod from her.

He gave her his full attention then, and brought his gaze up and over her. A tortured kind of anxiety kneaded away at his insides, but he kept his features carefully blank, as befitted the stoicism of his race.

Haiya, how he wanted to tell her of his decision this afternoon, his change of mind. He wanted her to know of his realization, of the conversation between him and the shadow, so that she might feel more comfortable here with him.

But he could not relate the whole of it to her. Not yet.

Tradition and social custom demanded he settle the matter first with Blue Raven Woman and her family. Moral obligation dictated he keep his own counsel until the details of the estrangement with the other woman were determined.

Still, no manner of rigorous training could keep him from desiring to comfort Rebecca, to tell her all that was in his heart. He might not be able to say the words, but he could let his actions speak for him, and he smiled at her with a sincerity that was as beautiful as it was honest.

He said, "Today you looked more fair than anyone of my acquaintance." Unwittingly, he raised his chin a notch. "Today you looked more Indian than white. You looked as though you belong here, but think not that it is this alone that makes you beautiful." He came to squat down beside her and ran his fingers over her cheek. He continued, "It is the essence of your spirit, the goodness of your heart, I think, that causes the blood in my veins to surge. It is not often that while here in camp we may be alone, so let us take and keep this night to ourselves, to remember it always." He swallowed, before he entreated, "Stay here with me."

And though he had been speaking of the evening yet ahead of them, he let the double-edged meaning of his words stand there between them.

She must have felt it, too, for she shut her eyes and bent her head into his hand, where it still remained on her cheek. She rubbed against it tenderly, and he knew strong emotion filled her spirit.

Still, she said, "I . . . you know I welcome you home."

"*Aa*," he said, "home."

"Still," she said, "you know that I cannot stay here forever, and I . . ." She couldn't finish.

Admiration surged through him; admiration for her strength, her spirit, and her weakness. He said, "I understand."

She opened her eyes wide and stared at him. She asked, "You do?"

He nodded.

She jerked her head away, staring out toward the tepee lining, and she said, "Oh, Night Thunder, what are we going to do now? You know how I feel about you, yet you know also that I cannot stay here for long."

"*Aa*," he said, "I understand." How he desired to tell her all that had transpired this day, all the knowledge that burned deeply within him, and it was only the strictness of his Indian training that kept him from saying to her what he knew she needed to hear. Still, though he could not speak the words, he tried to comfort her and said, "I would ask you to trust me. I would do all that I can to keep you from hurt, you know this?"

She nodded.

"Then you must trust me. I promise you I will find a way to keep you here and make you happy."

She looked back at him, her look tortured. "But I could never be contented if you marry Blue Raven Woman."

"I know this."

"Then how can you say—"

"Trust me."

"But I—"

"I promise this to you. I will find a way."

She wanted to argue with him, he could see it there, reflected in her eyes, but she held her peace.

Haiya, had he ever known anyone more beautiful, anyone whose courage inspired greater strength within him, anyone who tried his imagination more than she did? He decided that he had not.

Haiya, he wanted to show her the vastness of his love, too. Slowly he admired the gentle curves of her body, while images of how she looked naked filled his mind.

He reminded himself dutifully that this was a Sun Dance camp and that he had certain obligations and rites to uphold, to perform. Wasn't there a dance of the *Kuk-kuiks',* the Pigeons' Society, this night? He should attend. He knew it.

But suddenly nothing else mattered.

He loved this woman, and his heart demanded that he show her his devotion. Plus, he could not recall any strict rules on *not* making love to one's wife when in the Sun Dance camp.

Haiya, it was true: there was nothing that need stop him from his desire, nothing. He took Rebecca in his arms.

Aa, sweet medicine, her skin felt as soft as the finest buckskin, and her breasts pushed against him, driving him quietly crazy. He lay her beneath him, the downy softness of a buffalo robe cushioning her backside.

He became instantly ready for her, too. But, he realized, such things meant little to him at this moment. He wasn't certain when it had happened, but his own needs had become secondary to hers. She was all that mattered.

He wanted her to know his love; he wanted her to savor it, to believe in him, never to doubt the depths of his feelings for her.

Though he might not be able to tell her with words what she wanted to hear, at least with his body he would communicate all that was his to share within his heart. He would keep telling her in this manner until there could be no uncertainty in her mind.

She responded to him, too, he noted. She touched him, the action of her fingertips sending shivers up and down his body. Her lips nibbled at him, raining kisses over him, onto his neck, his chest, on downward toward his stomach. He sucked in his breath. Sweet medicine, he didn't know if he could endure such pleasant torture.

She moved further down his body. What was she doing?

He wasn't left long to ponder it. Imitating what he had done to her, she reversed their positions until he lay beneath her. Mischievously, she sent him a quick smile before she bent to him, taking the whole of his swollen stiffness into the soft recesses of her mouth.

Instantly the warm moisture of her touch filled every part of his body, and though he stoically tried to keep his reaction to a minimum, he could barely hold back the sound of a moan which escaped him unheeded. He shut his eyes that he might cherish the pleasure of it, of her more thoroughly, but it was useless. Dizzying sensations overwhelmed him.

She ran her tongue over his swollen flesh and the movement sent a tingling clear down to the arches of his feet. A frenzied excitement began to ache within him and a fire flicked to sudden life. *Aa*, how he yearned to return the gesture to her. The thought of how he would love her filled his consciousness until it became almost impossible to hold himself motionless. At last, he could stand it no more and he reversed their positions, placing her so that she lay beneath him once again.

He brought his hands up to roam over her breasts, while he arranged himself between her legs, her femininity at last revealed to him.

He bent to her, his tongue discovering her, as she had so recently done to him. *Aa*, the intoxicating taste of her. How he loved her. Joy burst within him as her gentle whimpers, her soft, high-pitched moans, reached his ears, its effect almost pitching him over the edge of his reserve.

But he held himself back. While her sweetened reaction was so very good, he still desired more. He yearned for her, for who and what she was. He needed to be one with her, to feel the warmth of her, the essence of her being, entwined with him.

She jerked and he could feel her body tripping on the edge of the precipice where he had taken her. He hurried her on toward it, his actions giving her wings to soar, while he, in turn, savored the exotic taste of her.

He could not remember ever being so stimulated by a woman, and he knew in his heart that it was love, pure and simple, that gave such intensity to their pleasure. This was no mere sex act. What he felt, what she felt, came from the heart, from the joining of two people together, to share in each other's lives forever.

He let her linger in the misty ecstasy of her pleasure for a while longer before he came up onto his forearms over her, the warmth of his gaze touching her everywhere.

His eyes met the golden essence of hers and he smiled; she returned it wholeheartedly.

He said, "*Kitsikakomimmo*, I love you."

And she replied, "*Kitsikakomimmotsspoaa-wa, aisskahs*, you are loved, always."

His stomach tightened to hear her say it, and with no more than a quick glance downward, he joined his body with hers.

Aa, he smiled as she opened to him, the softness of her flesh welcoming him as though he were returning home. His pleasure increased, if that were possible, and he began to move within her, though he never again looked away from her. As though mesmerized, they stared into one another's eyes, tender smiles passing from one to the other.

He couldn't remember when he had felt more

jubilant, so free. The warmth of her, the raw sweetness of her nature, reached out to him, encompassing and cradling him, taking what he had to give her and giving him what he needed most.

Did she feel it? Was she, too, experiencing the uniting of their spirits, the culmination of their love? He moved within her and with her, intending to give her as much satisfaction as he took.

On and on toward a finite conclusion they struggled, their eyes locked lovingly with one another.

It was beautiful, wonderful, incredible. Never had he felt such oneness with another person, and as they climbed toward the finale, he knew in an instant that he understood her—pure, simple understanding.

And as his seed spilled within her, he thought again of how he loved her. All of her; exactly who and what she was.

And the oddest thing was that he knew she had experienced exactly as he had. How could she not?

Their paths were irreversibly intertwined. For all time, he knew.

It was an overpowering experience, even for him, a medicine man of his people and, as he took the weight of his body off her, moving to the side and taking her in his arms, he began to make plans. He would bring her happiness, he decided. He promised it to himself.

Haiya, he would show her all of his world; he would ensure her happiness here with him. It was the last thought he had before he drifted off to a pleasant sleep.

* * *

"He said that our daughter must not marry Night Thunder. The medicine man said that we should have consulted him as soon as she had been given the vision. But it is not too late. He said that we must end this vow between Night Thunder and our daughter."

Morning Child Woman gasped, "But the pledge, the oath between you and Night Thunder's father . . ."

Her husband shrugged, and jerking his head sharply to the left, stared off to the side of their lodge before he turned back, drawing another puff on his pipe. "He said that Sun wills our daughter to find a husband elsewhere. You know that as Sun wills, we must try to do."

Morning Child Woman clasped her hand over her mouth. Eyes wide, she said, "*Kyai-yo*, how can it be? Night Thunder will be stricken with grief. He, who now has a wife who does not know our ways. He, who now needs our daughter more than ever to help his new wife." She glanced cautiously at her husband. "You know that he could become angry with us."

"*Aa*, it is almost certain that he will."

"My husband, what are we to do?"

The old man didn't answer right away, but after a few more puffs on his pipe, he continued, "As you know, these things must be handled in the right way. One cannot break a pledge without making a sacrifice. Perhaps it would be best if I were to seek out the medicine man. He will know the right way to ensure that Sun knows my heart is good. I will also ask the medicine man to tell Night Thunder of all that has happened. In this way, Night Thunder would realize there was good reason for us to break the pledge." He paused, his jaw becoming firm with resolve. "*Aa*, yes," he continued, "I will speak to the medicine man, perhaps give him my new bow."

"*Kyai-yo*! You speak wisely, my husband."

The old man gave his wife a discerning glimpse. "But until I speak with the medicine man, we must persuade our daughter to help Night Thunder and his new wife in any way that she can, that he not become too angry with us."

"*Aa*, yes," replied the wife. "Our daughter already helps his new wife, very much. She is fond of the white woman and has given her many presents; she even gave her the honour of becoming her sister."

"Sister?"

Morning Child Woman clasped her hand over her mouth. "Did I not tell you?"

"You know that making the white woman her sister gives Night Thunder even more right to marry our daughter."

"But our daughter did not know then that she would not become a wife to Night Thunder."

The old man grunted. "Perhaps I should give the medicine man a new pony, also, so that he will seek out Night Thunder at once and be done with this thing."

"*Aa*, yes, my husband. That might be prudent."

"Humph. I must hasten to do this with all possible speed."

Morning Child Woman nodded. "But what shall we tell our daughter?"

The old man became silent for several moments

more. He sat, reflected in thought, until in due time, he voiced, "We must say nothing of it to her until the medicine man has settled matters with Night Thunder. You know that she already favors someone else. What if she were to run away with him, whom she loves, as we know many young girls are prone to do—before I can speak with the medicine man and make the proper sacrifices? Night Thunder would have every right to become angry with us. And we would lose our honour here in our own camp if this happened." The old man sighed. "No, maybe I will give the medicine man more than one pony, that he might search out Night Thunder at once."

"*Aa*, yes, my husband, again you speak wisely. Should I also make a robe for the medicine man that he might favor our cause more quickly?"

The old man nodded. "It would be good."

"Then I will set to the matter at once," said Morning Child Woman, and pulled out her parfleche full of quills and beads.

However, she did not need her husband reminding her to keep her tongue quiet on the matter. Didn't their reputation as a family of honour and fair-mindedness depend upon their daughter's level head and Night Thunder's goodwill?

She would speak of this to no one.

The two men sat across from each other in silence, a fire of dying embers between them.

Blue Raven Woman's father, Little Elk, puffed on a pipe and passed it to Night Thunder, the younger man taking a whiff and sending it back, as was the custom.

At last the old man began the talk, speaking slowly as though he chose every word carefully. "Happy is my heart to see you here, son of my friend."

Night Thunder nodded appropriately.

"My home is yours," said Little Elk. "Speak freely here."

"*Soka'pii-wa*, it is good," said Night Thunder. "I have come to you on a matter of importance. I have come to speak to you about my marriage to Blue Raven Woman."

The elder man nodded as though Night Thunder had uttered something profound. "*Sok, sok,* good, good . . ."

"*Aa,* yes, it is good, but . . ."

Little Elk again bobbed his head.

Night Thunder cleared his throat and began, "About my marriage to your daughter. There are, I think, things we must discuss." He gestured around him, to the tepee lining, and said, "I have no lodge in which to keep her—"

The old man nodded. "You need a new lodge?"

Surprised at being interrupted, Night Thunder blinked. He said, "*Saa,* no, that is not what I am trying to say. I—"

"Blue Raven Woman will come and help your wife make new a lodge for you. Beautiful new lodge. You only needed to ask. We will send our daughter. *Aa,* yes."

Night Thunder became slightly baffled. It was not an Indian custom to intrude into another's speech. He said, a little more cautiously, "*Saa,* no, that is not necessary."

"Whatever it is you need, you have only to ask."

Night Thunder sent the old man an odd look. This confrontation was not going as he had planned. Night Thunder had sought out the lodge of Blue Raven Woman's parents, that he might tell Little Elk of his decision: the pact between himself and their daughter must come to an end. But he'd not been able to get the words past his tongue. Perhaps he hadn't stated his cause with enough intention? He began again, "My new wife has many strange ways ... and among them is an unusual idea about the lodge and about marriage and other women." Night Thunder paused to choose his words carefully.

The old gentleman asked, "Has our medicine man talked with you?"

Night Thunder shook his head. "I have not seen him since the afternoon of the Dog Society dance."

"Humph," said Little Elk. "My daughter is at your will to do whatever is necessary to help your wife set up her lodge. You need only to ask and my daughter will instruct her."

"*Aa*, yes, Blue Raven Woman has been a great help to me and to my new wife—"

"Can be greater help if you need it."

Night Thunder's expression became a trifle more bewildered. Why was this becoming so difficult? "About your daughter ... I think she will make a good wife, but—"

"*Sok, sok*, good, good," the older man gestured toward himself. "Me ... your father ... good friends. Made pact many, many years ago. Long ago. Many, many years ago."

"*Aa*, yes."

"Many years ago," Little Elk reiterated. A long

pause followed, and then suddenly, as though the older man had only thought of it, he added, "You need something else from my daughter?"

Clearly baffled now, Night Thunder felt his head grow light, and he said, "*Saa*, no, it is only that I do not believe that your daughter and I—"

"You have only to ask. She will help you in any way that she can. You know this?"

"*Aa*, yes, she is most generous, most kind." This was not going well at all. It was particularly odd, too, because the old gentleman kept interrupting him. An Indian would usually listen with patience—even to an enemy—before intruding upon him, even if it took an entire day for the other man to finish.

Perhaps Night Thunder needed more time to practice his speech?

Maybe. Still, he would try again. He said, "You and my father made the pact between myself and Blue Raven Woman long ago . . ."

"Humph."

"Have you considered what might happen if Blue Raven Woman and I were not to marry?"

A look of pure horror crossed the elder man's countenance, and Night Thunder cringed. "I spoke not of this. My daughter, our family, have been more than willing to keep the pact—"

"*Aa, aa, sok, sok*, good, good, but—"

"Always, we keep you in our hearts. Have not there been other suitors for her? Have not we turned them away? Have we not kept our honour and yours, also?"

Night Thunder, now utterly confounded, said, "I doubt not your honour."

Little Elk nodded. "*Sok, sok,* my daughter will come to your wife and instruct her in all our ways. Have you not seen already that she works well with her?"

"*Aa, aa,* yes, yes, I have, but—"

Little Elk suddenly tapped his pipe against the stone altar which sat next to the fire, a signal that their talk was at an end.

So soon? Night Thunder hadn't yet been able to put his cause before the older gentleman. More puzzled than upset, Night Thunder arose, having no choice for the moment but to leave.

"*Sok, sok,*" said the old gentleman, as Night Thunder stooped over to exit the tepee. "Any help you need from my daughter, you ask. We will ensure she gives you. Anything."

Night Thunder blinked twice, the look upon his face one of pure bafflement, before he said, "*Soka'pii-wa,* it is good." And, bending at the waist, he took his leave of the elder man's lodge.

Night Thunder straightened up once outside, giving the lodge a quick, pondering glance, as though it were the tepee puzzling him, instead of Blue Raven Woman's father.

It should have been an easy thing to have handled. *I no longer wish to fulfill the pact.* He had been on the verge of saying the words several times, yet for some reason, Little Elk had made it impossible for him to utter them.

Was it his speech that had failed him, or was his medicine becoming weak? Didn't a medicine man often, of necessity, have to go away, alone, to renew his medicine? The problem had to be one or the other, didn't it? Perhaps he should consult with the medicine man to discover which it was.

The medicine man.

Aa, yes, that was the path he should take. Was it not an important matter to end a pledge in the right manner? Perhaps he had not yet performed enough sacrifice? In his eagerness to please Rebecca, had he forgotten this?

Mayhap it would be good, then, if he were to scour his pony herd for his best mounts, that he might give them to the medicine man in order to secure his advice.

Aa, yes, good plan.

With renewed purpose, Night Thunder strode out toward the wild horse herds.

Chapter 20

Two of his own ponies and three from Blue Raven Woman's father stood outside the medicine man's lodge, along with a new robe from Morning Child Woman and a new bow and quiver full of arrows from Little Elk.

Night Thunder watched the old medicine man now, as the elder emerged from his lodge, the wise old man not appearing in the least startled by what he saw. He inspected first one pony, then another, looking well over his payment.

Payment for what?

The medicine man grinned and turning slightly, sent Night Thunder a cheeky smile, as though he had known all along that Night Thunder watched him.

What was occurring here?

Night Thunder understood why he had given his best mounts to the medicine man, but why Blue Raven Woman's parents?

They didn't suspect his intentions, did they? Did they know somehow that he planned to end the pledge? And if they did, what then? Were they even now seeking the medicine man's help in concocting a spell?

No, it couldn't be. The medicine man would not turn his powers upon one from their own tribe, especially when Night Thunder was to be the next medicine man. It was well known that using bad medicine eventually dwindled one's own power. It was not something a man did aimlessly or often.

But if not that, then what?

Night Thunder shrugged. It mattered little to him. He supposed he would find out what it was about in due time.

Walking back to his own lodge, he pulled back the tepee flap and bent to enter, moving forward to his own side of the lodge. He sat to await the summons from Old Lone Bull, the medicine man. He knew it would come soon.

His soft robe couch comforted him and he picked up his pipe, filling it with sacred tobacco. Lighting his pipe absentmindedly, he put his attention onto other things.

A few days had passed now and he was becoming more and more anxious to be done with the pledge. He ached to tell Rebecca of his newest intentions, to set her mind at ease over Blue Raven Woman. He needed his own mind free to ponder the mysteries of other things—the ghosts, for instance. Why did they follow him? What did they want? Was it only to tell him he should have only one wife? He didn't think so.

However, he had not been able to think of anything else but Rebecca, the pledge, this puzzlement over why he could not simply end it.

And though his need was great, he could not

speak of these things to Rebecca. Not until he had settled things with the medicine man and with Blue Raven Woman's parents.

Such was the way of tradition since "time before mind." He could not change it.

He heard a movement outside and Rebecca, stooping down, stepped into their lodge. He grimaced. How was he to explain his presence in the lodge at this hour of the day? Hadn't his wife become accustomed to his being out, either on the hunt, or with the other men, preparing for the secret ceremonies of the Sun Dance? Wouldn't she become curious?

He could only hope that Rebecca didn't recognize his ponies, hadn't spotted them in front of the medicine man's tepee. He did not know how he would explain that.

Coming farther into the lodge, she said, "Blue Raven Woman tells me that two of your ponies are tied in front of the medicine man's lodge. Is there a reason for this?"

He froze. "*Aa*, yes, there is."

He could perceive her eagerness to have him continue, to have him enlighten her about what he did, but he deliberately kept his silence, drawing a long puff upon his pipe instead.

"And . . . ?"

He glanced toward her as innocently as possible and repeated, "And . . . ?"

"Why have you given the medicine man your ponies? There isn't anything wrong, is there?"

He stuck out his chin and set his lips together. "There is nothing wrong."

"That is good."

She made her way to the women's part of the lodge and sat down, taking up a buffalo bone to stir the soup which sat stewing over the altar's cooking stones. She asked, "What are you doing here in our lodge at this time of day?"

He cringed, though he kept his features carefully blank. What could he tell her that was the truth, yet did not go against custom?

I await a conference with the medicine man. He has said that he will talk to me on a matter of great importance."

"I see," she acknowledged. "Do you know what that matter is?"

He shrugged, hoping she would cease her questions. But it was not to be.

"Is it about your pledge to Blue Raven Woman that sends you to the medicine man?"

Night Thunder almost choked, so great was his shock. Had she taken to reading his thoughts? He repeated, though somewhat lamely, "Pledge?"

Rebecca gave him the "look" woman has given man since time immemorial, when she perceives that he is, perhaps, stalling—which of course he was.

Night Thunder tried to ignore her.

She reminded him, "Pledge? Yes, Night Thunder. The vow that keeps you and me from being happily married?"

He supposed he should not have tried to evade her questions, even though he still could not tell her what he intended to do. Yet he also did not want Rebecca to anguish any more over a marriage that would never take place. Not after he had shared so much of himself with her. Still, he must say something and so, taking one last puff on his pipe, he confessed, "I would do all I can to make you happy."

"Even give up your honour?"

He gave her a curious glance. He said, "*Aa*, yes, even that."

"Humph," said Rebecca. "Is this wise?"

"Do not worry. The medicine man will tell me the best way to make you happy. I promise you this."

"What if I tell you that I do not believe you should give up your honour?"

Night Thunder couldn't have felt more puzzled if Rebecca had suddenly sprouted horns and pawed at the ground like an angry bull.

Still, he recovered enough to say, "You wish me to *marry* Blue Raven Woman?"

Night Thunder watched as a delicate pink stole across Rebecca's cheeks. She said, "No, I do not wish that. It's only that . . . I know that you have a responsibility to the people, as their next medicine man. What would happen if you did something that caused others to think bad things of you?"

"A man cannot live his life in fear of other people."

"No," she said, "you are right. But still, one must be careful of tradition, mustn't one?"

Night Thunder nodded, more than a little cautious. Where was this talk leading?

She said, "I have been thinking."

Haiya, thought Night Thunder, this sounded serious.

"Blue Raven Woman is a wonderful person and

I can understand why you would want her for a wife."

"*Aa, aa.*"

"But I stand in your way, don't I?"

It took him some little time to say, "I would not put it that way."

But Rebecca went on as if she hadn't heard him, "And Blue Raven Woman was, after all, expecting to be your sits-beside-him wife."

He shrugged.

"Have you wondered if perhaps it might be better, if I . . . if you . . . if we went back to the fort now?"

His stomach dropped and it was all he could do to keep the shock of what she had suggested from showing upon his countenance. Even knowing that their return had always been a possibility, to hear her voice it . . .

"Is it this that you desire?"

She stole a glimpse at him, then quickly looked away. "No," she said, "it is not. But I also would not want to cause anguish to you and your people. Also," she added, "I have come to care for Blue Raven Woman."

He took a deep breath, held it momentarily, then let it out slowly. He said, "I do not wish to lose you."

"Nor I you."

"Then we must wait."

"But I do not want to cause you or anyone else concern or grief."

"If you left me, my heart would become frozen and my life would be as barren and cold as the land under a winter storm."

She hid her eyes from him. She said softly, "But what would happen to you, to Blue Raven Woman, if you took back your pledge? Would not you lose your honour and she her means of protection?"

He didn't answer.

"And yet," she continued, "I cannot stay here if you marry her."

His breath caught in his throat. But he forced himself to say, "There will be a way. I promise this to you. Be patient for a few more suns, or days. Can you do this?"

She appeared noncommittal. She said, "I am uncertain, Night Thunder. I feel I am only causing you and others problems."

"Perhaps we require these 'problems' in order that we be happy."

Silence, until at last she said, "I do not know."

He cut a swift glimpse at her and said, "Stay until the end of the Sun Dance. Share my life with me until then. And if, by that time, I have become unable to find a way to make you happy, I will return you to the fort. This I promise you."

She stared off away from him.

He jut out his chin, waiting.

At last, she said, "All right. I will wait, Night Thunder. But I think it will end in the same way."

He bent his head and closed his eyes for a moment. At least she had agreed to stay long enough for him to disentangle himself from this thing. But with all possible speed, he knew he must hasten to the medicine man, that he present his problem.

Night Thunder put out the fire in his pipe and came to his feet. He must act.

It was not his place to seek out the medicine man. The wise old one knew he needed an audience. But Night Thunder could no longer wait.

He didn't dare look at Rebecca as he took a step toward their lodge's entrance. He did not wish her to see the emotion he could not easily hide.

He looked at her from over his shoulder, however, before he left the lodge. He said, "You know that I love you."

She nodded. "Aye. And I love you."

He set his features to show nothing. Then he said, "There will be a way. I promise this to you. You must be patient."

Again she nodded and said, "I will try."

He drew a breath of relief. It was something.

He stepped outside and stole a look toward Sun, which shone directly above him. Shaking his head, he was about to turn away when out of the corner of his eye he caught a movement. He turned his head, then, only to run directly into the tortured— the jealous—stare of another man within the camp . . . Singing Bull.

With some apprehension, Night Thunder scrutinized the young brave, wishing he could give his blessings to the young man to go ahead and court Blue Raven Woman.

From what he knew of the young Singing Bull, the man was honest, honourable, and brave. Singing Bull would make Blue Raven Woman a good husband. If only Night Thunder could convince the young man and Blue Raven Woman's parents of this, his task in putting the pledge behind him might be considerably quicker.

Hmmm . . .

Singing Bull, courting Blue Raven Woman, with his, Night Thunder's approval? If Blue Raven Woman's parents were to realize that Night Thunder approved the match? Whimsical thought, or sudden inspiration?

It might or might not work, but it would give Night Thunder something he could do until he was at last able to counsel with the medicine man.

Putting determination into his step, he approached the jealous young man.

"You need to give more than horses, if you want to win her hand."

Singing Bull made a face. "She said that it makes no difference. She must do as her father says."

"It will still make a favorable impression, and this is important. This I promise you. But you are right, we must think of some reason why her parents cannot refuse your suit." Night Thunder frowned. "There must be a way."

Night Thunder stood with Singing Bull just outside the Sun Dance encampment. The two of them had been hunting together that morning, having captured a fine-looking elk. Singing Bull had given it to Blue Raven Woman's parents, as he and Night Thunder had agreed.

"She is promised to you," said the young suitor, "and says that nothing can change it."

"Something can be done about it, I am certain. We only need to find an act that you do that will be so wonderful, her parents will have no choice but to accept you. You have her approval?"

Singing Bull gave Night Thunder a veiled gaze, looking as though he were uncertain he wanted to answer. He responded cautiously, "One can never be certain with a woman."

"That is true, my friend, that is true. But, come now, I have seen her looking at you. A young woman does not cast her eyes in a man's direction unless she is interested. You know this."

The other man shrugged.

"Have you met her at the stream when she goes to collect water?"

Again Singing Bull looked wary. Noncommittally, he answered, "Many of the young men go to the water to meet their beloved. I would not ruin her reputation." Singing Bull frowned, his expression becoming grim, and he commented, "I know what you told me about yourself and Blue Raven Woman. I know that you think she favors me. But what I do not know is why you do not simply tell her parents that you wish to end the marriage plans. It would make my own suit easier."

"A pledge that has been in place for so long must be dealt with in the right way, lest bad luck befall all of us," said Night Thunder. "A man does not wish to anger the shadows of those departed, nor does he wish Sun to shine upon him with disfavor, as you know would happen if one does not handle this with the proper ceremony. It will happen. I only await the medicine man's decision on how to do it without risk to Blue Raven Woman, her parents, or my own relatives."

Singing Bull nodded.

Night Thunder looked sullen. "There must be something here, something that I have not yet considered. What did you say happened when you brought the elk to her?"

"Her parents gazed at me as though I were an enemy creeping upon them in the night."

"Humph. Mayhap I had better give the medicine man another pony that he might see me more quickly."

"Perhaps."

"There must be something I am overlooking."

"If you are, my friend," said Singing Bull, "then I too am unaware of it."

The two men continued to talk, continued to plot, as Night Thunder placed his robe around Singing Bull—as friends will often do when in the Sun Dance camp. Together the men stumbled out onto the open prairie, where their conversation would be continued.

What was Night Thunder doing with Singing Bull? Was it true? Was he trying to make the other man court Blue Raven Woman, because of her? Was this what she had forced Night Thunder to do?

Rebecca lingered near the bushes where she had hidden herself, listening. Perhaps it would be better for all involved if she left quickly. Her heart missed a beat at the thought. Leave Night Thunder? Truly?

Aye, she thought. It was for the best.

But how could she do it?

Rebecca could not find her way to the fort on her own. She did not know the way, nor did she have the ability to survive on the plains for the length of time necessary to get there. Hadn't she also agreed to stay here until the end of the Sun Dance?

But she did not want to be the ruin of those around her.

Besides, there was another reason that made her need to get away all the greater—a reason she had better hide from Night Thunder.

It was all much too complicated, and it made her mind spin to think about it.

Taking her shawl and placing it over the top of her head, she turned away from the sight of the two men, retracing her steps to her lodge.

Chapter 21

$\sim\!\!\infty\!\!\sim$

Evening had descended upon the village as Night Thunder entered the medicine man's lodge. Immediately he was assailed by the scents of sage, sweet grass, and the incense of *katoya*, sweet pine.

Old Lone Bull sat toward the back of the tepee, his hands taking hold of his pipe, that he might ready it for the ceremony.

"*Haiya*, my son," said the wizened old man. "It has been too long since we last talked."

"*Aa*, my father, it is so."

"Come, take a seat, and let me pass the pipe to you so that you will know that when we talk, we will speak only the truth to each other."

Night Thunder nodded and took his seat on the old man's left.

Though not truly father and son, many of the younger men called the old ones by the term "Father," as was custom. Besides, this particular medicine man had been Night Thunder's teacher in the medicine ways for many years, and the two were probably closer than the more formal relationship of father and son.

Nothing was said or done until the medicine man had prayed—first to Sun, then to wind maker, *Ai-sopwom-stan*, to the thunder, *Sis-tse-kom*, and to the lightning, *Puh-pom'*. The pipe was lit, smoked, passed to Night Thunder, passed back.

In due time, Old Lone Bull began to speak, saying, with some amusement, "I am the possessor of many fine gifts these days."

"*Aa*, yes, I have seen that is true."

Chuckling slightly, the old man said, "You know that the parents of Blue Raven Woman have given me many ponies?"

"I have seen that."

"Do you know why?"

Night Thunder shrugged. "I do not."

Old Lone Bull heaved a deep sigh. He said, "I have many quarrels to resolve between some of our people. A holy man's work in a Sun Dance camp is great."

"*Hie, hie*, it is true."

"And yet all people must be seen, all things must be attended to."

"*Hie, hie*."

"You are to be the next medicine man of our people."

"*Aa*, yes, that is as it has been planned."

The old man gave him a wizened look from beneath his lashes before next he said, "Then it is only right, is it not, that I ask you what you would do about a particular problem between some of our people? Many are the mysterious tests that I have given you over several of our great suns, but

I think it only right that I put to you another test and see how it is that you would handle a civil matter that is arising amongst our people."

Night Thunder nodded, though he remained slightly surprised.

The elder continued, "In a camp of our allies, there is a family of some importance who made a pledge with another family, many, many great suns ago. So long ago has it been that many of the people who made the compact are no longer living. It is possible that both families may wish to resolve this vow. It is also possible that both do not know how to do it while still keeping their honour."

Night Thunder bobbed his head.

"Each may hesitate to tell the other of his desire to end the pledge, afraid of offending or angering the other."

Again Night Thunder nodded.

"What would you do to help these people? Do you think that they should keep the pledge, though many lives have changed since when it was made? Do you think they should dissolve the promise with little or no sacrifice? Would a mere few gifts bring about a great solution? What say you, my son? What would you do?"

Night Thunder stared into the old man's discerning eyes. He grinned slightly. "Do you speak of my own problem?"

The old man raised his eyebrows. His eyes twinkled, but without answering Night Thunder's question, he prodded, "Have you a similar difficulty?"

"*Aa*, my father, I do."

"Well, come now, my son, forget your own troubles for a moment and tell me how you would handle this matter."

Night Thunder sat reflected in thought for a moment. "I think that both families should make some sacrifice to ensure that Sun will shine down gladly upon them and their decision. Then they should seek out one another and settle the matter however they feel is right. Perhaps gifts will be enough, maybe not."

"*Aa*, my son, you speak wisely. But there is one other problem."

"What is that?"

"One of the obstacles involves a woman—a good woman. Even if a sacrifice is made, the woman would lose a provider. What is to be done about the woman?"

"Cannot the one family take her as a second or third wife?"

"*Saa*, no, not in this case."

"Then the one family should find a provider for her as one of their gifts. It is only right that it should be this way."

"*Aa*, again, my son, you speak with the wisdom of a man of your people. I will hasten to find these people and inform them of what they should do. Now, tell me, what is it that brings you to my lodge, bearing me gifts?"

Night Thunder grinned and stared away. He said, "It is nothing. I have my answer, now, before I even ask you the question."

"And so it is with the medicine ways," said Old Lone Bull, and tipping the ashes of the pipe upon the altar stone, signaled the end of their talk.

Night Thunder left and hastened to his own lodge. He would begin preparations for the sacrifice even this night.

Night Thunder awakened to the sound of what must have been thousands of buffalo hoofs running over the dry, hard land, resembling thunder, echoing in the distance. The earth shook under the weight of their sheer numbers. Possessions tied to the tepee lining fell to the floor and lodge poles trembled.

Night Thunder sat up, observing that Rebecca, amazingly enough, continued to sleep. But he could only spare her a cursory glance. Grabbing hold of his breechcloth and tying it on, he stepped quickly outside his lodge, finding the camp already in chaos.

All other things forgotten, the people dashed to and fro. The presence of buffalo, this close to the Sun Dance village, bespoke a good omen: no one, not even the old people, would remember a time when buffalo had come so near a Sun Dance. Perhaps Sun had already decided to honour them.

Excitement filled the camp. It took hold of Night Thunder, while contrarily, he despaired. Hadn't he only begun preparation for a sacrifice? Would he again have to put off what needed to be done in order to secure his and Rebecca's future?

Yet he knew that the secret societies, the dances, each and every ritual, would be abandoned for the stretch of a few days, as all the bands of the tribes would go upon the hunt. No warrior would be allowed to remain idle, not when the winter stores of food lay just beyond their camp.

Buffalo birds, a particular kind of fowl that lives off the backs of buffalo, had appeared now on the southern perimeter of the camp, pronouncing the presence of the buffalo more efficiently than any camp crier could have.

Scouts had already been sent out and had arrived back saying that they had seen the buffalo— tens of thousands of them. The buffalo, however, had scented the people and were hurriedly taking flight to the south.

All the chiefs, united in one massive decision, ordered the camps to make ready for the hunt.

Night Thunder returned to his own lodge, entering and staring at his pipe, the knives, his medicine bags and flints which he had set out in order to begin his sacrifice this day. It would all have to wait.

"*Kayiiwa*," Rebecca greeted him. "What is it?"

"Buffalo," he replied, "close enough to the camp that we are going to have a run."

"A run?"

"The people will go to bring back much buffalo meat for the camp. Prepare yourself to come with me."

"Prepare?"

"*Aa*, you will be needed to skin the animals and obtain the meat so that it can be brought back to camp. Go to Blue Raven Woman and ask her to help you."

"But I had planned to tan a hide this day."

He darted her a quick yet sympathetic glance. "I too had many plans for this day, but they will have to wait. The buffalo are here now and the chiefs have ordered a great hunt. The hide you intended to tan will be here when we return and you can do it then. With all there is to do, Blue Raven Woman will need your help to butcher the buffalo cows that we kill.''

He had knelt down to where he had placed his knives, his pipe, and his medicine bags, carefully returning them to a safe place. He had taken out his paints. Beginning the process of mixing the paints, Night Thunder did not notice Rebecca's look of horror.

He chanced a quick glimpse up at her now, and what he saw surprised him. ''What causes you to look . . . so fearful?''

''You . . . ,'' she stuttered, ''you expect me to take the meat off the buffalo?''

He didn't even look up from what he was doing. He asked, ''*Aa*, yes, we would not waste the meat—''

''I could never do that.''

''*Tsa*, what?'' He glanced up at her again.

''I could never take the meat from an animal.''

''Have you never butchered a buffalo?''

''No, I have not.''

Unconsciously he raised his chin, though he cautioned himself to let not a flicker of emotion cross his face. How, he wondered, did a society manage to raise a woman without the knowledge of how to obtain the meat or the skin from an animal? Strange. How did the white man's family survive the harsh winters without these skills?

There was no time to ponder the mystery of it, however. He suggested, ''Go to Blue Raven Woman and ask her to help you with it. This will be your first hunt and you will not be expected to do much. And she will teach you all you need to know."

Rebecca agreed.

She paused for a moment, and he felt her watching him. He waited, willing her silently to speak. He was rewarded for his patience, for she began to talk to him. "There was something I wanted to tell you," she said.

He had dipped a finger into his paint bowl. Glancing up at her, he sketched a round circle of blue upon his cheek. He said, "Tell it to me now while I paint my body for the hunt. I will listen."

She paused, staring at him oddly before she voiced at last, "Later." She brought a hand up to her stomach to massage it, before she stated again, "Later, after the hunt, I will tell you. For now, it is enough to know that we will have a large store of food for the winter."

He grinned at her then and went back to his work, his fingers working quickly at mixing the paint. His spirits began to lift.

Blue Raven Woman helped her mother sharpen the buffalo knives, while Rebecca tied small children onto the ponies' withers, as instructed, pushing the babies' feet under the saddle girths and securing them so that the children might not fall even if a horse should break into a trot.

The whole camp stirred in excitement and all the people—men, women, children, and even babies—prepared for the hunt.

Word had been passed from camp to camp that one of the scouts had discovered a white buffalo among the herd—a strong sign of luck, Rebecca had learned. Bets had begun to fly immediately from lodge to lodge, even the old people arguing over which tribe would be the one to secure the white hide.

Rebecca could little understand such a custom and she asked Blue Raven Woman about it. Blue Raven Woman had given her a strange look before asking, "Do you truly not know?"

Rebecca shook her head.

"The white buffalo is a sacred thing to the people, given to us by Sun. When it is killed, the skin is tanned in the best way possible and is given to Sun to be hung on a post at the Sun Dance. Once it is given to Sun, no one—not even an enemy tribe—will touch the skin again. It belongs to Sun."

Rebecca listened in silence, making no comment, even though she knew she could never share these beliefs. She did, however, have another question. "But why are all the warriors vying with one another as to who will be the one to kill it?"

"It is because the warrior who kills it receives special favor from Sun; his tribe, too. All his friends and his family will have luck," said Blue Raven Woman. "So you can see that each warrior will want to be the one to take it, that he might be the one to give it to Sun as an offering for himself, for his people."

"And no one will ever touch the skin after it is given in this . . . ceremony?"

Blue Raven Woman shook her head.

"Never?"

"Medicine men are allowed to cut strips off the skin so that they may wrap their medicine pipes

in it or make a band for their heads during ceremonies, that Sun might shine more favorably upon
them. But that is all."

"I see," acknowledged Rebecca. "Will we hunt
no other animal besides the white buffalo, then?"

"We go to hunt many buffalo. All the people go.
There will be many buffalo killed and many full
stomachs this winter because of this. It is a good
thing that is happening for the people. I cannot
remember a time when buffalo have come so close
to the Sun Dance camp, and never one with a
white buffalo. This is a special Sun Dance camp, I
think."

"*Aa*, yes," said Rebecca, "you could be right."

"*Aa*, I think that I am. But come, we must catch
up with the others. Do you see that already people
are leaving to follow the herd? We will take this
smaller lodge of my mother's instead of your
larger one, that we might carry more meat back to
camp. *Poohsap-oo-t*, come, and let us take the lodge
poles down."

Rebecca nodded and, standing off to the side,
grabbed hold of the pole Blue Raven Woman
worked over, and within a matter of minutes, the
lodge had been dismantled and placed travois-
style upon a pony.

Chapter 22

Night Thunder had painted his face and chest blue and white. He dotted white onto his cheeks, forehead, and chin and circled them with blue, the design given to him in a vision. He stood at the side of his pony, painting his mount, the final act in preparation for the hunt. He would pay tribute to his best buffalo pony by depicting it in much the same manner that he had himself.

He had already sketched blue and white circles around the horse's eyes. Now he was attending to the horse's flanks, creating the same blue and white pattern that he wore upon his own body.

Their tribe had been on the buffalo's trail for a little over a sun, or a day, and finally, the herd in sight, they were ready to begin.

Rebecca stood behind Night Thunder as he crouched down, drawing a series of blue circles and streaks down his pony's leg. Though he was more than aware of her presence near him, he said little to her, his attention centered upon the symbols he painted.

In due course, however, she spoke to him, saying, "Blue Raven Woman told me that hunting the buffalo is dangerous."

Night Thunder didn't answer at once. He continued his work, rising up onto his feet to draw a another circle around one of his pony's eyes. After a moment, he said, "Often a warrior's life is in danger, even in camp. Never do we know when and from where the enemy could strike at us, and we must always be prepared. Would you rather not have food for the winter?"

"It isn't that," she said. "It's only that . . . well, could we not find a better, safer way to get the food supplies that are needed?"

He thought for a moment. "In the past," he said, "we have had a *piskun*, where the people run the buffalo over a cliff or into a pen where the animals are slaughtered. But we do not like to do this too often, too many are killed this way—more than the people can use. And even in luring the animals into a *piskun*, there is danger. Better it is that we hunt and kill the buffalo this way, that our friends the buffalo may continue to flourish upon our land."

"But there are so many of them; surely you needn't worry about how many buffalo you kill, do you?"

Night Thunder shrugged. "Our wise men say change is coming. And our wise men tell us that we must take from the buffalo only what we need."

From out of the corner of his eye, he observed Rebecca stare away from him. The ripple of a warm chinook breeze blew in, and he watched her as the wind suddenly swept into her face, pushing back her hair. It reminded him of how she had looked a few nights previous, as she had lain beneath him, and his breath caught in his throat.

She seemed to want to continue to argue with him, though, and she said, "Promise me that you will be alert today, that you will not take any unnecessary chances."

"Chances," he mimicked, "what are these 'chances'?"

She narrowed her eyes at him, placed her hands on her hips and said, "You know very well what chances are."

He grinned as he gave her a quick look. Had she been more observant, she might have noted a twinkle reflected in his eye before he began to talk. But he could tell that she was preoccupied, so he said, "I will try not to ride too many bulls, that you should worry about me."

"Ride bulls? What bulls?"

Night Thunder gave her a wide-eyed stare. "Buffalo bulls."

"Surely you jest."

"What is this 'jest'?" he inquired. "I do not know what this is, but *aa*, yes, have you never heard that the Indian must ride to its death every buffalo that he shoots—before the cow can be butchered?"

Rebecca turned her attention on him and gave him a weary gaze. "I have never heard of such a ridiculous thing."

Night Thunder grunted. "An Indian cannot eat the meat of such a bull or cow that has not been ridden. Bad medicine," he said, keeping his countenance serious. "Very bad medicine, indeed. Indians ride the cows all time. Must ride buffalo before we butcher them, or buffalo get mad at us and never return. People go hungry then."

She gave him another suspicious look, but he hid his face from her so she would not be able to see directly into his eyes.

Someone called to him—Singing Bull—and Night Thunder handed his pony's reins to Rebecca. He said, "I go now. Keep close to Blue Raven Woman, and stay away from the buffalo until they are killed and ready to be butchered."

He turned to leave, but she caught his arm, staying him. "Night Thunder," she asked, "do you tease me? About the buffalo?"

At last he smiled; he couldn't help himself. But all he said was, "Ask Blue Raven Woman to tell you if I make joke or not. But see this lasso?"

She nodded.

"I catch many buffalo to ride with this."

She rolled her eyes at him, and he laughed. "Watch carefully to see if we Indians ride these buffalo."

"I do not want you riding them."

"No?" He grinned at her. "Here, take this horse. He is my best buffalo pony. He knows what to do. You tell him to keep me safe and keep me from riding the wild buffalo. He will do it."

Rebecca opened her mouth to say something else, but Night Thunder added, a note of humor in his voice, "Tell him in good Blackfoot. He understands not the words of the white man."

"Humph," Rebecca responded. But as she studied the horse, noting a look of unusual intelligence in its eyes, she said to it, "*Matsiw-ohkit-opii-wa*, he is the rider of a *fine* horse." She petted the pony's nose, then in Blackfoot, said, "I'm making it your responsibility, now, to bring my husband back to me safe and unharmed." She added, under her breath, "And keep him away from riding those buffalo."

The pony whinnied softly as though he had understood each and every word, and Rebecca smiled.

Night Thunder sat several feet above the prairie, squatting down upon the lower edge of a butte. The warm air pushed his hair into his face, but he had tied its long strands back into three braids, two at the side of his face and one straight down his back. No jewelry adorned his appearance this day, nor heavy clothing—Night Thunder settling for breechcloth and moccasins alone, nothing extra to get in his way. The warming rays of Sun shone down upon him, the feel of them giving him courage. He waited for the signal to begin the hunt and as he sat, lit his pipe that he might wile away the warm day, his eyes ever scanning the horizon.

As he looked out upon the land, his heart expanded in his chest and he breathed in deeply. Everywhere as far as the eye could see were buffalo—so many, one couldn't count them. The ever-present wind rushed by him, seeming to whisper something in its wake. But he could not understand the words, and he gave up trying.

A peacefulness settled over him. This was the home that he loved: the land, the wind, the thunder, the lightning. A part of him reached out to the ends of the horizon, and he felt himself expand, his thoughts gaining space so that they did not bother him so much. Thus he sat for quite a while.

He brought his gaze back, after a time, closer to the butte, and peered into the buffalo herds. Try as he might, he could not discern a white buffalo. There were simply too many of them and a white one would have faded into the herds and landscape.

He waited for the signal to be given so that he could begin the run on the herd. Not until that signal came could he or anyone else begin the hunt, lest they disturb the herd before all was ready. No one would be allowed to scare the animals before the proper time, sending them away. Such an action might leave their tribes with nothing—no meat and no winter stores.

To the southeast of him, he discerned a commotion and noted that several warriors had already begun the hunt.

"It must be the white buffalo," he said to himself. No one would have begun the chase before the signal was given; not unless there were some unusual circumstance to cause it, and a white buffalo was circumstance enough.

The riders, the buffalo, were no more than dark specks to his eyes, yet, *aa*, yes, there it was, out in front of the hunters. The white buffalo.

Emptying his pipe and wrapping it up quickly, Night Thunder put it away and jumped onto his pony, setting it into motion and riding out in a quickened trot to intercept the herd. He would catch that white one.

It took him little time to maneuver himself onto a slight elevation in the land, which seemed to be near where the frightened buffalo would have to pass. The wind blew in his face, carrying his scent away from the approach of the buffalo, and he knew the herd would most likely not get wind of him.

He took himself behind the slight elevation, dismounted, and crawling up to the top of the hill, peered over the hill. Patiently he waited ... and waited.

The ground shook with the thunder of a thousand hooves coming his way. Still he waited.

Finally the buffalo were almost upon him and he ran to his horse, mounted it again, and sent it into a mad dash toward the herd of buffalo, his pony as excited as he, needing little if any whipping or direction.

Thump, thump went the hooves of his pony, and with his intrusion into their midst, buffalo scattered everywhere. Still, guiding his mount with nothing more than his knees, he rode toward the white buffalo, that animal so quick, he could barely catch it. Onward, with more speed, his trained pony caught up to it, the horse bringing him close to the animal. With a quick bolt in toward the buffalo's left shoulder, his mount gave Night Thunder a good shot at the animal.

Fluk went his arrow, the tip of the steel-like blade sinking deep into the heart of the buffalo. Blood gorged from the animal's nostrils, but the buffalo, as a species, were gallant, and though fatally wounded, would not give up so easily. The white buffalo rolled; it wobbled, mooed, and struggled valiantly before it stopped, finally falling over onto its side.

Night Thunder jumped from his pony and glanced around him, just in time to see Singing Bull running toward him.

Singing Bull? Had that been Singing Bull who had come upon him from over his shoulder? Was this even Singing Bull's arrow lying here on the ground next to his?

Night Thunder had little time to think. Still, he knew what needed to be done.

Picking up Singing Bull's arrow, Night Thunder pulled his own from the buffalo's ribs, positioning the other man's arrow in its place.

The young Indian brave rushed up to him. After only a moment's hesitation, Night Thunder said, "Your luck is good this day, my friend. It was your arrow that brought down the buffalo."

Singing Bull looked doubtful. But Night Thunder gestured toward the animal as though to say, "Look for yourself."

Sure enough, Singing Bull glanced at the animal and could not deny the evidence. There was his arrow in the ribs of the white cow.

"It was my shot that brought down the cow? But I thought I had seen yours make the mark."

Night Thunder simply gestured toward the buffalo.

Suddenly the import of what had happened, the honour bestowed upon him for what he had done, took effect upon the young warrior, and Singing Bull began to tremble. He pulled out his knife to attempt to skin the hide, but the young man shook so badly, he could not accomplish the task. Night Thunder took the knife from him and began the slaughter.

"Be careful. Know that you do the work for the sacredness of Sun," Singing Bull said.

Night Thunder made a slit and handed Singing Bull the tongue of the cow, not that anyone would eat the prize; to do so would be a sacrilege. The meat of the tongue, however, would be dried and given in ceremony, along with the white robe, to Sun.

Others began to gather around them, to pay tribute to their catch. But just before they came upon them, Night Thunder said to Singing Bull, "Go to the parents of your beloved. I think they will look with great favor upon your suit, now."

Singing Bull drew in his breath, a startled look coming onto his countenance. "You are right, my friend. This is the chance we sought. No longer can her parents deny me the right to ask for her. And no one will think bad things of me, of her, of you."

"*Aa*," said Night Thunder. "Take Blue Raven Woman to you, then, and be true to her. She is a good woman."

"I will always treat her well. I promise. She will remain in my heart all my life."

Night Thunder touched the other man on the shoulder and nodded. "I know, my friend. I know."

Perhaps because he sensed the regard of another upon him, Night Thunder turned his head, his attention diverted.

Aa. Rebecca watched him, over the wide stretch of the plains. The wind blew back her hair and she stared at him for a long time. Beside her lay a buffalo cow. Blue Raven Woman worked over it, taking off its hide and its meat.

And though he knew she was too far away, he wondered if Rebecca had seen what he had done.

He had freed Blue Raven Woman so that she and Singing Bull could marry, and in doing so had freed himself. It only remained now for him to tell Rebecca. His heart gladdened and he felt as though he might burst.

He only prayed that this gesture would be enough to make her want to stay with him, that she would be happy with him in their life here.

He would tell her at once.

But first, his eyes scanned the horizon, he had to take down a few more buffalo so that his and Rebecca's lodge would be filled with meat this winter. He could not afford to waste this opportunity.

So decided, Night Thunder jumped back onto his buffalo pony, and, casting one last glance at Rebecca, rode out, back into the buffalo herd.

Rebecca gazed at Night Thunder. How she loved him. Her stomach twisted with her need to be with him, to love him. Oh, how she wanted to be able to stay here with him. How she wanted, needed, to spend the rest of her life here, with him.

But, her tortured soul reminded her, she couldn't. He belonged to Blue Raven Woman, the sweet girl Rebecca had tried to hate, but could not. Besides, didn't Rebecca have her own dreams, her own path to follow?

Confused, Rebecca turned away. She would help Blue Raven Woman.

"Excuse me, ma'am."

Rebecca spun around to stare behind her. What was this? Someone had spoken to her in English? Was she hearing things?

But there stood a man behind her: a white man, holding a dust-covered hat in his hand.

He repeated, "Excuse me, ma'am. Is yer name Rebecca?"

Rebecca nodded. It was all she seemed capable of doing at the moment.

"Yer employer, Katrina Wellington, has sent me here ta find ya and bring ya home."

Rebecca still couldn't find her voice.

"Ma'am?"

At last Rebecca recovered enough to ask, "Your name, sir?"

"Robert, ma'am. Robert Clark. Yer employer has hired me an' a couple of me friends ta find ya. If ya want ta get yer things together, we can take ya back ta the fort."

Rebecca peered around her, toward the spot where Night Thunder had been, but he had already disappeared back into the herd of buffalo.

Leave her husband?

This wasn't what she wanted. She glanced at Blue Raven Woman again. Or was it? Wasn't this the opportunity she had been seeking? Hadn't she only this morning realized that she needed to cease bringing hurt to Blue Raven Woman and Night Thunder? And here was her solution. These men could take her home.

Home? Was the fort her home? It didn't feel like it. Yet what could she do? Hadn't she known for some time now that her stay here with Night

Thunder would end soon? Hadn't she been thinking about finding a way to leave? It was only that
she had expected to have a few more days—perhaps a month—with Night Thunder.

She drew a deep breath and asked, "How is Katrina?"

"She was well, ma'am, last time I seen her. She's
done married that Indian brave that took her ta
her uncle, though."

Rebecca smiled. "Has she?"

He nodded.

"How did you find me?"

"I knows that the Sun Dance camp is held here
every year and I figured that if that brave found
ya and saved ya, he'd bring you here. I's right,
wasn't I?"

Rebecca gave him a weak smile. "You were
right."

"You's ready to go?"

Did she want to go? No . . . yes . . . She brought
her hands up to cover her mouth, as she had seen
so many Blackfoot women do, when under the
weight of great emotion.

The wind blew in her face once again, bringing
with it the gentle scent of sage grass and prairie,
the scent she would always associate with Night
Thunder. She didn't want to go, not really. In her
heart, she wanted to stay here with her love.

But surely not with Blue Raven Woman as his
woman, too.

Her head began to ache with her thoughts.
Didn't he intend to do something about his engagement? Something that might bring him disfavor with his people?

She had to go, didn't she? Besides, there was another reason why leaving had become so necessary. Rebecca clutched at her stomach.

Wasn't there another life to take into account now, too? Hadn't it only been a few mornings previous that she had become aware that her menses were two months overdue? Hadn't she been going to tell Night Thunder of it, but failed?

That issue settled it for her, making up her mind, and she said to the white man, "You will have to give me a few days to prepare. Can you do this?"

The man looked suddenly nervous. He commented, "Will yer Indian man allow ya to leave?"

Swaying sightly, Rebecca nodded. "There will be no problem there. He has been intending to take me back as soon as the Sun Dance camp breaks."

"Ya sure, ma'am?"

Rebecca nodded again. She said, "You go on back to camp. I have things to finish here, and then I will tell my husband—"

"Yer husband? Ma'am, he mighten not like the idea of me takin' ya—"

"He will not object. Please, I need some time now to finish what I've begun here. You go on back to camp and wait for me there."

The man nodded. "Yes, ma'am. I's will, but . . ."

"It will be fine, Mr. Clark, I promise you."

The man turned then and stepping up to his horse, mounted quickly. Along with his pack horse and one other animal, he trotted in the direction of the camp.

What was she to do?

She had to leave, didn't she? This wasn't really her rightful home, was it?

Besides, hadn't Night Thunder once told her that any child of their union would be considered his to keep? His to take from her? Better that he never know, wasn't it?

Tears dammed up behind her eyes and it was all she could do to keep them from spilling over onto her cheeks.

Truth was, she didn't want to leave, no matter all the reasons why she should. But did her feelings matter in this? Didn't she have to consider her child, her beliefs, her convictions?

Taking a deep breath and squaring her shoulders, she walked slowly toward Blue Raven Woman. But she stopped suddenly. What would she say to her?

Nothing. She had nothing to say. Rebecca turned then and trudged ahead of her aimlessly, looking at the cows lying stretched out across the plains, catching sight now and again of the arrows entrenched in the cows, trying to find Night Thunder's own special arrow, so that she could begin the skinning process on her own. Wasn't that what Blue Raven Woman had told her to do?

She came upon a big buffalo—a cow, most likely. She stared at the arrow, carefully noting its design and colors. Slowly she pulled it out.

It was Night Thunder's.

But where was he? Wasn't he supposed to ride the buffalo before the skinning process began? Or had he only been teasing her? Most likely he had been merely jesting with her, but still . . .

What if it were true, and if she began to skin

this cow, she would bring bad medicine to the people of his tribe?

She should have asked Blue Raven Woman about it, as Night Thunder had instructed her to do. Where was the young Indian maiden?

Rebecca glanced behind her.

Blue Raven Woman sat by a cow, a good distance away from Rebecca, still butchering the animal.

Rebecca shouted at her. "Is someone supposed to be riding this buffalo, now?"

Blue Raven Woman didn't hear her.

Rebecca glanced down at the woolly cow. What did it matter? The cow was dead. There surely could be no danger in sitting on it now, could there? And then she could start to skin it without fear of doing something bad to the people.

Rebecca gathered her courage and forced herself to approach the cow, throwing her legs over its rangy back. She had just dug her hands deep into its woolly fur when suddenly the cow moved.

Wasn't the buffalo dead?

The animal suddenly struggled to its feet, Rebecca perched atop it. She screamed, she couldn't help herself, and dug her hands even more deeply into its wool. She took a strong hold.

The animal pawed at the ground. Wasn't this a cow?

Dear God, no. This was a young bull.

No sooner had the bull come to its feet than it began to race away, wildly running to and fro, Rebecca upon its back.

She screamed again.

She heard shouts, heard the thunder of the buffalo's hooves. Did anyone know she was in trouble?

She became dimly aware of low-pitched shouting, though she couldn't make out the words, and she screamed once more.

Was that Night Thunder's voice she heard shouting out to her, "Stay with the animal. Don't let go"?

How could she let go? Didn't her life depend upon her staying her seat?

A pony raced right up beside her, pitched in toward the buffalo's left side. Someone pointed an arrow at her. She screeched again.

On and on the frenzied buffalo sped, Rebecca only half aware that several horsemen followed her.

Finally someone put a shot into the bull's head. Nothing happened. Another shot to the head. Still nothing. Two more shots.

The buffalo hit the ground and with a wild scream, Rebecca flew through the air, her hands coming up and over her stomach for protection. She came down on the hard ground, hitting her head, screaming again, and then, nothing.

Rising above her body, she became aware of herself sprawled out on the prairie, Night Thunder having sprinted to her side. He spoke words of English to her. What was he saying? She tried to listen.

"Don't leave me," he pleaded with her, and she heard him, though not with her physical body's ears. Had she died? "Come back to me," he begged her. "Think of yourself, of me, of how lonely I will be without you. Rebecca, I love you."

She remembered no more. She smacked back into the body, taking on its pain, so much so that she passed out from the stress of it.

But at least the body began to breathe again ... though she was not aware of it. All she knew was how very tired she had become and how very much she hurt.

Chapter 23

~~~

Tom-toms had been booming out a steady beat throughout the day. Children had been holding contests of courage and skill all morning long, while large crowds of men had gathered around one another, practicing the rhythmic steps of their "secret society dances."

At least, that was what Blue Raven Woman had said they were doing.

Rebecca was sitting outside her lodge on this sunny afternoon, bending over the task of removing the hair from a skin Night Thunder had produced for her. Blue Raven Woman had exclaimed over the article, saying the deerskin would make the best clothing, once it had been "Indian worked." Indians, Rebecca had quickly learned, did not really tan hides, as the western world thought of it; the Indian worked and worked the hide, with ashes, with buffalo brains, with scrapers. It was moistened, rolled up to dry, moistened again, stretched, scraped again, pulled through a rawhide loop, stretched again.

Hard work.

But rarely was it left to one to do it alone. Mothers, aunts, sisters, friends would all gather round to help, making the chore more social event than task. And no one worked longer than they felt was good or necessary.

Today, however, Rebecca appeared to be working alone, the others busy with preparations for the big Sun Dance, whatever kind of dance that was.

Every now and then Rebecca would look upward to catch whatever activity took place around her, and she did so now.

To her right she saw old men, with gatherings of children around them; to her left, women, sitting around a large robe, sewing, perhaps even discussing some ancient legend, or maybe speculating upon the love life of their young people. The laughter of many people's voices joined the rhythmic throb of the drums, played in accompaniment to the intoxicating melody of a song being sung.

Rebecca had realized that she was growing accustomed to such things as these and would feel lost to awaken each morning without hearing the chattering of the birds, the stirrings of the camp to life, the voice of some old woman reciting to Sun the names of her grandchildren, the camp crier as he went through the village encouraging others to awaken.

So, too, would she miss the smell of smoke and the beginnings of preparation for their morning meal. She would miss Night Thunder's teasing her about the silly customs he kept making up.

Rebecca would have to admit, too—and she grimaced as she thought if it—that she would miss

Blue Raven Woman and the girl's constant cheer. Strange, that Rebecca should have become so attached to these things so quickly and to the other woman in so short a time.

Yet she had.

But why would she miss them? Was there some reason she would never experience them again? She couldn't remember.

Blue Raven Woman approached her.

"*Nit-ik-oht-yaahs-i'taki k-ikaa o'too-hs-yi*, I'm glad you have arrived," Rebecca said.

"*Sok sok*, good, good."

Blue Raven Woman took a seat beside Rebecca. After a moment, the other woman said, "*Kit-ik-a-sok-a'po'taki*, you work very well," and gestured toward the skin in Rebecca's grasp.

"*Iniiyi'taki*, thank you."

Blue Raven Woman stared around her and Rebecca began to suspect that something was bothering the other woman.

Rebecca didn't at once ask the Indian girl any questions about what it might be. As she had found was customary, she worked quietly for a while, hoping the other woman would start the conversation.

But when more silence followed and still Blue Raven Woman did not appear to have courage to speak, Rebecca asked, "Is something troubling you?"

Immediately tears formed in Blue Raven Woman's eyes, though she turned her head away that Rebecca not see it.

Rebecca grasped the other young woman's shoulder. "*Tsa*, what is it?"

Silence followed as Rebecca observed Blue Raven Woman attempt to bring herself under control. At last, the Indian girl began, "I come here to beg a favor of you."

"Of me?"

Blue Raven Woman nodded.

"Of course," said Rebecca. "*Tsa*, what is it that you would like to ask me?"

"I need you to ask Night Thunder to speed the marriage between himself and me."

Speed? Rebecca's insides dropped as though she sailed through the air. Had she heard the other woman correctly? Rebecca couldn't speak.

"Know that I would not ask if it were not important."

The young woman must have sensed something amiss, for the Indian girl glanced at Rebecca briefly and asked, "You would welcome me into your family, would you not?"

Rebecca nodded.

Silence ensued.

At length, Rebecca found the courage to ask, "Is there some reason, now, that you are asking me this?"

Blue Raven Woman nodded, but didn't enlighten Rebecca as to what was that reason. And Rebecca couldn't find the right words to ask. All she knew was that she couldn't let Blue Raven Woman marry her husband.

"No," Rebecca tried to talk, to form the words, but somehow her lips wouldn't move. She tried again, this time in Blackfoot, "*Saa*, no," but all she managed was a small whimper.

Why couldn't she speak?

Someone took hold of her hand. "Rebecca, wake up," someone whispered in her ear. Night Thunder? Someone put something—a salve?—onto her head and made it ache again. Rattles shook over her, tom-toms beat beside her—she heard them, as well as the wail of a voice singing something that sounded, even to her untrained ears, like a lament.

She cried out, but then stopped, the energy expended in doing this too much. Taking a long breath, she went back to her dreams—or were they nightmares?

Someone held her hand. Someone had moved her so that she lay in the sun.

Rebecca struggled toward consciousness but couldn't open her eyes, nor did her lips work. She could utter nothing.

She dimly heard the sounds of people all around her, but she couldn't focus on them.

She heard noises, a huge commotion, and then in Blackfoot someone said to her, "Twelve of our young warriors are coming racing into the Sun Dance camp." It was the voice of her Indian "mother," Blue Raven Woman's mother. Was she also the one who held her hand? How Rebecca wished she could ask the questions, but nothing in her body seemed to work. The voice went on, "They drag behind them the evergreens that they have only cut this morning. See there," a shadow passed before Rebecca's closed eyes, "the medicine man has given the signal and now the young men throw the evergreens over the Sun Dance lodge. And now here come two of the women from the Blood tribe with the eagle's nest. Soon the medicine man will place that nest at the top of the Sun Dance pole."

The woman asked, "Can you hear what I say?"

Rebecca couldn't answer.

"Wiggle your fingers against my hand if you can understand me."

Rebecca tried, but her hand seemed not to work. She must have accomplished something, however, because Morning Child Woman said, "That is good."

"Sun is now directly overhead and the medicine man is finally giving the signal that the Sun Dance lodge be erected."

Suddenly it seemed as though the world were coming to an end. Never had Rebecca heard such noise, yet still she couldn't come fully awake.

Morning Child Woman continued, "There must be a hundred warriors now rushing into the camp. Can you hear them?" Rebecca tried to wiggle her fingers. "They are galloping all around the Sun Dance and they are yelling and shooting, showing Sun how proud we are to be doing honour to him this day."

Soon the odor of gun smoke and powder reached out to Rebecca, yet still she could not force her eyes open.

"And here come the Sun Dance women—they who have sponsored this dance for the people. There is your sister, Blue Raven Woman. Can you see her? She has been fasting for these past few days that she honour you. As soon as you became ill, she announced that she too would be one of those to give the Sun Dance, that you might re-

cover. After today, you will see. Sun will heal
you."

It seemed too much an effort for Rebecca even
to think of contradicting the woman, and so she
did nothing more than breathe evenly.

"There is Blue Raven Woman now, taking her
seat next to the medicine man. Before her will
come all the braves who are to dance to honour
Sun this day, one of them your husband, Night
Thunder. He dances for you that Sun might reach
out to you and bring you back to us."

Night Thunder. Rebecca's heart filled with a
warmth and a joy she hadn't felt for many days.
Night Thunder was dancing for her? Dancing?

"Do you see her now, she is painting black the
faces and the wrists of the young men. Hold on.
Soon the dance will begin and you will start to feel
better."

Would she?

"Now the medicine man has grabbed the eagle's
nest and is painting the black circles around the
hole where the Sun Dance pole is to go. It is done.
Now he has placed the blanket over himself and
is fastening the eagle's nest to the pole. Soon, my
daughter. Soon. Take heart."

Rebecca tried to respond. She couldn't. Her
body wouldn't obey her commands.

"Five of our braves have now rushed to the pole
and are placing it in the hole, with the medicine
man still atop it. *Aa*, yes, he does not fall. All is
well. The Sun Dance will continue. Now, here
come the young men who are to dance. Do you
see him, he who is your husband? He stands tall.
He stands ready to dance. This is the second time

he has danced for Sun. You should be proud of him. *Aa*, very proud."

Rebecca wanted to agree, but all she could do was wiggle her fingers in her "mother's" hand.

"*Aa*, yes, you care for him deeply. I can tell. Now it is his turn to stand in front of the medicine man. The medicine man is running his knife into your husband's left breast . . ."

He was what? Rebecca tried to object. What was wrong with her body that it didn't respond?

"Now he runs another gash alongside that one and he is placing the rawhide thong into the cuts. Night Thunder has not made a sound. He is a brave man. Now the medicine man is repeating the procedure on the other side of Night Thunder's chest. There is only one part left before they begin dancing and that is to tie the thong onto the Sun Dance pole. It is done. Your husband is yet awake and has not made a sound or fainted. He is a brave man."

Or very stupid, thought Rebecca. But she couldn't talk. She could do nothing but listen in helpless attention.

"Now he starts to dance, hoping to pull free of the thong. Soon, my daughter, soon, you will be well. You will see. Their torture, their giving something of themselves, will appeal to Sun, and he will heal you. I have seen this thing happen many times."

Rebecca's hand remained in the other woman's, listening to her commentary on the dance and on Night Thunder. Time passed, minutes turned to hours, and still the young men danced, as told to her by Morning Child Woman. One by one the warriors had pulled free of the bonds which held them, or had passed out from the effort.

It seemed to Rebecca much too long to be torturing oneself, no matter the reason why, yet Night Thunder still danced, having not yet freed himself from the bonds, or having fainted as her "mother" had commented.

"Night Thunder is the only one left, now," said Morning Child Woman. "All the rest have jerked themselves free or collapsed. Here goes the medicine man to the pole to attach the thong to a horse that it might release your husband of the bond. He is still awake. He has still not gotten free. Now the medicine man is backing the horse up and he will soon make the horse charge—"

Whoosh.

As the sickening sound of tearing flesh split the air, Rebecca came suddenly awake, her eyes flying open in terror.

What had happened to her husband?

"Is he all right?" These, the first words out of her mouth, seemed to startled her "mother." But Rebecca rejoiced in the fact that her voice worked, her body again responded to her command.

She raised one of her hands up in front of her face, wiggling her fingers, then stared into the eyes of her Indian "mother." Why did her "mother" cry?

"Your husband is fine." The woman's voice broke, but still she continued, "The medicine man is giving him herbs for his wound and Night Thunder will rest, but Sun has heard his plea. He has healed you. You have come back to us, my daughter."

And the strangest thing happened right then and there: for the first time since coming to the Indian encampment, Rebecca looked at the other woman as though she were exactly that—her mother.

Rebecca let out her breath in one long, drawn-out sigh. "What happened to me?"

"Do you not remember your fall from the buffalo?"

"Buffalo . . . ?Aye, I remember, but . . ."

"Sun almost took you from us."

Aye, he almost had. "I need to see him."

Morning Child Woman seemed momentarily taken aback. She asked, "Sun?"

"No, I need to see Night Thunder."

Morning Child Woman nodded. "We will go to him at once, my daughter. We will get you there to him."

Rebecca tried to sit up; she was too weak to accomplish it on her own, however. Morning Child Woman helped her up, Rebecca placing her weight upon her mother, as Rebecca gazed out into the Sun Dance circle, seeing the people gradually leaving the area. Rebecca asked, "How long have I been unconscious?"

Morning Child Woman made a sign with her hands, then spoke, "Seven days you have been gone from us and we did not know if you would ever awaken. But now, Sun has healed you, do you see? Here you are again, with us."

Rebecca smiled. It felt good to be alive, to feel her body again respond to her own will, and as she breathed in the fresh prairie air, she felt herself gain strength. She asked, "Could you help me up and walk with me so that I may go to my husband?"

Morning Child Woman agreed eagerly, and nodding toward another—perhaps Morning Child Woman's sister—the two women assisted Rebecca, enabling her to stand up on her feet.

The three of them began to leave the Sun Dance circle, stepping through the Indian encampment with Morning Child Woman and the other woman's help. Rebecca received several gestures of friendship, she noted, from more people than she cared to count—people coming up to her to reassure her that they were pleased that she had "come back" to them.

Rebecca's heart constricted. Many of these people she had met only briefly, yet each one seemed honestly concerned for her welfare. She grimaced. How could she have ever thought these people savage? More kindness and consideration were being bestowed upon her now than she had ever experienced in the "civilized" world.

She asked, as they made their way through the camp, "What were you talking about when you told me that my husband was dancing for me? And your daughter, did you say Blue Raven Woman was a part of this?"

Morning Child Woman seemed puzzled, as she asked, "Do you truly not know?"

Rebecca shook her head.

"Then I will tell you my daughter, that you understand what has taken place here today. Sun took you away from us," Morning Child began. "There was nothing we could do. Night Thunder gave our medicine man many horses to save you.

Night Thunder has sat with you every night, caring not for his own needs, not eating, not sleeping. Blue Raven Woman sat with you, too, and bathed you when Night Thunder was gone to hunt. But nothing we have done brought you back to us. That was when Night Thunder begged Sun and asked Old Man to heal you if he would give of himself in the Dance to honour Sun. He beseeched Sun to take his pain instead of yours, and to make you whole again.

"My daughter, Blue Raven Woman, heard of this pledge Night Thunder made to Sun and implored Sun to return you, too. My daughter also loves her white sister and asked Sun that if she also made a sacrifice, fasting and praying for many days, would he bring you back to us? It is an honour that she has given you, given us. Because she has helped to sponsor the Sun Dance, others have been made into warriors. And Sun has shone kindly upon us this day. He has made many more warriors to defend our people and he has given you back to us."

Rebecca's heart filled with emotion as she listened to the old woman's words, and she felt tears well up in her eyes.

The women brought her to her own lodge, and as Rebecca entered the tepee, the feeling of coming home and of belonging here swept over her.

Her husband lay upon his sleeping robes, there on his side of the lodge, Blue Raven Woman at his side, attending to his wounds. As she entered, Night Thunder looked up at Rebecca, his dark eyes seeking out hers.

Weakly he asked, "Are you real or shadow?"

She said, her voice barely working, "I am real."

He sighed. "It is true, then. Sun healed you. You have come back to me?"

"I am here," Rebecca reassured him, and moved further into the lodge, rushing to him, as well as she was able. She bent over him.

"It was my fault what happened to you," he explained to her.

"Sh-h-h," she responded. She touched his lips with her finger.

But he wouldn't be quieted. He said, "I should not have left you without ensuring that you knew I was teasing you."

"You told me to ask Blue Raven Woman. I should have."

"But I—"

"How could you have known that your crazy woman would take it into her head to ride a buffalo?"

He reached for her hand. "It is good now. Sun heard my pleas—and Blue Raven Woman's. You have been returned to us."

Rebecca shut her eyes, fighting to keep back the tears. But it was useless. One streamed down her face, even as she hardened herself against it. She didn't hear Blue Raven Woman, Morning Child Woman, and her sister slip out of the lodge.

Rebecca said, "I love you, my husband. I love you. Do not ever forget it."

Twice he opened his mouth to speak, twice no words would come, until at length he was able to say, "How could I forget, when you have taken my heart from me?" He squeezed her hand and shut his eyes. Several tortured minutes passed before he continued, "I am tired now from the dance. But I will be well in a few suns, and then I will tell you about my marriage to Blue Raven Woman . . . I . . . there is something . . ." He nodded off, but came to moments later, only to say, "Something I must tell you about my marriage. Do not worry. I would not have you . . ." He shut his eyes, but before he drifted off to sleep, she heard him say, "*Ikakomimmawa kitana*, your daughter is loved."

Night Thunder lay before her, his eyes closed in sleep.

Rebecca bathed his chest with the rawhide rag Blue Raven Woman had left behind. The sweet scent of the herbs used to freshen the water reminded her of the same scent that had been used to wash her own injuries, and she felt her head begin to ache.

What had he been about to say? Something about his marriage to Blue Raven Woman? He hadn't married the Indian woman already, had he? He wouldn't have done that, would he?

And what had he meant, "Your daughter is loved"?

Did he mean, was he trying to tell her, that he loved Blue Raven Woman? Rebecca already knew that Blue Raven Woman loved him. Hadn't the girl said as much?

Briefly Rebecca shut her eyes, trying to make sense of it. But her head hurt and the effort seemed enormous.

What a mess. Rebecca loved Blue Raven Woman; she also loved her husband and would not share him. She couldn't, could she?

Rebecca brought her hand up to massage her forehead.

Briefly, she wondered, could she share her husband?

Her stomach twisted at the thought, her pulse rate increased, and a sense of dread filled her being.

She had her answer: no, she could not. She might love Blue Raven Woman, might even think of her as a sister, but she would not share her man with another woman.

Never.

Rebecca raised her chin.

She had to leave. She *had* to. It was the only choice left for her. Before Night Thunder became well enough to prevent it. And he would try to prevent it, she was certain.

She would no longer stand in the way of these two people coming together, nor would she continue to bring hurt to these two who had shown her nothing but kindness.

No longer would she think of herself as the woman who had taken Blue Raven Woman's man from her; no longer would she worry that she was causing Night Thunder to sacrifice his honour.

Was her own heart so special that she could not break it in order that she keep these two people safe? After all, hadn't Night Thunder risked all for her? Hadn't Blue Raven Woman?

It was the only way. She had to leave quickly, too, before he guessed at her secret. Before he came to know that she was pregnant. Wouldn't he then demand that the baby stay here with him? Hadn't he said as much? And wouldn't Rebecca then *have* to stay here, ruining the lives of all those around her? Because she knew she'd never be able to leave her own baby.

Another thought crossed her mind.

She was still pregnant, wasn't she? Surely she hadn't lost the baby. Wouldn't Morning Child Woman have told her about it if she had?

Her head began to ache so critically that she knew she had to rest. But the last thought she had before she lay down beside her husband was whether or not Robert Clark still remained in the Indian camp, awaiting her decision.

She would make enquiries tomorrow . . . about that . . . about the baby . . .

Tomorrow . . .

Chapter 24

She stole out of camp the next day. Robert Clark had been only too willing to leave quickly and she had needed to get away before Night Thunder became well enough to suspect what she planned. But in doing so, Rebecca had become completely dejected. One day passed into the next and it became impossible to think in the present. Everywhere, everything around her reminded her of Night Thunder. The prairie, the wind, the very scents of the air. Would she ever get him out of her mind? Was she going to have to return to the east in order to do so?

Night Thunder . . .

She saw him around every bend, over the top of every elevation, behind every tree. She dreamed of him, longed for him, listened for his voice on the wind.

And she realized, she would go on loving him—no matter if or when he married another, no matter where her life took her from this moment forward. Always, she would love him.

She had been on the trail with Robert Clark and

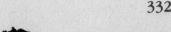

his two friends for over a week and she had to admit that the three men were kind, though they often gave her strange looks, perhaps wondering why she rarely spoke to them or answered their questions. But they neither said nor did anything to make her nervous.

Their party traveled mostly at night, the men telling her that even though she had lived among the Blackfeet, that tribe and others in the vicinity remained antagonistic toward the white man.

It was safer that they travel at night.

Rebecca had simply nodded agreement. She didn't care. Nothing appeared to matter to her anymore, and she wondered if it might not have been better if she'd stayed in the camp and let Night Thunder marry the other woman.

Her life wouldn't have been so bad, would it?

But at times like this, reason would again come to her rescue and she would affirm once more what she knew in her heart: she could not have suffered it. Her convictions wouldn't allow her such an arrangement. Always, she would berate herself, think less of herself. Surely that was no way in which to live.

No, she had made the right choice. She would return to her own world, to her mistress and her friend Katrina. She would go again to the east, perhaps even venture across the ocean to Ireland. Though oddly, the prospect of doing that no longer held the gladness in her heart that it once had.

She wanted her life back. Wanted her husband back.

But she could not have it, or him.

Her thoughts caused her anguish, and she told herself that she would live through this—for herself, for her baby.

Her baby. A part of Night Thunder. Rebecca's heart softened and she could little understand the pleasure that the thought gave her. Perhaps because she knew that she would always have a part of him, there within her child. Her child would be a testimony to the love she felt for Night Thunder, the love they had shared.

It would have to be enough.

Night seemed to come early, spreading around them like darkened mist, with only Old Woman, the moon, and the stars to guide them.

Old Woman. Had she even begun to think like an Indian?

What was it Night Thunder had said? Spirits are everywhere, but there is only one Creator? Was Old Woman a spirit? What would happen to her if she, a white woman, appealed to Old Woman for advice?

Nonsense.

Rebecca trudged on ahead with the others, her pony snorting at her as though the animal knew her thoughts.

The sound of drums, far off in the distance, came to her softly at first, easing her tension so much so that Rebecca didn't register the clamor of them until several minutes later. Suddenly she listened more intently.

Indian drums?

She asked the man ahead of her, "Do you hear it?"

At first, the man had seemed startled that she

had taken to talking to him, but he recovered swiftly enough, and looking over his shoulder, had asked, "Hear what, ma'am?"

"The drums," she responded. "Let us stop for a moment."

"Now, ma'am, we can't be doing that."

But Rebecca wouldn't be put off. She reined in her horse, the others having no choice but to do the same. She said, "Sh-h-h. Do you hear it?"

The men listened. "No, ma'am, I don't hear nothing. Does any of you fellas?"

"No," replied one, then the other.

"But it's right there," she insisted, "not too distant from us. Shouldn't we investigate it and see about it?"

"No, ma'am. We needs ta get ya back ta the fort in one piece, now."

"But I hear it. Please, let us go and see about it."

The man in front of her sighed and turned back toward her. He said, "Jack, ya get yerself ta go with her, see if there's any Injuns over that way. We'll wait here for ya."

Jack, the man in back of her, simply nodded and took the lead, saying only briefly to her, "Come on, ma'am."

She went.

Strikes The Bear jumped upon his pony.

"Where do you go, my cousin?" Night Thunder had barely recovered enough to stand. But upon witnessing the other man mount his pony, he had pulled himself up from his bed. He now strode up to the man.

Strikes The Bear sneered, "It is nothing to you."

Pretending more strength than he felt, Night Thunder said, "It is everything to me if you go to hunt my wife."

Strikes The Bear growled. "She is nothing to you now. She has left you. No longer is she Blackfoot."

"She is Blackfoot and I will go and get her and bring her back. By the laws of our tribe, you have no right to find her and use her, if it is still revenge that you seek."

"You have no right to tell me what I can do. She is *white*, or are your eyes so blind to her that you cannot see it?"

"*Aa*, my cousin, she is white."

"And did not white people kill my wife? Did not white people abuse her? Did not white people cause me all of my pain? I hate all white people."

A crowd of people had gathered around the two men, listening, murmurs of awe or perhaps dissatisfaction on their lips.

But Night Thunder ignored them. He mimicked. "You hate all white people?"

"They killed my wife. Have I not the right?"

"Do you hate even those traders who give us the beads and the guns and the steel flints?"

"Humph." Strikes The Bear jerked back his head.

Night Thunder went on, "I say it was only a few who did this to your wife, my cousin. Do not we also have those among us who do bad things? If I were to believe as you say, would that not make all of us bad, too?"

The larger man growled.

Night Thunder continued, "Why do you not

seek to discover the identity of those few who did this thing to you and have your revenge upon them, and only them? Is this not your duty? Not to seek out one with the same colour of skin who knows not the injustice done to your wife."

Strikes The Bear dismounted, and shouting, he took a few steps toward Night Thunder. He said, "You speak as a coward who cannot let go of a woman who does not want him."

Night Thunder ignored the insult and said, "I speak as a man about his *Blackfoot* wife. *Blackfoot*, I say. For you to seek revenge upon her is to do harm to the people and act as a murderer. Do you seek the sure justice of being labeled a murderer?"

Strikes The Bear howled.

Night Thunder continued, though, sweeping his arms around the circle of people. "What manner of this? Is a person now good or bad according to his skin colour? Is an Indian now not bad when he kills one of our own? Is a white man now bad when he trades with us the guns and blankets that we need? I say this is foolish. A person is a person of worth or not, depending upon his honour and his character, not his type of skin. How can those of us pretend to say that we are brothers to the wind, to the bear, to the wolf, and to all things around us, and forget that we are also brother to our own kind? Are we as a people to forget that there are only few who do terrible things, white man or red?"

Night Thunder had no more than finished when a sudden wind swept up behind him, rushing howling across the prairie. And for those who lived and breathed upon the prairie, there was another name put to this sort of wind—a spirit wind. Voices could be heard from above it, old voices, speaking in tongues no one could understand—no one but a medicine man.

Tepees around them rocked and tilted in the gale, and still the voices continued, swelling, getting louder until at last, with a sudden jerk, the tepees around them came flying off their pegs.

Into this chaos stepped Old Lone Bull, the tribal medicine man, his wise, aged eyes scanning first Night Thunder, then Strikes The Bear. The old man raised his rattles toward the sky and sang out his medicine song until the wind quieted.

At length, he spoke, saying to one and all, "I have talked to the spirits and they have answered me. Know this. The spirits have decreed that Night Thunder's plea, and his plea alone, has been heard; we will do the white woman no harm. She has become a part of our tribe as much as anyone here. Go back to your lodges, now. There is nothing more here to see."

Strikes The Bear screamed, and as though unable to accept the truth of the statement, hurled himself forward, pulling a knife and lunging at Night Thunder.

But the big Indian never made contact. In midair, the spirit wind whipped toward him, as though it were a living thing. It propelled the Indian upward, taking him into its whirlwind, carrying Strikes The Bear from the crowd, and dumping him out onto the prairie.

At such a fantastic sight, murmurs of wonder and fear swept through the crowd. But the medicine man continued to speak to them, pressing his point: "Know that the spirits have spoken. Go against their desires at your own risk."

But though he might have spoken out against what Strikes The Bear had attempted to do, the medicine man left, going out on the prairie to the man, and touching him on the shoulder, he said, "Come, I see many ponies in your herd. Perhaps we can make enough payment to the spirits in order that we discover the identity of those who wronged your wife."

Night Thunder watched the big Indian rise to his feet, then saw the other man glance around the crowd, but all that was said was, "*Soka'pii-wa*, it is good."

Night Thunder heaved out a sigh. It was time. He was well enough; his body needed to recover no further before he went after his wife, if for no other reason than to ensure that she arrived at the fort safely.

He braced himself against what he might find, for she might not wish to see him or come back to him. And if it were true, if she no longer wished the protection of his lodge, there would be little he could do about it.

He began to move away from the crowd. The spirits, however, were not finished with him.

Whipping back into the encampment, the whirlwind came to twirl before him, not moving away, not ceasing its spin, but remaining before Night Thunder. Night Thunder attempted to move away. The whirlwind went with him, and Night Thunder had no choice but to turn and confront it.

Gradually the whirlwind began to take form,

turning into a being Night Thunder had already encountered: the old man.

Misty substance shrouded the old man, and as Night Thunder began to speak, a sudden, forceful gale sped toward him, pushing at him as though he stood in the midst of a thunderstorm. Weak though he was, he stood his ground, letting the strong currents push back his hair, his clothes.

His courage never deserting him he said, "Old man. We meet again."

The old man paced toward Night Thunder on feet that never once touched the ground.

"What is it you want from me?"

"*Waapo'to*, freedom for my people," the old man said.

"Freedom? I have not that power."

"Have you not?"

"I know not the ceremony to free yours from the bonds that hold them."

The old man came to stand before Night Thunder. Reaching out a hand, the spirit touched the younger man, the feel of it, Night Thunder thought, like that of a cold, shivering mist.

"Many years ago, in time before mind," said the old man, "your people killed mine in a terrible fight over a woman. Decided I then, for all time, to seek out yours and kill them. I was young and foolish. I was not good. Killed I your people, many of them. At last, though, your people sought out me and killed me and mine. They took our legs, our arms, our hearts. We could not walk to our ancestors."

"You have legs now."

"But not the will. I am forever lost from my

wife, the heart of me. It is she that I seek."

Night Thunder said, "I have not seen her."

The old man stared up at him with eyes, sad. "Find the one that you love and bring her back to you. *Mat'-ah-kwi tam-ap-i-ni-po-ke-mi-o-sin*, not found is happiness without woman."

Night Thunder opened his mouth to say more, but it was useless. The spirit of the old man had disappeared as quickly as it had come.

The people stared at Night Thunder for many moments, stunned at what they had seen. At last, however, Night Thunder found the strength to move, and strode toward the pony herd, to find and prepare his own mount.

He hadn't needed the old man to tell him to go and find his wife. Nonetheless, he now felt driven to do just that.

Rebecca was afraid. Without Night Thunder to guide her and protect her, she had little courage to confront these spirits, if that was what these were.

She could see them there, on the plains; she could hear them, the steady drum, the ghostly sound of their singing, the thump of their feet. There, under the silvery strands of moonlight.

She said to her companion, "Do you see them, now?"

"No, ma'am, I don't see nothing."

"Come," she said, "follow me."

She dismounted, bringing her horse forward with her. "There they are, there in the distance. They're having a dance."

The man looked at her strangely.

"Ma'am, I still don't see nothing."

What was it that Night Thunder had told her, that few people could see the shadows of the dead?

She said to her companion, "I understand. You wait here for me. I will go on."

"I can't allow that, ma'am. I been told to accompany ya."

"Then come on with me. Let's move closer."

An ethereal quality of the drums called to her, the singing enchanted her. She had to be closer to it. Why, she did not know. But she suspected that it was because the spirits, the singing, even the dancing reminded her of Night Thunder.

She stepped toward them, not caring whether her escort continued on with her or not.

Closer she came, closer and closer, her fear a tangible thing. But she would not stop.

Finally she stood at the outskirts of their encampment.

Said she in Blackfoot, as loudly as she was able, "Who are you?"

No answer.

"Why do you follow me?"

Again, no answer. No change.

"What do you want from me, from my husband, Night Thunder?"

A brief silence and then, "Do you believe now that he is your husband?"

Who had spoken to her? It had been a baritone voice. Was it one of the braves, or perhaps the old man? The same one who had married her to Night Thunder, he who had spoken to Night Thunder at the Dog Society dance?

She answered, though not aloud, "Aye, my husband."

"Then why did you leave him?"

"If you be truly shadows of the dead, then you know why." Her words were in thought only and she wondered that she could carry on a conversation such as this. Yet she did.

"He loves Blue Raven Woman," the old man said.

"Do you think I do not know that?"

"But only as a man might love his sister."

Was it true? And even if it were true, did it matter? "Still," thought Rebecca, "Night Thunder has his honour to keep. And you must know that Blue Raven Woman loves him."

"As a sister loves a brother."

Hope suddenly flared within her. But she dared not hope too well. Not yet. She asked, in thought alone, "Why do you care? Why are you here?"

"Some things you will have to discover on your own."

The drums crescendoed, becoming louder and louder until they sounded deafening, and wind rushed toward her as though it were a tornado, howling around her, blowing her dress, her hair forward. Bells and jangles on the dancers' feet jingled in time to the beat, though the dancers began to part, the wind sweeping in among them and into the center.

She caught her breath.

A long figure stood in the midst of the center, his form as misty as that of the old man.

Night Thunder?

"No," she screamed. "He isn't dead, is he?" she asked the old man.

Night Thunder spoke, "I am alive."

"In shadow form only?" she asked.

"A medicine man has many mysterious powers. One of them is to be able to take form elsewhere. I have come to find you, to ask you to come back to me."

Said she, "I . . . I cannot. I would not bring hurt to you."

"How is it that you hurt me?" he asked, beckoning her forward.

She took one step toward him. She couldn't help herself. "I asked you to give up your honour, to put Blue Raven Woman from you."

"Worry no more. She is married."

"No." Rebecca backed away. "You married her when I was ill?"

"She is married to Singing Bull. It happened while you were gone from us in spirit." Again Night Thunder beckoned her forward.

"Singing Bull?" she asked. "I do not know him."

"And yet Blue Raven Woman has been in love with him for many years, and he with her."

"Did you know it all this time?"

"*Saa*, no, I have only discovered it."

"But your pledge, hers . . ."

"Was never made by the two of us. Our parents made the vow, and all are glad now that it is broken. My heart, hers, have been caught up elsewhere. The spirits of my father and mother can now rest easy." Again he bid Rebecca to come forward. "My heart has been sad since you left."

Rebecca shut her eyes. "I cannot believe any of this."

"Come here to me."

As though mesmerized, she did as he beckoned, the line of dancers parting for her.

Drums increased their beat, sounding faster and faster, and as she swayed forward, the singing grew louder.

She stepped up to him quickly, the drums urging her on, and he took her in his arms, as though he were made of substance instead of shadowy mist.

"*Kitsikakomimmo*, I love you. I will always love you, no matter the flesh, no matter where or what we are. Come back to me. Spend your life with me."

She swayed to the beat of the drums, to the beat of what must have been his heart, hers. She said, "I will."

He threw his robe over her, then, enveloping her in its nebulous fragrance as he kissed her, his lips touching hers as though he were truly there with her.

And just as quickly as they had come to her, the shadows of the dead disappeared, Night Thunder with them.

She stopped, completely still, listening.

Had she really seen them? Was it only her imagination?

She touched her fingers to her lips. No, it had been real. As real as the lingering scent that had been caught in the prairie winds.

She would return to Night Thunder.

She would ask Robert Clark to take her back immediately.

Turning, she paced to the place where she had left her horse, not at all surprised to discover that the man, and the animals, who had accompanied her here had fled.

Curiously, she smiled.

Chapter 25

Long Flagpole, as the Indians called it, or Fort Union, stood before her, its walls looking more prison to Rebecca, at the moment, than haven. Horses, enclosed within an unsightly corral, munched on the rich though dry prairie grass, while further away, cows swished their tails and glared at the newcomers.

The manure and sickening sweet smell of the steers suddenly struck Rebecca as they rode past them, and she could barely refrain from holding her nose. Why had she never noticed their unsightly odor before? Or more important, when had she become more accustomed to the stronger scent of the buffalo?

None of the graceful Indian tepees dotted the landscape around the fort at this time of year, either, which would have made a more welcoming homecoming. Rebecca sighed, resigned.

Robert Clark had refused to take her back to the Indian encampment, and Rebecca had needed to comfort herself with the knowledge that if Katrina were still at Fort Union, then White Eagle, Katrina's husband, would be there, too, and he would take her back to Night Thunder.

It was this thought alone that had given her courage to continue on with their trek.

Fort Union's gates opened to them at once, without requiring then to announce themselves.

Rebecca rode in with the three men, uncertain of what awaited her. Perhaps because she hadn't expected much, she was greatly surprised to be met by not only her employer, Katrina, but with Katrina's husband, White Eagle. Also present were another white woman, a beautiful redheaded white woman, and another Indian whom Rebecca did not recognize. Two elder gentlemen joined the party also, all of them forming a welcoming line. Who were these people? Europeans, and in particular European women, were rare in this part of the country.

No matter, Rebecca sent Katrina a happy smile, and quickly dismounting, the two women embraced one another.

"I have been so worried about you," said Katrina, Rebecca's mistress.

As her blond hair curled around her face in neat order, Katrina appeared just as Rebecca remembered her, and Rebecca smiled at this mistress who had long ago become her friend.

"And I am glad to see you, too. Thank you for sending these men to find me."

"Of course. Come, let me introduce you to my friends." Katrina, her arm around Rebecca's waist, led her toward the assembled group. "You know White Eagle, of course." The Indian man nodded recognition to her. "And this lady here is Lady

Genevieve, and her husband, Gray Hawk; her father, Viscount Rohan. Lady Genevieve and her father have come here from England, originally to study the dialects of the Indians."

Rebecca nodded toward them all. Viscount Rohan took her hand into his and kissed the back of it, causing Rebecca to smile.

Not a single emotion crossed either Indian's face, though Rebecca, seemingly attuned to the Indian character by now, could sense their puzzlement over the viscount's strange behavior. A man, stooping over a woman's hand? Where was the man's sense of honour?

However, she could little consider such thoughts as Katrina was continuing, "And this gentleman here is my uncle, trader Wellington."

"How do you do?"

"Pleasured, ma'am, pleasured." The elder man took her hand into his and kissed it.

Katrina hardly missed a beat as she went on to say, "But come, now, let the men care for your horse and anything else you have brought with you while Genevieve and I escort you into the fort. You must be exhausted."

Was she? She had become so used to physical activity that she had begun to give her body little thought.

Rebecca went with her friend, though. It would be good to chat with the others for a while, to become accustomed to speaking in English again and to learn about what was happening in the "States," as the frontiersmen called it, referring to the United States as though it were a foreign country.

Then, once they were all settled, perhaps she would ask Katrina to persuade her husband to accompany her back to the Indian village. Back to her love, Night Thunder.

"Where is Night Thunder?" asked Katrina. "I thought he might have come with you."

The two women sat in the drawing room of the bourgeois house, sipping tea and coffee.

"Night Thunder is still in his village, I believe," said Rebecca. "I left in a bit of a hurry."

"You did?"

Rebecca nodded briefly, glancing away.

"And . . . ?"

"And what?"

"What happened between you and Night Thunder? He did save you from the Assiniboin, did he not?"

"They were Blackfoot Indians that took me—the Blood tribe."

"Then that must have been easier for him."

"Or harder."

For all that Katrina bore the distinctive blond hair, her eyes were quite dark, and they stared into Rebecca's own now. She asked, "What do you mean?"

Rebecca drew a long breath. "Night Thunder couldn't be fighting them over me, now, could he? They were from his own tribe."

Katrina gave her an odd sort of smile. "Then how did he save you?"

"He . . . well, he married me."

"He what?"

"No, no, he didn't really marry me. He only pretended it."

"Pretended? He lied about it? But he is a medicine man, isn't he?"

"Not yet," said Rebecca. "He will be when their current medicine man can no longer function."

"Goodness," said Katrina. "I have never heard of such a thing. He must think highly of you to have done this for you."

Rebecca paused. "I think so."

"Then what are you doing here without him? Why did you leave in a hurry? He did marry you, in fact, did he not?"

Rebecca cleared her throat and stared away. She said, "Aye, he did, but . . ."

"But what?

"He . . ." Rebecca looked back at Katrina. "He was engaged to marry another, and I thought it best if I were to leave."

"Hmmm," said Katrina. "The plot thickens."

"Doesn't it?" Rebecca smiled.

"What happened?"

"I left so that he could marry the other woman. Oh, Katrina, it's all so complicated. I want White Eagle to take me back to Night Thunder's camp. Do you think you could convince him to do that? And before the snow comes?"

Katrina smiled, a rare, secretive smile. She said, "I think I might be able to do something to . . . influence him."

Rebecca grinned. "I bet you can," and seeing the flush upon Katrina's face, Rebecca added, "My, but you haven't said a thing about you and White Eagle. Won't you tell me what has happened to you? I had heard that you and White Eagle married."

Katrina nodded.

"And weren't you hating your uncle, now? If I remember correctly, the last time I saw you, you were intent on having your revenge on him for demanding you come into this country. Has that changed, too?"

Katrina smiled. "Yes, it seems I misunderstood a lot. But now, as you can see, all is well."

"Aye," said Rebecca. "I can see that. All, that is, except Night Thunder . . ."

Katrina took hold of her hand. "Then we'll have to take care of that, won't we? I will talk to White Eagle at once and we will prepare to go."

"We?"

"You don't think I'd let you go back into Indian country without me, do you? And my uncle loves that part of the country better than any other. I would assume, too, that Genevieve and her husband will want to go with us; probably, too, her father. We'll make quite a party, won't we?"

Rebecca grinned. Two women of the upper class gentry, traveling over the wilderness with their Indian husbands? Rebecca certainly did not want to miss seeing this. She said, "We'll make quite a sight, at that."

The two women looked at each other, and at the same time started to giggle as though they were children.

"White Eagle says he will take you to the Indian camp, but that we cannot go until we have a celebration."

"A celebration? Of what?"

"Of your return, of course." It was Lady Genevieve speaking, and Rebecca chanced to catch a glimpse of the beautiful lady, so delicately dressed, so very genteel.

It was hard for Rebecca to comprehend that these two women who sat with her were married to Indians . . . plains Indians. Yet one had only to see the two of them to realize that they were both happy.

That Katrina's uncle and Lady Genevieve's father had both sanctioned the marriages probably helped to strengthen the unions, but Rebecca felt sure that both ladies would have followed their hearts, no matter the urgings of their patriarchs.

Rebecca grinned. "Are we to celebrate my return only to have me leave at once?"

"It seems only right to me," answered Katrina.

"That's the way I see it, too," said Genevieve.

All three of them were seated out doors, a blanket thrown over the dry ground. Two days had passed since she had arrived back at the fort. Two days during which Rebecca had been anxiously awaiting word from White Eagle.

"My husband says there are to be special guests at our celebration," Lady Genevieve said, a note of secrecy in her voice.

But Rebecca cared little. She only wanted to leave with all haste, and hurry back to Night Thunder. "Is that so?"

Lady Genevieve nodded, but Katrina went on, in the same sort of tone that Lady Genevieve had used, "Indians do nothing, you will find, without a great deal of ceremony. It makes living with them all the more interesting . . . and exciting."

"Does it?" asked Rebecca. "It is good to see you so happy, Miss Katrina."

Katrina raised her brows. "Since when do you call me Miss Katrina? I thought we had been all through that."

"And please do call me Genny," said Lady Genevieve. "It seems so much of a warmer name, somehow. And it's so silly, here in the States, to keep the title of Lady, is it not?"

Rebecca smiled. She said, "Genny *does* seem much more a casual name, and it fits in a bit more with the setting here, I do agree."

"There, now, do you see? Already we're going to be grand friends, we three."

All three women grinned.

"There, now that the celebration has been settled, why don't we start to make plans for the ball?"

Rebecca's eyes flew wide. "A ball?"

Katrina stared at her. "Of course, a ball, silly. How else did you think we were going to celebrate?"

"I thought we were going to have a small party."

"Then you thought incorrectly," said Genevieve. "If we are all to travel to the Indian villages and stay there, then we shall have to say our farewells in proper style, don't you think? And a proper ball will do it well. Shall we start the preparations?"

Rebecca was more than happy to agree.

* * *

Dusk descended upon the land, while gaiety filled the home of the fort's bourgeois.

Torches had been lit, transforming the entire house into a bright and lively ballroom. Chandeliers from up above dripped wax into a glass circle laid out on the floor, and dancers swayed to the music of a quadrille. Several fiddles had been found plus a guitar and a clavichord. Strange symphony, strange setting, and equally strange dancers. Yet it was satisfying for all that.

Only three white woman had taken to the floor in dance, as they were the only white women in the fort. But there were more women dancing, the rest Indian wives of the employees.

Rebecca stood amazed at how her Indian counterparts had taken to the dance of the quadrille. How they could leap and shuffle, their husbands picking them up and swinging them round and round and high into the air.

They were all chattering, too, and laughing like all young ladies anywhere in the world would do.

Oddly, Rebecca found she missed the drums and the Indian melodies set in a minor key, but she kept that knowledge to herself.

She had just finished a dance with an employee of the fort, but her mind had been only half on what she was doing. She needed time to pull her thoughts together.

She missed Night Thunder. Funny, that here, at last, she was attending a ball thrown in her honour, something she had yearned for all her life, yet all she could do tonight was think about Night Thunder, missing him.

She wished to be on the trail, instead of here,

making her way back to him. But Katrina's husband, White Eagle, had insisted upon the ball. It was all Rebecca could do to pretend to be enjoying herself.

She smiled as yet another young man came up and asked her for the pleasure of a dance. She flicked open the fan in her hand and fanned it back and forth in front of her face furiously.

"Please forgive me, sir," she said, "but I must sit out this dance." She ran a gloved hand over her brow, pretending fatigue, when what she really wanted to do was run outside, find a good mount, and be on her way back to Night Thunder.

Luckily, the young man did not know this and took her refusal good-naturedly, sauntering away.

"*Ki-tak-stai pes-ka*'?" Rebecca started at the words, spoken in a baritone voice so achingly familiar.

She spun around.

What was this? It couldn't be, and yet . . .

Was it truly Night Thunder standing before her? Night Thunder, in the flesh, not an apparition?

But my, what a figure he cut.

He stood before her in trousers and waistcoat, boots and top hat and white gloves. His hair had been pulled back, away from his face.

He bowed to her formally, saying again,"*Ki-tak-stai pes-ka*'? Will you dance?"

She felt herself grow faint. What was this?

He smiled at her. "Did you not tell me that it was at one of these balls that you would meet your future husband, the man you would love all your life?" And he repeated, "*Ki-tak-stai pes-ka*'?"

She couldn't speak.

How had he gotten here? And so quickly? He hadn't followed her, had he?

But her voice seemed unable to work and so she did the only thing possible: she placed her gloved hand into his.

The musicians struck up a waltz and he led her out onto the dance floor.

Dip, sway, twirl. They floated around the dance floor. Step, step, spin.

At last it finally occurred to her and she couldn't help asking, "How have you learned the waltz?"

He grinned down at her. "I have been practicing since I arrived here."

"And how long have you been here at the fort?"

"Since two days before you arrived. I have been here five days."

She frowned up at him. "Have you? And why did you not come to me right away?"

He shrugged. "I wished to surprise you with the ball."

"The ball?" she asked. "I thought it was White Eagle's idea to have this."

Night Thunder grinned. "White Eagle is a good friend."

"And has everyone known you were here but me?"

Night Thunder had the grace to look chagrined. "I wanted to surprise you."

She murmured softly, "You have."

He stared down into her eyes, the music swirling around them. Step, step, sway, step, twirl; round and round, it was as though they were floating.

He said, "I love you, Rebecca. I want you with

me. I want you to be a part of my life."

She smiled. "And I love you. I will."

He grinned, she did, too, and they floated around the floor until Rebecca voiced, "There are some things I must ask you, my husband. I had the oddest experience on the trail."

He smiled at her, and he said, "I know. But first, there are others here whom you might enjoy seeing."

"Are there, now?"

"Look over there to that corner," he tilted his head. "See who is there?"

She looked. Blue Raven Woman sat in the corner with a few other Indian women, all of them chattering, talking, and laughing.

"You brought Blue Raven Woman here?"

"*Aa*, yes, I did. Her and her husband."

"Her husband? Singing Bull?"

"*Aa*," he said, "Singing Bull."

"Then it was real, that night upon the prairie. You were there."

"I was there."

"But how?"

"A medicine man is supposed to protect his secrets. Know though that a medicine man can sometimes, during moments of great need, project his image and his thoughts across distances. I wanted you to know that Blue Raven Woman had taken another as husband; one whom she has loved for many years."

Rebecca closed her eyes. "Then there really isn't any reason why we can't—"

He whispered in her ear. "There is not."

"Oh, Night Thunder." She couldn't help herself.

She drew herself even closer into his arms. "I have been so silly."

He laughed then and twirled her into a series of turns, their gazes locked, each smiling into the other's eyes.

After some moments, however, he asked her, "Why did you leave me? I had wanted to tell you that I had decided not to marry Blue Raven Woman, but I could not tell you of my plans until I had settled the matter with her and her parents."

"You had been?" And she suddenly remembered the conversation she had heard between Night Thunder and Singing Bull.

He nodded. "But by the time I had resolved that matter, you had gone." He asked again, "Why did you leave me? Did you not know of my feelings for you?"

"I . . . suppose that . . . aye, I did, but I . . . you had said something about her, about Blue Raven Woman the night when you were resting from the Sun Dance."

"I did?"

"Aye."

"In my sleep?"

"Aye."

"And what did I say?"

"Don't you know?"

"*Saa*, I do not."

"You said you loved someone's daughter, and I could only think you meant Blue Raven Woman. There were so many other reasons why I thought I should leave—for her sake, for yours. It seemed the best thing to do for everybody."

He smiled and pulled her in closer. He said,

KAREN KAY

"*Aa*, yes, my wife. We have both been silly. I should have confided in you at once. But I thought I could not."

She nodded. "I understand."

"But do you not know?" he continued, "Do you not know that it is *you* who is the daughter of Sun? He has given you back to us, and by doing so has made you his daughter. It was you that I spoke of. I was telling you that I love you."

"Oh, Night Thunder." She threw herself against him and he accepted her weight, swinging her around and around, until their dizzying laughter could be heard across the dance floor.

"Goodness," she said. "Why did I not become aware of this before now?"

"What?"

"Do you not see?" she said. "I knew I would meet my love, the man I would marry, at a dance. Do you not remember the first time we met?"

It took him a moment, but all at once he grinned. "*Sina-paskan*, the dance of the Sioux, that night when I tricked you into a kiss."

"Aye, do you see? I should have known it all along. It was then that I met the man I was to marry."

He laughed.

"You are not the only one who has some surprises," she said and, glancing down, held her hand to her belly. "I, too, have something to tell you. Soon," she voiced, her eyes beaming up at him with happiness, "you will be a father."

His face alit all at once with more joy than she had ever witnessed in him, and his eyes filled with such love, she was left in no doubt as to his feelings for her, for their child.

And as the two of them stepped off the dance floor, in order to converse more privately, Blue Raven Woman and Singing Bull took to the dance to try their hand in the white man's waltz. Meanwhile, White Eagle and Katrina, Gray Hawk and Genevieve all stepped around the floor to the ever-thrilling three-quarter beat, and the shadow of the old man stood in the corner, watching the proceedings with a sad-sweet smile.

He had done well, thought the old man. Because of the good deed done for these two here tonight, all his people had been allowed to complete their journey to the Sand Hills, there to join their relatives, and he had ensured the safety of the *Pikuni* by uniting the white woman with the medicine man.

Rebecca would bring great happiness to the young medicine man, the two of them and their friends helping the tribes through times that would seem to hold nothing but bleakness.

Aa, yes, he had done well.

If only . . .

Someday, he thought; someday, he would find his wife, who had been lost to him for so long.

But for now he was happy.

The tribes would survive. And these here tonight would thrive for all of their lives in happiness.

All was as it should be.

Alas! Alas! Why could not this simple life have continued? Why must the railroads, and the swarms of settlers, have invaded that wonderful land, and robbed its lords of all that made life worth living? They knew not care, nor hunger, nor want of any kind. From my window here I hear the roar of the great city, and see the crowds hurrying by. The day is bitterly cold, yet the majority of the passersby, women as well as men, are thinly clad, and their faces are thin, and their eyes express sad thoughts. Many of them have no warm shelter from the storm, know not where they can get a little food, although they would gladly work for it with all their strength. The are "bound to the wheel," and there is no escape from it except by death. And this is civilization! I, for one, maintain that there is no satisfaction, no happiness in it. The Indians of the plains back in those days of which I write alone knew what was perfect content and happiness, and that, we are told, is the chief end aim of men—to be free from want, and worry, and care. Civilization will never furnish it, except to the very, very few.

—JAMES WILLARD SCHULTZ, *My Life as an Indian*

Glossary

This note appears in my first book in the Blackfoot Warrior series. It is repeated here, with a few other definitions added, so as to bring a better understanding to the work and to define certain words which might otherwise be hard to find.

At the time when this story takes place, there were three different tribes of Indians that together comprised the Blackfeet or Blackfoot Nation: the Piegan, or *Pikuni*, their name in the Blackfoot language; the Blood or *Kainah*, and the Blackfoot proper or *Siksika*.

The *Piegan*, which is pronounced Pay-gan, were also divided into the Northern and Southern bands.

All three of these tribes were independent and were known by the early trappers by their own individual tribal names. But because the three shared the same language, intermarried, and went to war with the same enemies, it became more common, as time went on, to call these people under one name, the Blackfeet or Siksikauw.

At this time, the time of my story, the names Blackfoot and Blackfeet were used interchangeably, meaning one and the same groups of people.

However, during reservation days (the story goes, as I was told it), the U.S. government utilized a misnomer, calling the tribe of the Southern Piegan, or *Pikuni*, the "Blackfeet." This designation stuck, and to this day, this tribe resides in northern Montana on the Blackfeet reservation, and are referred to, by the government, as the Blackfeet (although they are really the Southern Piegan or *Pikuni*).

Consequently, when we speak today of the Blackfoot tribes, or the Siksika Nation as a whole, we talk of four different tribes: the Blackfoot, Blood, and *Piegan* bands in Canada, and the Blackfeet in Montana. Thus, today when referring to the "Blackfeet," one is speaking of the band of Indians in Montana (on the Blackfeet reservation), whereas the name "Blackfoot" refers to the band of Indians in Alberta, Canada (on the Blackfoot reserve).

If this seems confusing to you, I can assure you, it baffled me.

Thus, in my story, because the Blackfeet and Blackfoot names were interchangeable at this moment in history, I have used "Blackfeet" as a noun ("I went to visit the Blackfeet"), and "Blackfoot" as an adjective ("I went to Blackfoot country"). I did this for no other reason than consistency.

I am also including some definitions of common Indian words, as well as some newer Irish terms for this, the third book in the Blackfoot Warrior series. I hope this will help toward further understanding.

Afeared—an Irish way of saying afraid.

Algonquin—"member of a group of Indian tribes formerly of the Ottowa River valley in southeastern Canada. Also, Algonquian—widespread American-Indian language family spoken from Labrador westward to the Rockies and southward to Illinois and North Carolina." *The Scribner-Bantam English Dictionary, 1977.* Some of the tribes which spoke this language were the Cheyenne, Blackfeet, Arapaho, Shawnee, and Ottawa:

Assiniboin Indians—a tribe of Indians whose territory bordered the Blackfeet on the east. These Indians were at war with the Blackfeet.

The Backbone of the World—term used by the Blackfeet to indicate the Rocky Mountains.

Coup—a term used widespread by the Indians to mean a deed of valor.

Cree—a tribe of Indians closely associated with the Assiniboin, whose territory bordered the Blackfeet on the east.

Crow—a tribe of Indians that inhabited that part of the northern United States, around the upper

Yellowstone River. They were at war with the Blackfeet.

Dog Society Dance—a dance given by the Dog Society of the Blackfeet. These different societies denoted different social strata.

Duggins—an Irish term meaning rags.

Gros Ventre—a tribe of Indians which neighbored the Blackfeet.

Kit Fox Society—all Indian tribes had different societies for men and for women. They denoted different social strata. Prince Maximilian, who visited Blackfoot country in the early 1830s, was probably the first white man to observe the different Blackfoot societies. He noted that there were seven of these societies and that each of them had their own dances and songs, as well as their own regalia.

Medicine—described by George Catlin in his book *Letters and Notes on the Manners, Customs, and Conditions of North American Indians*, " 'Medicine' is a great word in this country; ... The word medicine, in its common acceptation here, means *mystery*, and nothing else; and in that sense I *shall* use it very frequently in my Notes and Indian Manners and Customs. The fur traders in this country are nearly all French; and in their language, a doctor or physician, is called *'medecin.'* The Indian country is full of doctors; and as they are all magicians, and skilled, or profess to be skilled, in many mysteries, the word 'medecin' has become habitually applied to every thing mysterious or unaccountable; . . ."

More-than-friend—in most Indian tribes, a more-than-friend refers to friends of the same gender who have made a pact to fight together and hunt together, etc. in an effort to increase both persons' potential of survival. Such is a friend, but more. It was expected that if one of them had troubles, so, too, did the other take on those troubles as his own, helping to find solutions.

Parfleches—a bag fashioned out of buffalo hide and used by the Indians to store clothing, food and other articles. An Indian used parfleches much as the white man uses a chest of drawers. They were often highly decorated and some were sewn in patterns "owned" by a particular family, thus easily recognized.

Rock of Cashel—an Irish saying which usually goes, "As firm as the Rock of Cashel."

Scalplocks—can be a reference to hair at the top of one's head—that part that was most often "scalped." Or this can refer to hair which adorns Indian clothing, on shirts and leggings, etc.

Sits-beside-him woman or *wife*—in Indian tribes that practiced polygamy, this referred to the favored wife, usually the first wife. She directed all the other wives and had the right to sit next to her husband at important meetings.

Snakes—this refers to the Shoshoni or Snake Indians. They bordered the Blackfeet on the south and west and were traditional enemies of the Blackfeet.

Sun Dance—in Blackfoot society, a religious ceremony where the warriors show honor to Sun and where a warrior becomes a man. Many warriors received a vision during these ceremonies.

Sun Dance camp—this was a camp where all the Blackfeet tribes came together in celebration, usually in August. The camp would last as long as a month, sometimes less. There was always good feeling and great celebration, including many different dances performed every night, as well as secret society dances and celebrations.

Wheen—an Irish word meaning a small quantity of something.

Dear Reader,

Karen Ranney's love stories are so filled with passion and emotion, that once you open one of her Avon books I can't imagine you'll want to put it down. In next month's MY BELOVED, Karen spins an unforgettable love story between the convent-bred Juliana and Sebastian, a man haunted by the demons of his past. Wed when they were mere children, Sebastian refuses to share a bed with his wife. Can she break down the walls that keep them from surrendering to a passion neither can deny?

Readers of contemporary romance won't want to miss Patti Berg's delicious WIFE FOR A DAY. Samantha Jones needs money desperately, so when she meets millionaire Jack Remington she agrees to his wild proposal—pretend to be his fiancee for one night...no hanky-panky allowed. But when the night is over Samantha finds it nearly impossible to say goodbye...

THE MACKENZIES are one of Avon's most beloved series, and now Ana Leigh brings you another one of these wild-western men: JAKE. Jake Carrington is determined to win pert Beth MacKenzie any way he can...even luring her into marriage with a proposition she cannot refuse.

A dashing rogue, a young Duchess, and a Regency setting all add up to another fresh, exciting love story by Malia Martin, THE DUKE'S RETURN. Sara Whitney has no desire to marry again, especially not to rakish Trevor Phillips...but she has no choice but to surrender herself to him.

I know you're going to love each of these unforgettable Avon romances. And, until next month, I wish you happy reading!

Lucia Macro

Lucia Macro
Senior Editor

ael 0799

Avon Romances—
the best in exceptional authors
and unforgettable novels!